ALSO BY ELLEN MEISTER

The Other Life

The Smart One

Secret Confessions of the Applewood PTA

Farewell,
DOROTHY PARKER

Ellen Meister

G. P. PUTNAM'S SONS
NEW YORK

G. P. PUTNAM'S SONS
Publishers Since 1838
Published by the Penguin Group
Penguin Group (USA) Inc., 375 Hudson Street,
New York, New York 10014, USA

USA / Canada / UK / Ireland / Australia / New Zealand / India / South Africa / China

Penguin Books Ltd, Registered Offices: 80 Strand, London WC2R 0RL, England
For more information about the Penguin Group visit penguin.com

Library of Congress Cataloging-in-Publication Data

Meister, Ellen.
Farewell, Dorothy Parker / by Ellen Meister.
p.   cm.
ISBN 978-0-399-15907-7
1. Parker, Dorothy, 1893–1967—Fiction.   2. Self-realization in women—Fiction.
3. Women authors—Fiction.   4. Film critics—Fiction.   5. Spirits—Fiction.   I. Title.
PS3613.E4355F37   2013   2012039838
813'.6—dc23

Printed in the United States of America
1   3   5   7   9   10   8   6   4   2

Book design by Jennifer Daddio/Bookmark Design & Media Inc.

This is a work of fiction. Names, characters, places, and incidents either are the product
of the author's imagination or are used fictitiously, and any resemblance to actual persons,
living or dead, businesses, companies, events, or locales is entirely coincidental.

THIS BOOK IS DEDICATED TO

Betty Mogavero

IN LOVING MEMORY

The first thing I do in the morning is brush
my teeth and sharpen my tongue.

—DOROTHY PARKER

FAREWELL, DOROTHY PARKER

Chapter 1

Violet Epps stood before the maître d' in the lobby lounge of the Algonquin Hotel, waiting to be noticed. She cleared her throat and he looked up, glancing right past her.

"Who's next?" he said.

Me, she thought. *Me.* But before she could summon the courage to get the single syllable across her tongue, a young man behind her spoke up.

"We have a reservation," he said, putting his arm around the pretty girl at his side. "Dr. Walker."

Doctor my ass, Violet thought. Guy was maybe twenty-three years old, probably a waiter who just walked over from his afternoon class at the Actors Studio.

Violet closed her eyes and tried to find the gumption she needed to speak up and tell the maître d' she was there first. But as usual, social anxiety paralyzed her vocal cords. Too bad she couldn't channel Dorothy Parker the way she did at work.

Violet Epps was a thirty-seven-year-old movie critic whose withering zingers were inspired by the famous wit who had made the Algonquin Hotel her home for many years. Dorothy Parker was Violet's hero, and not just for her scathing reviews, clever jokes, quotable poetry, and insightful short stories but for her potent social courage. The diminutive Mrs. Parker, as she was often called, was so commanding that even her friends thought of her as larger than life.

So far, Violet had been successful in summoning her muse only when writing her movie reviews. In her personal life, she was held captive by her own timidity. Today, she hoped, would be different. She was meeting her boyfriend, Carl, for dinner, and needed to tell him it was over. She had tried this once before—just a few weeks ago—and failed. Worse, Carl had made a strong case that the only problem with their relationship was that they didn't spend enough time with each other. He even managed to convince her that if they were together more he would drink less. And so she caved, agreeing to let him move in with her. In two short days it would be happening. Everything in the "apartment" he rented in the basement of his parents' home would be loaded into a U-Haul and moved to her house.

As the maître d' led the young couple to their table, Violet glanced inside her oversized handbag, where a tiny bundle of fur lay sleeping. It was Woollcott, a funny-looking little dog who had survived the car crash that killed her sister and brother-in-law. Violet had petitioned for temporary custody of her thirteen-year-old niece, who had also survived the accident, but wound up with the dog.

Violet knew that Dorothy Parker, whose most famous quotes were uttered right here in this room, would have made a glib joke about the trade-off. After all, it was life's most painful events that brought out Mrs. Parker's famously wicked sense of humor—like the time she responded to an unwanted pregnancy by saying, *That's what I get for putting all my eggs in one bastard.*

Violet gave Woollcott a pat. He was, she had discovered, a mellow companion who had a calming effect on her nerves. That was why she had decided to sneak him into this meeting with Carl; if she couldn't channel Dorothy Parker from the hallowed walls of the Algonquin Hotel, at least she had this little dog to help steady her.

A grab from behind gave Violet a start. It was Carl. She pulled his hands from her waist.

"Hey, babe," he said. "Where's our table? Didn't you tell them who you were?"

"You scared me," she said.

"But I was just horsing around."

Violet sighed. What did one thing have to do with the other? Surely she was entitled to be startled regardless of the intent.

But that was Carl. He was so sure he never did anything wrong that you couldn't suggest otherwise without feeling like you had done something truly villainous.

Violet shook her head. This relationship was not just dead. It was starting to rot.

They had met three years ago at a crafts fair in Stony Brook, Long Island, and Violet was immediately intrigued, as he was the opposite of her rigid ex-husband. Carl McDonald was an artist and looked the part, with a messy mass of long wiry locks, parted in the middle. He was thickset with large hands and bitten nails, which usually had paint embedded deep in the cuticles. Carl had carved out a niche for himself painting nostalgically kitschy designs on small pieces of furniture, and eked out a living selling his work in cramped booths at local shows. Recently, he launched a Web site to try to broaden his customer base.

He was handsome in an offbeat way, and Violet, God help her, loved his disheveled-artist look and the intensity of his dark blue eyes. Yes, he was different, but that was why she felt so immediately electrified. Here was a man with passion—someone who could love. But when they met, she was still on the rebound of her failed marriage and got involved way too soon. What seemed like disarming emotional honesty in the beginning revealed itself to be nothing more than a self-involved kind of neediness. And then there was the drinking.

She leaned in to take a whiff, hoping he hadn't stopped someplace for a shot or two on his way to meet her. He misinterpreted her body language and responded by kissing her on the mouth with passion more appropriate for a private room than a hotel lobby.

She pushed him away before her body had a chance to react. She was, she believed, too easily stimulated by the smallest touch. "How much did you have to drink?"

"Nothing. Just two little Bud Lights." He snapped his fingers at the maître d'.

Violet cringed. "Don't *do* that," she whispered. "For God's sake."

"Can I help you?" the host asked. He was classically handsome—almost a central-casting version of a maître d', Violet thought—with dark hair, rigid posture, and a wisp of Middle Eastern accent.

"Reservation for Violet Epps," Carl said to him, pronouncing her name loudly enough for several diners to overhear. This was typical. He loved having a well-known girlfriend and always thought it was a good idea to use her celebrity to their advantage.

"Yes, of course," the host answered. "Right this way."

A few heads turned as they were led to the Round Table Room, which was really just a section in the back of the open lobby. As they made their way past people relaxing in the overstuffed chairs and sofas of the hotel's famous lounge, Violet heard someone quoting from one of her crankier reviews: *The best thing I can say about* By the Long-hairs *is that people who have been given two months to live might be dead before it comes out on DVD.*

Violet squirmed. It wasn't the notoriety that made her uncomfortable. In fact, she liked being cited in newspaper ads and didn't even mind getting trashed online. But being recognized in public was a horror-film double feature compared to seeing her name in print. She let her hair fall in front of her face.

"Your server will be right with you," the maître d' said, as they took their seats.

"Could someone get me a Dewar's, rocks?" Carl asked.

The host bowed and left. Violet balanced her open bag on her lap and petted Woollcott.

Carl leaned over the table to get a look. "You brought that ugly mutt with you?"

"He's not ugly," Violet argued, though she knew she would have a hard time defending that position under cross-examination. He was, without a doubt, one of the oddest-looking dogs she had ever seen. In addition to the dull beige fur that stuck out in every direction, he had a pushed-in snout, round bulgy eyes set too far apart, and a nose and mouth cramped too close together. And though he was her niece's dog, Violet was the one who had named him. She took one peek at his face and decided he looked like Alexander Woollcott, the famous theater critic of the 1920s and founding member of the Algonquin Round Table—the group of wits who met daily for lunch at this very spot.

But unlike his vinegary namesake, this Woollcott was so sweet and docile she considered him the world's most perfect pet. Without opening his eyes he stuck out his pink tongue and licked her hand. She rubbed his ear.

"I have to talk to you about something," she said to Carl. "Something important."

"Is it the garage?" he said. "Because—"

"It's not the garage." Ever since she agreed to let him move in, Carl had been badgering her about the detached garage, which he thought would make a perfect studio for him. But it was crammed full of family possessions Violet was not prepared to part with.

"It's just that there would be so much room in there if we got rid of all that—"

"Carl," she said, and then hesitated. There was simply no way she was letting him do this. "I can't—"

"I'll rent the truck for an extra day and put the stuff in storage myself."

"Wait," she said. "Please." She petted Woollcott again and tried to find the words. She put her head in her hands and mumbled, more to herself than to him, "This isn't working."

"What's the matter? Did I do something wrong? Are you mad about the beer?"

Yes, I'm mad about the beer, she thought. I'm mad that you can always find time to get a buzz on but can never find time to come with me to one of my screenings. I'm mad that it's always about you and *your* needs, and never about mine. I'm mad that—

"Because you know I love you," he said, "right?"

Irrelevant, Violet thought.

"And anyway," he continued, "I really don't drink that much."

You do.

"You're just hung up on the drinking thing."

I am not.

He reached over and took her hand. "On account of your sister's accident."

Okay, so maybe he had a point. She pulled her hand away.

"And what about Delaney?" she asked, referring to her niece.

"What about her?"

"I need a stable environment for her."

"I know I kind of got off on the wrong foot with her," he said, "but she'll warm up to me. I'm great with kids."

Just say it, she told herself. Three simple words: *It's over, Carl.* Then get up and leave. She stroked Woollcott. He picked up his head and looked at her, then gave her hand a lick and went back to sleep. Things were so beautifully simple in a dog's world. Love, food, slumber.

"This is not . . ." She paused and swallowed, struggling to finish the sentence as she anticipated his reaction. Please, God, she thought, don't let him freak out.

"Not what?" he asked.

Violet closed her eyes and tried to summon strength from her surroundings. She imagined the room abuzz with chatter as the members of the Algonquin Round Table ate and drank and traded quips. They were a group of writers and actors who met here for lunch every day for ten years, and their bon mots were printed in newspapers, laughed at over morning coffee, repeated in offices, and celebrated in speakeasies. But the most often quoted of them all was Dorothy Parker. Violet could envision the tiny brunette wedged between the rotund Alexander Woollcott and the very tall Robert Sherwood. And though physically dwarfed by the two men, her presence was gargantuan.

In contrast, Violet did her best to be invisible in a crowd. On the rare occasion that she actually accepted a social invitation, Violet managed to slink her way from the door to the host and back out again without being noticed. And if anyone did happen to spy the lanky woman with the hair in her face, they never would have suspected she was the often-quoted Violet Epps, whose passionate praise shouted from so many full-page movie ads, and whose searing swipes lit up the blogosphere.

Help me, she thought, and envisioned her muse turning her head. Violet looked straight into Dorothy Parker's eyes, and for a moment the scene was so vivid she could swear she smelled gin and cigarettes. Was it her imagination? She took a deep breath. It was strangely powerful, and yet she couldn't shake the feeling that she was smelling history. Where was it coming from? She sniffed her blouse.

"What's wrong?" Carl asked.

Violet looked around. "Is someone smoking?"

"I don't smell anything."

She took another whiff. The scent was gone. Maybe it *was* her imagination after all.

She leaned back in her seat. When the waiter came with Carl's scotch and asked her if she wanted something from the bar, Violet pulled her handbag closer and waved him away.

"What were you trying to say before?" Carl asked.

She stared into his drink, thinking about her niece. You can do this, she told herself. Just say it. She swallowed hard, rehearsed the words in her head, asked Dorothy for strength, and then tried to spit it out.

"You," she said, and choked. *C'mon, words.*

"Me what?" Carl said.

"You can't."

"I can't *what*?"

Violet shut her eyes tight. "You can't move in this weekend." There. She did it. She did it, and she wouldn't back down.

"You want me to *postpone* the move?"

"Not postpone—"

"Good," he said. "Because I would probably lose my deposit on the truck."

"I mean, you can't move in *period.*"

He laughed. "Okay, I get it. I won't pressure you about the garage anymore. At least for now." He snapped his fingers at the waiter. "Can we see menus, please?"

Violet rubbed her forehead. Please, Dorothy, she thought. Help me out here. Give me *something.*

She looked up and saw two men approaching their table—the maître d' and an official-looking man in an expensive suit. The floor shook with their footsteps, and Violet knew she was in trouble. These men were on a mission, and it could be only one thing. The dog. The waiter must have seen him when he delivered Carl's drink, and now she was busted. Violet knew it would do no good to try to make a case that Dorothy Parker brought her little toy poodle to lunch at the Algonquin almost daily for ten years. They were going to throw her out.

Damn it, Dorothy, she thought. I ask for help and this is what you send?

She quickly threw a cloth napkin over her open bag, her hands trembling. The thought of making a scene terrified her. Please, she thought, let it be over quickly. I'll just grab my bag and leave.

"Ms. Epps?" the maître d' said. "I'd like to introduce Barry Beeman, general manager of the Algonquin."

The suited man thrust his hand at Violet, and she shook it. "It's such a pleasure to meet you," he said. "Here at the Algonquin we're big fans of the reviewer who's been called 'the modern Dorothy Parker,' and we'd be honored to have you sign our priceless guest book." He leaned over and placed an antique leather-bound volume in front of her.

"Guest book?" she said.

"It belonged to Percy Coates," he began, and Violet nodded. She knew he had been the manager of the hotel when it became a literary landmark. "All the original members of the Algonquin Round Table signed it, and over the years we have asked specific notable representatives of the literary establishment to add their names—"

"Literary establishment?" Violet said, her face burning with embarrassment. Dear God, all she did was write snarky two-paragraph reviews for a weekly entertainment magazine. "I hardly think—"

He put an expensive pen in her hand and carefully opened the cover of the book. There, on the very first page, were the actual signatures of the men and women who had made the hotel so famous. Violet got dizzy just thinking about it—all these people in the flesh, holding this same book and signing it. The first was George S. Kaufman, who had a special place in her heart because she was a Marx Brothers fan and he had written three of their funniest movies. He was followed by humorist Robert Benchley, who was Dorothy Parker's best friend, and then Franklin P. Adams, whose newspaper column quoted the group almost daily. Harold Ross, founder of a tiny magazine he called *The New Yorker*, was on the list. Violet remembered reading that he had hired Dorothy Parker to write reviews, and once found her at a speakeasy in the middle of a workday. Her excuse? *Someone was using the pencil.*

Of course, Alexander Woollcott, who presided over the whole affair, was on the list, and so was Edna Ferber, who wrote *Showboat.* Then, right under Robert Sherwood, was the one name she had hoped to see.

"Dorothy Parker," she whispered. Violet put her hand over the name and could swear she felt a comforting warmth rising from it, as if the famous wit was trying to reach out and touch her.

"Some say she still haunts this room," Mr. Beeman said.

I believe she does, Violet thought.

In fact, there was a powerful force emanating from the signature, and the longer Violet held her hand there, the stronger it got, until her fingers prickled with the strangest sensation—tingly and hot like she was touching a sparkler.

Her fingers started to burn, and she wanted to pull her hand away, but she willed herself to be brave, take a chance, see what happened next.

And then. The strange heat moved up her arms and shot through her body with so much force she had to grab on to the table.

"Oh!" she cried.

"What is it?" Carl said. "What's wrong?"

"I don't know."

He reached over and touched her cheek. "You're ice cold," he said.

No, she thought. I'm burning up. But she let go of the table to touch her own face and realized he was right. She was red hot and ice cold at the same time.

Then she was swept up by a terrible wave, as the two forces seemed to meet and clash, resulting in nausea so overwhelming Violet thought she must surely be dying.

The nausea continued to build until she could no longer endure it and the light began to disappear from her world. Thank God, she thought. Thank God I'm fainting. At last she passed out, carried off in beautiful, blessed unconsciousness.

Still, even in her blackness she heard the voices of the men around her. *Are you okay? Ms. Epps, are you all right? Maybe we should call an ambulance. Violet, wake up. Violet!*

No, no, she thought. Leave me alone. Let me stay in this faraway place.

And then another voice spoke to her. A woman's voice.

Don't be a coward. It's your moment.

Violet opened her eyes, and the sickness compressed itself into a tiny tight ball right behind her navel. She looked around the room, and it was as if the light had changed in a way that altered her focus. Everything was crisper, like she had just put on stronger glasses.

She stared straight at Carl. With her new vision, he looked smaller, weaker.

"There's my baby," he said, with a grin so condescending she wanted to spit.

"She's okay," the maître d' announced. "Thank goodness. Ms. Epps, is there anything we can get you?"

Violet didn't take her eyes off Carl. "A loaded pistol."

"What are you talking about?" Carl said.

"Us. We're over."

Carl turned to the general manager. "Maybe you *should* call an ambulance. Something's wrong. I don't like the way she sounds."

"And I don't like the way you look," she said.

"Violet, what's wrong with you?"

She removed the napkin that covered her bag. "Don't get up," she said, as she reached in to give Woollcott one reassuring pat. But as soon as her fingers grazed his warm body, the hot sparklers returned to her fingertips and sent a charge of static to the unsuspecting animal. Yet something more than electricity passed between them. The knot behind her navel shot from her like a bolt and split in two, zapping the dog and the guest book. Immediately, the room seemed to soften and change. Woollcott growled.

"Is that a *dog*?" the man in the suit asked.

"He's very docile," Carl said, reaching across to give him a pet.

Before he could make contact, Woollcott jumped from her bag to the table and sunk his sharp little teeth into the artist's fingers.

"Fuck!" Carl said, and pushed the dog right into his scotch, which knocked over. Violet quickly slammed shut the ancient leather-bound guest book to protect it. Woollcott released Carl's hand, leapt from the table to the floor, and ran, scurrying around chairs, past customers and between waiters, as he headed for the door.

"I'm so sorry!" Violet said to Barry Beeman and the maître d'. "Woollcott!" she shouted, and before anyone could notice, she slipped the guest book into her bag and ran off after him.

Chapter 2

"Settle down," Violet said. "I can't hear myself think."

But the little dog continued to bark and yip as if he was, well, possessed, running in frantic circles around her kitchen table, where the Algonquin guest book lay.

Violet couldn't believe she had actually stolen it. She had never done anything like that in her life. But then again, she had never had an experience as terrifying and exhilarating as those few moments in the Algonquin. If she opened the book now, would it happen again? Violet put her head in her hands. Couldn't that dog be quiet for a second so she could get ahold of herself and reason it all out?

"Come here, boy," she said, but he ignored her and kept yelping.

She picked up his leash and jangled it. "How about a walk?" That usually got his immediate attention, but not today. "A treat?" she asked, opening the cabinet where she kept his Milk-Bones. She shook the box, but even that got no response.

Violet paced. She didn't understand what was going on with the poor little dog and didn't know how to get him to settle down. One thing she did know without question—the force that had seized her at the Algonquin was Dorothy Parker.

And now that force was captured in the guest book.

As tempted as she was to open it, she couldn't bear the thought of feeling as sick as she did in the restaurant, but, oh, the power! With

Dorothy Parker's spirit compressed into a tight ball at the center of her soul, she was as courageous as she had always dreamed of being.

The phone rang, though she could barely hear it over the incessant high-pitched barking. Knowing Woollcott would follow, she picked up the book and carried it into the study, a dark, cozy room off the foyer her sister had restored to its original charm, repairing and refinishing the ancient oak paneling and recessed bookcases. It was a small space, furnished with a settee, an old desk, two antique wingback chairs facing the stone fireplace, and loads of books. Except for the anachronistic laptop she kept on the desk, entering the room always felt like taking a step back to another century.

She tossed the hefty tome onto one of the chairs and a cloud of dust wafted up, followed by a pang of guilt. This house had meant so much to Ivy. Violet needed to do a better job of keeping the place in good order.

Woollcott, oblivious to her shortcomings as a housekeeper, jumped onto the seat and put his head on the cover of the book. At last he was quiet.

Violet went back into the kitchen and listened as her answering machine clicked on.

Hey, baby, it's Carl. Why aren't you answering your cell phone? And what the hell happened to you in the restaurant? I guess you're a little wigged out about moving in together, but I promise it'll all be okay. We'll talk about it more on Sunday when we're unpacking, okay? Hope your back is feeling strong, because mine isn't. And my fingers hurt where that crazy little dog bit me, but I put on some ointment and bandages, and now all I need is a kiss. Love ya!

"Shit," she said, and grabbed for the phone. It was Friday evening and he was planning to move in on Sunday morning. She couldn't put this off another minute. She had to tell him it was over.

"Carl," she said, "you still there?"

"Hi, baby."

Violet heard the tap-tap-tap of Woollcott's nails on the tile as he came back into the kitchen. He sat at her feet and rubbed his face against her leg. "You're better, huh?" she said, giving him a gentle scratch behind the ears.

"Much better," Carl said. "I think the Neosporin helped."

"I was talking to Woollcott."

"I'm the one who got bitten, and you're worried about the dog?"

"He hasn't been . . . himself," she said.

"I noticed. He nearly took my fingers off."

Violet rolled her eyes. She knew Carl hadn't been badly hurt. "Well, thank goodness he didn't," she said. "Thank goodness it's just a tiny wound."

"It's not that tiny," he said. "My mother thinks I should get a tetanus shot."

His mother. When Violet first started dating Carl, she thought his attachment to his parents was charmingly eccentric. But now she realized how arrested his development really was. If he moved in with her, he would bring that neediness with him, making Violet the mother figure. It was the last thing she wanted from a man.

"I . . . never finished what I was trying to tell you in the restaurant," she said.

"Yeah, what the hell happened to you in there?"

"Wait," she said. "I think I just heard something."

"Heard something?"

"In the house. It sounded like . . . like a little dog barking."

"Woollcott," he said. "Duh."

Violet bristled. Didn't he think she would know if it was her own dog? "Woollcott's right here with me," she said.

"Must be coming from outside."

That made more sense. She pulled out a kitchen chair and sat—she had to get this over with. "Okay, remember when I said you couldn't move in this weekend?"

"You were upset about the garage. I understand. You have a lot of family treasures in there. But maybe we can put a shed in the backyard."

"I don't want a shed, Carl."

"I saw some at Home Depot that were pretty attractive. They even have them with wood shingles."

"I don't care about wood shingles."

"Or a fiberglass one that looks like white clapboard siding."

"Carl, please. I have no interest in a shed."

"Don't be so stubborn," he said. "A shed is a perfect solution. You get to keep all your sister's stuff, and I get a studio."

This isn't about the fucking shed, she thought. This is about us. "Look," she said. "This isn't going to work."

"I bet there's room in the attic," he said.

"The attic?"

Violet heard something—something that definitely wasn't coming from outside. And it wasn't a dog.

"If it's empty—" Carl said.

"Shush," she said. "I think there's someone in the house."

Carl was still talking, so she took the phone away from her ear. And then she heard it. She heard it as clearly and distinctly as if there was a person in the next room.

Oh, for God's sake, said a woman's voice. *Just tell him to go to hell.*

The phone slipped from Violet's hand and hit the floor. She fumbled for it. "Carl?"

"What's going on?" he asked.

"I don't know," she said, her heart pounding. "Someone's here. I heard . . . a woman."

"First you heard a dog and now you hear a woman? Violet, are you okay?"

"I'm okay," she whispered, her hand over her mouth. "I'm going to investigate."

"If there's really someone there, don't you think you should call 911?"

"*Shh,*" she said, as she tiptoed out of the kitchen and toward the study.

The door was ajar, and she quietly pushed it open. The first thing she saw was the Algonquin guest book, open on the floor beside the wingback chair. And there, on the seat itself, where she had left Woollcott, was a cloud of dust far thicker than the one she had created when she tossed the book onto it. It seemed to hover several feet in the air with a distinct shape. As Violet stared, she could make out lines and shadows within the floating matter. It was like seeing a three-dimensional form take shape in one of those Magic Eye pictures you had to look at with a relaxed focus.

And then the particles settled themselves into a recognizable image. Violet blinked. She wasn't just looking at a mass of floating dust particles. She was looking at a pale gray suggestion of a small woman holding a French poodle on her lap. As she continued to stare, the vision got stronger, more vibrant, until it wasn't a vision at all but a real live person.

"You still there?" Carl asked, but Violet didn't answer him. She couldn't. She was paralyzed in place, unable to move or speak.

Then the apparition broke the silence.

"It's customary," the woman said, as she petted the small dog on her lap, "to offer a guest a drink."

Chapter 3

Violet hung up the phone without saying good-bye.

"Dorothy Parker?" she said to her guest. It came out as soft as vapor.

"And this is Cliché," Mrs. Parker said, introducing her poodle.

Violet stared, dumbstruck.

Dorothy Parker looked straight at her. "I don't believe I've had the pleasure."

"What?"

"Your name, miss."

"Uh, Violet. Violet Epps."

"The movie critic?"

Dizzy, Violet held on to the door frame. "You've heard of me?"

"One doesn't float about the dining rooms of the Algonquin for forty-five years without learning a thing or two."

Violet closed her eyes for a second, remembering the smell of gin and cigarettes that seemed to pass right through her just moments before the incident with the book. Had that been the spirit of Dorothy Parker?

"What are you—" she began. "How . . . ?"

"It's all tied to this awful thing," Mrs. Parker said, indicating the guest book, which lay open on the floor next to her. "My damned luck. I get to spend eternity with one book and it's a collection of signatures."

"I don't understand," Violet said.

"Percy Coates," she explained, referring to the erstwhile manager of the Algonquin, "was obsessed with two things—writers and death. He collected us in life, and tried his damnedest to collect us in death. His favorite medium, a Madame Lucescu, assured him that anyone who signed the book would be captured in it upon their death. But I'm the only one who stuck."

"Why you?"

"Long story, dear child. But it's my own stupid fault, I assure you."

Woollcott trotted into the room and parked himself at Violet's feet. He gave one of his quiet little yips, which was much more characteristic of him than the frantic barking he had been doing earlier. She bent to pick him up.

"And who is this charming creature?" Mrs. Parker asked.

"His name is Woollcott."

Violet saw the corners of Dorothy Parker's mouth curl as she recognized the name of her feisty friend and fellow theater critic.

"Then he must have quite a bite."

Violet couldn't suppress a smile, as a soft tingle of conspiratorial warmth relaxed her. "Not really," she said, "though my friend Carl might disagree."

"The handsome fellow with the messy hair?"

Violet nodded.

"In that case, I hope it was worse than his bark."

Yes, Violet thought. It's really her. She took a step forward for a closer look. "Are you . . . a spirit?"

"Something like that. Speaking of spirits, where's that drink?"

Violet wanted to touch her guest to see if she was flesh and blood, but she held back. "Can you do that? Can you . . . eat and drink and all that?"

"As long as the guest book is open I can take on a corporeal form.

All I have to do is hold still for a few minutes to let the matter settle together."

"And if the book is closed?"

Mrs. Parker shrugged. "It's rather like going to sleep."

Violet considered this for a moment. "Can you open and close the book whenever you want?"

"I cannot," Mrs. Parker said. "And there's the rub. I'm a damned prisoner. I can't even leave the confines of the room. Wherever the book is, I am. About that drink."

"Of course," Violet said. "Sorry." She didn't want to walk away, afraid that if she took her eyes off Dorothy Parker she would disappear. But she did as she was asked and went across the foyer to the living room, where Ivy and Neil kept their liquor cabinet.

"Gin okay?" Violet called.

"As long as it's not homemade."

Violet mixed gin and tonic in a highball glass. It was the first time she held a drink in her hand since the accident, and for a moment, she thought about *him*, the stranger in the pickup truck, and wondered what he had been drinking. They never did tell her the particulars, only that his blood alcohol level had been more than twice the legal limit. Back then, Violet had been burning to know every detail, as if that would help her make sense of it all. But, of course, it didn't really matter. Not one bit.

She came back into the study and handed the cocktail to her guest.

"Where's yours?" Mrs. Parker asked.

"Oh, I don't—"

"You're not going to make me drink alone, are you?"

Violet took the chair opposite her guest. "I'm sorry," she said. "I don't drink."

"I understand that's very fashionable now. Reformed drunks."

"Oh, I'm not a . . . an alcoholic. I just don't, that's all."

"Suit yourself," Mrs. Parker said, and took a dainty sip of her drink. "God, that's good. It's been so long."

"Is this the first time you've had a drink since . . ." She nodded toward the book.

"Since I died? Heavens, no. I've helped myself to more than a few cocktails behind the bar at the Algonquin, though I've learned to do it during the wee hours when no one's around." She took another sip. "I once made the mistake of materializing in front of a Guatemalan bellhop and the poor thing collapsed."

Violet nodded. She imagined that over the years there were times the guest book had been left open for days or even weeks, enabling Dorothy Parker to become a free spirit in the truest sense.

"Tell me about your young man," her guest said. "He seems like a faun's behind."

"Carl," Violet said. "He's not so bad, really. He's just . . . childish. And needy. And maybe a little lazy."

"I know the type. You'd probably wind up supporting him. What does he do?"

"He's an artist."

"God help us. I hope you're not in love with him."

"I was. Or at least I thought I was. But no. And I have to end it."

"Why don't you, then?"

She makes it sound so easy, Violet thought. "It's hard. I . . . I'm not very good with confrontations."

"So I noticed," Mrs. Parker said. "You seem to need a good deal of help."

"Is that why you came to me in the Algonquin?"

She took a few sips of her drink. "I knew I had to do something. And I couldn't very well crack you over the head with a bottle of whisky. So I took over. It would have worked, too, if you hadn't backed down."

"I know," she said. "I'm so ashamed."

Mrs. Parker waved away the remark. "People have done far worse, trust me."

"It's not just Carl, it's . . ." Violet paused and thought about the nervous meltdown in court that had cost her custody of her niece. And poor Delaney. She deserved better. "I've really made a mess of things."

"Join the club," Mrs. Parker said, and finished the last few drops in her glass. "Would you be a dear and fetch me another? And this time get one for yourself, as well. I insist."

"But—"

"I did you a favor, didn't I? At least I tried. Now, don't make a poor dead woman drink alone. One little cocktail never hurt anyone."

Violet took her guest's glass and went back to the bar. She did as she'd asked and poured herself a drink, too, despite the silent promise she had made at her sister's funeral. At the time it seemed like the best way to honor Ivy's memory. Now, though, she had to wonder. After all, it wasn't as if she was getting behind the wheel of a car. And anyway, maybe it would even do her some good. Maybe it would give her the courage to call Carl and end it once and for all. "Forgive me, Ivy," she whispered, as she took a small sip. "It's just this once."

"That's more like it," Mrs. Parker said when Violet come back with two drinks. "Now, have a seat and tell me more about how you've made a mess of things."

"I'd rather hear about you," Violet said. "I have so much to ask. I don't even know where to begin."

"Let's take turns, then," her guest said. "First me, then you."

Violet shrugged her assent.

Dorothy Parker scanned the room and peered out into the foyer. "Nice place. Is it yours?"

"It is now. My parents bought it figuring it would be a fun project. It needed a lot of work, and they were going to renovate. But . . . it didn't work out that way. Then after my mother died, my sister and her family moved in."

"When did your mother pass?"

"About ten years ago." It felt like yesterday. It felt like forever.

"So you were . . ."

"Twenty-seven," she said. Too young, she thought.

"Lucky girl."

"Lucky?"

"You had a mother, dear," Mrs. Parker said.

"Right, of course. You lost yours when you were very small."

"Yes, but she was quickly replaced by Lucrezia Borgia. Did your father remarry?"

"He's gone, too—about three years before my mother. That's why they never moved into this house. It was sudden. Dad was doing so well with his business, and this was where they were going to spend their golden years after he retired."

"You're from money, then?"

"Oh, no," Violet said, thinking about the wealthy people Dorothy Parker had known—old-money types with sprawling estates and servants' quarters. "At least not in the sense you're imagining. My dad was in manufacturing and did pretty well, but wasn't rich. Not *Gatsby* rich, anyway."

Mrs. Parker stroked her little poodle. "So you've read Scott."

"Scott," Violet repeated, smiling. "Of course. I mean, everyone has. You knew him, right? What was he like?"

"Handsome, bright. Charming when he wanted to be. I was never crazy about the wife."

"Zelda," Violet offered. "They say she was beautiful."

"In a vapid and petulant way, I suppose."

"What about Hemingway?"

"What about him?" Mrs. Parker asked.

"One of your biographers implied that you might have had a crush on him."

"Everyone had a crush on Hemingway," Mrs. Parker said. "He was a brute, but he had magnetism. And he could *write*."

"One of the truly great American novelists," Violet added.

"His novels were fine. But he could write the fucking bejeezus out of a short story."

Goose bumps. Her idol was talking about Ernest Hemingway . . . and cursing like a sailor, as she was known to do. People of every generation seemed to think their contemporaries practically invented swear words, but Dorothy Parker and her friends were dropping the f-bomb way back in the 1920s.

"What about the other members of the Algonquin Round Table?" Violet said. "Robert Benchley and George S. Kaufman and—"

"I believe it's my turn," Mrs. Parker said.

"Yes, of course. I'm sorry."

Mrs. Parker sighed. "Your apologies are starting to give me a headache."

"I'm—" Violet said, and caught herself. She remembered a conversation she had with Ivy a number of years ago. Her sister had suggested she try channeling a strong female movie character when she was feeling timid, but Violet had just reviewed *Kill Bill,* and all she could picture was Uma Thurman ripping out Daryl Hannah's eyeball with her fingers. That was a bit stronger than what she aspired to.

"You're right," she said to Dorothy Parker. "I have to work on that."

"Never mind," her guest said. "Tell me what you've made such a big mess of."

"That's a long story."

"All I've got is time. I'm rich with it. I'm the goddamn J. Paul Getty of time."

"Okay," Violet said, and took a deep breath, knowing it might feel good to talk to someone besides Carl and her lawyer about this. "A little over a year ago, my sister and her family were driving to visit friends of theirs upstate. But some loser with a pickup truck had decided that the best way to get through his impending dentist visit was to get plastered first. Only he never made it to his appointment. At eleven o'clock in the morning he got onto the Taconic Parkway headed in the wrong direction and had a head-on collision with a little family from Long Island. My brother-in-law was killed instantly."

Violet paused, remembering the call she got from the hospital. They didn't tell her over the phone that her sister was dead, but the coldest, darkest chill swept through her and she knew. In the months since, she could never remember the drive to the hospital or even the words the doctor used. But she could still feel his clammy hand on her shoulder. At the time, it was incomprehensible. How could this man be alive if the world had just ended?

Violet swallowed hard and continued. "My sister bled to death on the way to the hospital. Delaney, my niece, was in the backseat and survived with a broken arm and a chest contusion that did enough damage to her young heart to put her on medication for the rest of her life."

"And the drunk?"

"Dead. Shot through his windshield like a missile."

"That's one way to avoid a dentist appointment," Mrs. Parker said, and then shook her head and looked into her lap. "I'm rotten to the core."

"No, it's okay."

Mrs. Parker looked up. She was crying. "I'm so sorry," she said. She kissed Cliché on the top of the head. "Truly. Were you close with your sister?"

Violet took a sip of her drink. She didn't want to start crying. Not now. She wanted to get through this story and move on. "Very," she whispered, and drew a long, jagged breath. "They had been living here, in this house. So after the accident, I gave up my apartment and moved in to take care of my niece."

"So where is she?"

"That's the part I screwed up so badly. When the people at her school district told me I needed to be her legal guardian, I figured it was just a matter of paperwork and that a judge would rubber-stamp it. But Neil's parents—Delaney's grandparents—showed up at court with a lawyer. And not just any lawyer—a mountain of a guy with a shaved head and a European suit. He got right in my face and said, 'My clients just want what's best for the child, *Miss Epps* . . . or should I say *Ms.*?' He was so derisive, as if I could only be one of the two lowest forms of life— an unmarried woman or worse, a feminist. I realized later it was all theater meant to intimidate me, but at the time it worked like a charm. I freaked. I was so blindsided I couldn't talk. Not a word. I could barely even stand upright. So the judge set a date for a formal hearing to determine guardianship, and in the meantime . . . in the meantime he granted temporary custody to her grandparents." Violet paused to push at her cuticles. "It should have been me," she said softly. "She had stability here—her room, her house, her friends, her dog. If I had been able to utter a single word—"

"But you'll get her back, right?"

"Not if I have another meltdown in front of the judge."

"You have a lawyer now, yes?"

"I do, and she's good. But since Delaney's been living with her grandparents for a few months, it's not a slam dunk."

Mrs. Parker looked puzzled.

"A sure thing," Violet explained.

"I see," Mrs. Parker said. She petted Cliché as she considered this. "So you appear before the judge and go mute in terror and he decides you're too irrational to take care of a child and he grants permanent custody to the grandparents."

"That's right."

"Are you?"

"Irrational? No, I'm good with her. Maybe not perfect, but I'm learning. And Neil's parents are ghastly. Not that they don't mean well, but she's miserable there. Sandra, the grandmother, is a hypochondriac and a neurotic mess. And her husband, Malcolm, is in his own world. He used to be okay, but now that he's retired he devotes his spare time to a worthy cause—himself."

"What does the girl want?"

"She wants to move back here."

"Won't the judge honor her wishes?"

"The way I understand it," Violet said, "he'll take that into account, but it's not the deciding factor. So I'm going to need to do a hell of a lot better at the next hearing, or poor Delaney will be stuck."

"Well, then," Mrs. Parker said.

"Well, then what?"

"Well, then, we will just have to teach you to speak up for yourself." She held up her empty glass. "Let's have another drink."

Chapter 4

Teach her to speak up for herself? Yes, Violet thought. That was just what she needed. Of course, it wouldn't be easy. Violet had been suppressing her voice for decades.

She hadn't always been so timid. As a small child, Violet was so outspoken that her verbal brass became family legend. It was blown out of proportion, of course. To hear her relatives tell it, you would think she was the love child of Oscar Wilde and Fran Lebowitz—a neat trick in more ways than one. But in truth, she really *had* been a verbal prodigy, speaking in clear sentences at eighteen months, to the delight of her loving parents and any other adults who might be within earshot.

Unfortunately, the more praise she received, the angrier her older sister became. It was a perfect storm of sibling rivalry. By the time she turned five, Violet was running verbal rings around seven-year-old Ivy. Naturally, this infuriated the older sibling, who found every possible excuse to cut her little sister down. Still, Violet worshipped Ivy with an almost fanatical devotion.

Back then, she was too young to understand the reason for Ivy's animosity. In fact, Violet was so awed by her sister's talents that it never occurred to her that Ivy could be jealous. She just assumed everyone recognized that Ivy was the true genius. After all, making clever remarks was easy. But the ability to draw realistic horses and build intricate Lego structures and know right away where the jigsaw puzzle pieces went seemed like a miracle. Violet thought Ivy was a star.

And so the little sister continued to perform her verbal parlor tricks for the adults while dogging her sister for attention.

Until the day she went too far.

The girls were sitting at the kitchen table, doing homework. Ivy was struggling with her spelling, and their mother was trying to help her. Words like "dense" and "fence" were giving her trouble.

"Spell fence," their mother said.

"F-E-N-S-E?" asked Ivy.

"F-E-N-*C*-E," their mother corrected. "Now try to use it in a sentence with one of your other words."

"She's too *dense* to spell *fence*," Violet said, grinning. She expected her mother to roar with laughter, but she just looked at her crossly.

The next thing Violet knew, she was on the floor. Ivy had tipped over her chair and was standing over her, seething.

"Why'd you do that?" Violet said, rubbing the spot where the back of her head had hit the hard tile.

"I hate you!" Ivy said.

For a moment, Violet couldn't speak. She just lay there, her eyes filling with tears as she stared into her sister's angry face.

"I was just kidding," she said, but it was too late. Ivy had stormed out of the room. When Violet pounded on her bedroom door to try to apologize, she wouldn't answer. And the next morning at breakfast, Ivy acted as if Violet were invisible.

"I'm sorry!" Violet said. "Please talk to me. *Please!*"

But Ivy was stone-faced, staring at the back of her cereal box as if it were the only thing that mattered. She acted the same way that afternoon and evening. The next day was more of the same. And the next and the next. Ivy had completely stopped talking to her sister, and Violet was in agony. She cried. She pleaded. She apologized. Night after night she lay prostrate outside her sister's door, wailing and begging. But Ivy was resolute.

Their parents tried to intervene, but nothing they said or did would get Ivy to talk to her sister, or get Violet to stop her hysterics. She was no longer performing for her parents or even talking to her friends in school. Her existence had become pure misery, as nothing mattered but getting Ivy to speak to her again.

It was torture, pure torture. And little Violet knew that she had only herself to blame. The misery of self-loathing took root in her tender psyche and began to flourish. She was a horrible girl who had said a horrible thing, and now she was suffering horrible consequences.

One night, about three months later, as Violet lay in bed, her mother stroked her forehead and told her that if she left Ivy alone, she would come around.

"She will?" Violet said.

"I promise."

And so that's what she did. For the next two days, Violet didn't say a word to Ivy, and barely spoke at all to her parents.

Then, on the following day, a miracle happened. Violet was rummaging through the kitchen drawers, trying to find the Scotch tape she needed to complete a school project, when she heard a single word: "Here."

She looked up and saw her sister holding out her hand, the roll of Scotch tape resting on her palm like a peace offering.

And that was it. Within days, their relationship was back to normal, except for one thing—Violet promised herself she would never make a wisecrack again.

It was hard only for the first year or so. But every time she slipped, Ivy punished her with icy silence, and so Violet learned to keep it all locked inside a cold vault of shame. For a while, she missed the attention she used to get from the grown-ups. But even that paled in comparison to the joy of being back in Ivy's good graces.

Of course, as she matured and Ivy's flaws, shortcomings, and human frailties became clear to her, Violet stopped worshipping her sister as a goddess and they became friends on the equal, if sometimes rocky, footing of adulthood. Still, the fear of her own verbal power never diminished. And although a grown-up Violet was well aware that this single childhood trauma had been the cause of her social anxiety, her fears persisted.

Today, though, she wasn't going to think about that. She was simply going to bond with her Dorothy Parker in the one way she knew would do the trick. Violet took the bottle of gin from the liquor cabinet and poured two more drinks. And then, instead of putting it back on the shelf, carried it with her into the study, where her thirsty friend awaited her.

Chapter 5

The first thing Violet noticed was the grittiness beneath her lids. Then the pounding in her head. And finally the impossible stiffness in her neck. What the hell kind of position had she slept in? She opened her eyes and realized she'd spent the night passed out on the settee in the study. Only she couldn't quite put her finger on the reason.

Then she remembered. Or remembered most of it, anyway.

Woollcott was curled up on her chest, asleep, legs twitching in the happy frolics of doggy dreamland. She waited until his muscles settled and gently put him aside. Then she sat up and looked around. The wingback chair was empty, and the guest book was on the coffee table, closed.

Dorothy Parker had vanished.

Violet considered opening the book, just to be sure what happened yesterday wasn't her imagination. But she needed coffee first. She wasn't learning anything until she quieted the pounding in her head.

She shuffled into the kitchen and brewed enough for two, which might have felt silly if she wasn't so groggy. But she really *had* spent the night drinking with Dorothy Parker, hadn't she?

Violet leaned against the counter drinking her coffee, waiting for the caffeine to kick in and dissolve her cobwebs. The phone rang—too loudly—and she checked the caller ID: Carl. Damn. Tomorrow was move-in day, and she hadn't yet told him he wasn't welcome. Or, more precisely, she had, but not emphatically enough to get through his granite skull. She let the machine pick up, as she was still too foggy to deal with him.

Hey, babe, it's me. Where are you? Oh, maybe you left to get Delaney. Call you later.

Delaney. Right, it was Saturday. Violet looked at the clock. She didn't have much time.

She finished her coffee, poured two more, and carried them back into the study, still barely awake. Her plan was to set the cups down on the coffee table, then place the book on the chair, gently open it, and stand back. But when she reached the room she nearly dropped the cups.

"Good morning, dear." Mrs. Parker sat in the wingback chair, stroking Cliché and looking not the least bit hungover.

Surprised and confused, Violet tried to focus. Was Dorothy Parker able to materialize at will? Hadn't she explained that she couldn't appear unless the book was open? Then Violet realized a certain furry companion had nosed open the book the day before, and must have done it again.

"Woollcott?" Violet asked, indicating the open book on the coffee table.

"It seems I have a fan."

Violet handed her guest a cup of coffee and lowered herself into the other chair. Woollcott jumped onto her lap, and the two women sat facing each other, drinking their coffee and stroking their little dogs.

"What happened last night?" Violet said. "Who shut the book? It's all a blur."

"It was you, my dear."

"Me?" Violet closed her eyes, trying to remember. "God, I'm sorry," she finally said. "I guess that was rude."

"Not at all," Mrs. Parker said. "It was at my request. I finally found the perfect remedy for a hangover. I disappear, and when I return, I'm new again."

"Neat trick."

"Nevertheless, I don't recommend it. Death can be so"—she paused to blow across her hot coffee—"*inconvenient*. And yet it still beats living in Hollywood."

Violet laughed, remembering that Dorothy Parker had spent a number of years on the West Coast, writing movie scripts and fighting with studio heads. Once, in a snide reference to the power wielded by one of the most imperious moviemakers, Dorothy Parker had quipped that the streets in Hollywood were paved with Goldwyn.

Still later, she referred to another studio as "Twentieth Century Fucks."

Violet asked Dorothy Parker if she wanted something to eat.

"No need," she said. "That's another thing about death. Digestion becomes a mere nuisance." She looked hard at Violet. "Forgive me for not inquiring sooner, but were you ever married?"

"I'm divorced. Why do you ask?"

"Trying to figure out if I should call you *Miss* or *Mrs.*"

"I prefer *Ms.*, which doesn't signify either married or single. But you can just call me Violet."

"I shall call you Ms. Epps. And you may call me Mrs. Parker."

Violet bit her lip to hide her disappointment. She thought they would be friends.

"Oh, don't look so glum," Mrs. Parker said. "Some of my closest friends called me Mrs. Parker their whole lives. It's one of those customs that keeps the world a civilized place. And when you're as beastly inside as I am, you need all the civilization you can get."

The explanation appeased Violet, who related to the notion of feeling beastly inside. Perhaps it was one of the reasons she had always felt connected to this great lady. "Mrs. Parker," she said, trying it out, and decided it did indeed feel civilized.

Later, when Violet told her new houseguest that she had to leave to pick up her niece, Mrs. Parker insisted that the guest book remain open.

"So many books in this room," she said, "and it's been a long time since I've read." Violet couldn't see what harm it would do, especially since Mrs. Parker was confined to the study, so she agreed.

Now Violet sat in her parked car in front of the Webers' house, where her niece, Delaney, was currently living. She tapped twice on her horn, hoping Delaney would rush out so they could make a quick getaway. Any time Violet could pull away from the curb without having to face Sandra, she felt like throwing confetti.

Otherwise, she felt like throwing up.

The front door opened and Delaney ran out, backpack hooked over one shoulder, hair flying around her face. It was the same dark brown as her Aunt Violet's, but thick and wavy like her mother's. Violet's shiny hair hung straight and thin. And while she knew many people envied the silkiness of her long tresses—or at least said they did—Violet always coveted the full-bodied mane her sister had passed on to beautiful Delaney.

"Hurry up," Delaney said, lowering herself into the passenger seat and slamming the door, "before Lady Munchausen and Lord Sunkist come out."

The girl came up with new nicknames for her grandparents every few weeks. The current pair referred to her grandmother's neurotic hovering and her grandfather's newly acquired orange complexion—the result of an apparent addiction to self-tanning products.

The nickname habit had materialized after the accident. Delaney simply stopped using real names. For anyone. Her cardiologist,

Dr. Nichimov, became *Dr. Knock 'Em Off.* Her impulsive friend Ashley became *Rashly.* Others were less clever but just as steadfast. A close pal named Cynthia Chu became *C.C.*, and her Aunt Violet was simply *V.*

The only people she called by their real first names were her parents, Neil and Ivy. But, of course, that was to avoid referring to them as Mom and Dad.

Her therapist had explained that it was Delaney's way of distancing herself from emotional attachments. There was simply too much pain for the child to deal with. Violet was instructed not to press the issue—the girl would eventually come around on her own. So when Delaney started calling her *Aunt* V, instead of simply V, Violet was thrilled. Even an inch of progress felt like cause for celebration.

"You okay?" Violet asked.

"Better than you," Delaney said. "You look like crap, Aunt V."

"Good to see you, too. Buckle, please."

Before Violet could put the car in gear and go, Sandra scurried out the door, yelling, "Wait! Wait!" Violet gritted her teeth and watched as the short, bosomy woman ran toward them. The wind, Violet noticed, was no match for Sandra's Aqua Net, as her brittle, wheat-colored hair remained stationary.

"Just go," Delaney said.

"I can't."

"Shit," the girl whispered.

Sandra tapped on Delaney's window and pantomimed rolling it down.

Delaney pressed the button to open her window. "Are you lassoing something?" she asked her grandmother.

"What?"

Violet jabbed her niece with her elbow. "How are you, Sandra?" she said.

Sandra ignored her question. "I've had enough of your sass today, young lady," she said to Delaney.

"Let me move back home with Aunt V and I'll take my sass with me."

Sandra folded her arms. "She has a piano lesson at eleven tomorrow."

"Her piano lessons are on Thursday," Violet said.

"We changed her schedule."

"Why?" Violet asked, irritated. A Sunday-morning lesson would cut into their time together.

Sandra tsked. "Just make sure she's there on time."

Violet rolled her eyes. When had she ever been irresponsible about getting Delaney anyplace on time? "Of course," she said.

"The piano teacher hates when she's late."

"Don't worry," Violet said, her jaw tensing. "She won't be late."

"I'm not supposed to worry!" the older woman said to the heavens, and then addressed her granddaughter. "Did you pack your digoxin?"

"Duh."

"Don't forget to take it with dinner."

"I won't."

"Remind her," Sandra said to Violet.

"I will," Violet said.

"Promise?"

Violet gripped the steering wheel so tightly she felt like she could yank it from the car. She wasn't going to play this game—the game where Sandra is the only one responsible enough to care about Delaney's welfare.

"Chill out, Butch," Delaney said.

Sandra ignored the insulting nickname. "Promise me," she repeated to Violet, making it sound more like a command than a request.

Shove it up your sass, Violet thought. *I'm* the one who slept on the recliner in her hospital room for four straight days when we didn't know if she would make it. *I'm* the one who took her to three different pediatric cardiologists to find the best person to treat her. *I'm* the one who worked with a therapist to help coax her back into the world, inch by excruciating inch, when she wanted to curl up and die with grief. So don't make me *promise* to give her the goddamned medicine she needs for her poor broken heart.

"See you tomorrow," Violet said, hoping Sandra would back off from the car so she could pull away.

Delaney saw something that made her sink in her seat. "God, let's *go.*"

Violet looked toward the house to see what her niece was reacting to, and there stood Malcolm, smiling broadly enough to flash his newly bleached teeth against a glowing artificial complexion. God, he was an idiot, but so happy and guileless Violet couldn't help but have a soft spot for him.

"Wait a minute," he shouted, taking a careful step forward.

"What's on his feet?" Violet asked. He was shuffling forward in what looked like paper slippers.

"He just got a *pedicure*," Delaney said, rolling her eyes. "He gets *pedicures* now." She pronounced the word like it was covered with drain scum. "Could you gag?"

Yes, I could, Violet thought, feeling a little queasy at the image of some poor woman on her knees scraping at Malcolm's feet.

"Seen any good movies lately?" Malcolm said, when he reached the car.

It was his standard greeting to Violet, and, apparently, it never ceased to amuse him.

Violet forced a smile. "How've you been, Malcolm?"

"I got a new car," he said, pointing to a red SUV in the driveway.

"That's *yours*?" Violet was surprised. As long as she had known him, Malcolm never drove anything but pre-owned Lincolns.

"It's a RAV4," he said, beaming.

"I don't think I've ever seen one that color before."

"Salsa red. Special order." He looked as if he might burst with pride.

"Well, that's great. Congrats."

"Can we *go*?" Delaney asked.

Malcolm laughed. "Teenagers. Always in a hurry." He patted the top of the car as a signal to take off. "You two kids have fun," he said, and stepped back.

As Violet pulled away from the curb she heard Sandra yell, "Don't forget the digoxin!"

Chapter 6

"He's so clueless he can't even get a midlife crisis right," Delaney said when they were under way. "I mean, a RAV4? That's a lesbian car. Doesn't he know he's supposed to get a sports car when he's trying to impress chicks?"

Violet glanced at her niece and then back at the road. "A lesbian car? Where do you get this stuff?"

"It's common knowledge."

"Doubt that," Violet said, laughing. "And what do you mean, 'trying to impress chicks'? Malcolm is trying to impress chicks?"

"What do *you* think?"

Violet didn't consider herself naive, but it had never occurred to her that Malcolm might be on the make. "I think he's too impressed with himself to worry about what anyone else thinks," she said.

"Yesterday he came to my track meet. I wanted to *die.*"

"He's not *that* bad," Violet said.

"Aunt V, he was wearing *skinny jeans.*"

Violet almost did the driving equivalent of a spit-take, but somehow she managed to stay on the road. "He was not!"

"He was!"

She patted her niece's knee, laughing. "At least he's happy."

Delaney folded her arms and got quiet. Violet waited a few minutes for her to say something and finally asked if she was okay.

"Everyone deserves to be happy but me."

Coming from another kid it might have sounded like ordinary ado-lescent petulance, but Dr. Susan, Delaney's therapist, had explained that overcoming survivor's guilt was often a long process.

"Of course you deserve to be happy," Violet said.

"Then why am I living at Casa de la Puke?"

You shouldn't be, Violet thought. You should be living with me.

After the accident, Violet dropped everything in her life for Del-aney. There wasn't a moment of soul-searching about it, or even time to grieve her old lifestyle. She simply abandoned her Manhattan apartment to move into her sister's house and try her damnedest to give Delaney what she needed. Of course, what she needed most was the one thing Violet couldn't deliver—her loving parents. So she did everything else—took a hiatus from work, ignored phone calls from well-meaning friends, stopped everything and anything that didn't relate directly to Delaney's well-being. She barely even ate for three months.

And what did the Webers do? They hired a lawyer.

Of course, it wasn't just the unfairness that brought Violet's blood to near boiling, it was the threat to her niece's fragile progress. Violet knew, without equivocation, that Delaney was better off with her than she was with the Webers. Nothing else mattered.

She counted silently to ten so that she could respond calmly to her niece's question.

"You know I'm not allowed to talk about that, Del," she said.

She and the Webers were under strict orders from the judge not to discuss the custody battle with Delaney. It was tragic, because the girl needed to hear that her aunt was fighting for her. But if Violet brought it up she could jeopardize her case, and that would hurt even more.

Delaney breathed on the window and drew a frowny face with her finger.

"Woollcott'll be excited to see you," Violet said. The dog was her secret weapon. Delaney loved that little creature with all her heart, and the idea of seeing him was often enough to lift her from her funk.

"I brought him a new fish," she said. "Neon green."

Woollcott's favorite toy was a squeaky plastic clown fish, and Delaney adored going to the pet store to find more treasures for him.

"He'll love it," Violet said.

"Hey, what happened with Vincent van Loser?" Delaney said, using the nickname she had coined for Carl the first time she saw his artwork. "Did you give him the ax?"

"Not exactly," Violet said, and knew she needed to rectify that as soon as possible. Somehow she would have to find the strength to make it crystal clear. He could not move in. Not tomorrow. Not ever.

When they got to the house, Violet asked her niece to drag the trash cans into the backyard. It was a ruse so Violet could slip inside and close Dorothy Parker back into the guest book before Delaney came in.

As soon as Violet opened the front door she knew something wasn't right. From the foyer she could see straight into the study on the right, which looked empty. But there was noise coming from the living room across the hall. It sounded like humming.

Violet walked toward the sound and there was Dorothy Parker, laid out on the sofa, Cliché curled up in a ball by her feet. On the floor in front of her was a broken glass, an empty bottle of Beefeater gin, and the Algonquin guest book. A bottle of scotch was propped up next to her on the cushion.

"What the hell?" Violet said.

Dorothy Parker turned toward her, only one eye barely open. "Ms. Epps," she said, spreading her arms wide. "You have a very well-stocked bar, but you are going to need to purchase more gin."

Violet was horrified and perplexed. How did Dorothy Parker leave the study and get into this room? "I don't understand," she said.

Mrs. Parker struggled to sit up. "There's nothing wrong with scotch," she said. "But if one is drinking gin, one should *stay* with gin. It's just so ghastly to run out. One should *never* run out of gin." As she righted herself, the bottle of scotch next to her tipped over and began spilling onto the cushion. Violet quickly grabbed it and placed it on the bar.

Mrs. Parker didn't see the maneuver, and felt around the sofa for the bottle. "Hey, where did the scotch go?"

"How did you get out of the study?" Violet asked.

"I go where the book goes," Mrs. Parker said.

"But I thought you couldn't move it."

"I can't," she said, and reached toward the book to illustrate how her hand went right through it. "But I have a trick. Watch this." Dorothy Parker clapped her hands at Woollcott. "Come here, come here, little doggie." She picked him up, and Violet stepped forward in case she needed to snatch the dog to protect him from her drunk guest's hands. But Mrs. Parker simply nudged Woollcott against the book so that it inched forward.

"See?" she said. "My little friend here helps me out." She put him down and patted his head. "Good boy."

Violet heard the front door open and her niece call out. "Woollcott? Aunt V?"

Alarmed, Violet grabbed the guest book. "Sorry, Mrs. Parker," she said, and slammed the cover shut, closing her visitor inside.

Delaney appeared at the door of the room just as Dorothy Parker and her little dog disappeared. She stooped to pick up Woollcott, who had trotted over to her, wagging his tail madly. "Woolly Woolly Woollcott," she said, petting and kissing him. She surveyed the room. "Holy crap, Aunt V."

"Bad, huh? I, uh . . . had a few friends over last night."

Delaney picked up the empty gin bottle and turned it upside down to illustrate how dry it was. "A *few*?"

"Heavy drinkers."

"It stinks." She leaned over and picked up the Algonquin guest book. "And what's this?"

Violet grabbed it from her. "Nothing," she said. "A friend left it there. Why don't you take Woollcott for a nice walk and I'll get this place cleaned up."

Chapter 7

With Delaney gone, Violet paced up and down the hall, holding tightly to the phone, telling herself she could do this without Dorothy Parker's help. She would just tell Carl she was breaking up with him and that he couldn't move in tomorrow. If he objected she would stand firm. *We're done*, she would say. *Fini. The End. No epilogue. No sequel.*

But what if she couldn't? What if she froze . . . again? She pictured standing at the front door with Delaney in the morning as Carl pulled up with his moving van. What kind of message would she be sending to her niece about sticking up for yourself?

In some ways, the breakup with her husband, Andrew, had been easier. But, of course, she had gone through all her emotional trauma in the months leading up to the separation. After the tragic result of her pregnancy, Andrew had made the cruel decision that he didn't want children after all. It ripped through Violet like a knife. How could he change his mind about wanting a baby? How could he possibly not want to try again? At first, Violet tried to be understanding. She thought it was the grief talking and that he would change his mind when enough time had passed. But he didn't; all the talking and probing and crying went nowhere.

She went to her sister and brother-in-law for help, and Ivy had said, "I think it's a control thing. He likes being the one to call the shots, and this gives him ultimate power over the relationship."

Violet couldn't disagree. Not completely. But it didn't feel like the whole story.

"Maybe he decided he wants you to himself," Neil said. "Maybe he realizes a baby would take your attention away from him."

If only, Violet thought. Deep down, she knew that Andrew had started pulling away from her even before she got pregnant. And as the weeks went by, his stubbornness turned to animosity, until she could no longer ignore the reality: Andrew wasn't rejecting the idea of a baby. He was rejecting her.

And so, when she finally approached him about splitting up, she knew there would be no tears, no arguments, no ugly scenes. Indeed, he merely nodded and said that yes, it was probably for the best. That night he packed a suitcase and left. When she got home from work the next day, more of his things were gone. Two weeks later he took an apartment and sent Violet an e-mail listing the furniture, electronics, and other household items he thought he deserved. Violet wanted to be fair, but it seemed like he was trying to get his hands on every-thing that was new and expensive. She forwarded the e-mail to her sister, who replied, "Hire a lawyer *today*. Then change the locks and tell Andrew to fuck off."

And that's what she did, except for the part about telling Andrew to fuck off. On her lawyer's advice, she ignored the e-mail, and held on to everything in the apartment until they met with a mediator.

Looking back, it seemed like she had been so strong then. But in truth, she was still depressed from the loss of the baby, and Andrew's presence had only added to her misery. Besides, she felt like she was doing Andrew a favor. Clearly, he wanted out.

Thirteen months later—just when Violet was starting to feel like she might actually be able to get on with her life—she heard from a mutual friend that Andrew was engaged to a striking veterinarian named Deanna . . . and expecting a child. Violet tried to tell herself that she didn't care, that it had nothing to do with her, but the idea that he rushed headlong into the very life he had rejected with Violet felt like an assault. It was simply too much to bear. After spending a week in tears, she told her friends she was done with men. Done. They simply weren't worth the pain.

Then she met Carl.

At the time, he seemed like the antidote to Andrew—the kind of guy who would never hurt her. And now here she was, gearing up to hurt *him*.

Violet's heart felt heavy with guilt. She should have known from the start that this relationship wouldn't last. But was it all her fault? Surely it was opportunistic of Carl to try move the relationship to the next level when he knew she was in too fragile an emotional state to make any decisions about her life.

"Goddamn it," Violet said out loud. Guilt, she knew, was the worst reason to stay in a relationship. She went into the study and opened the guest book. Then she stood back as Dorothy Parker materialized in the wingback chair.

"Well, hello," Mrs. Parker said, as she smoothed her hair. "That was an abrupt dismissal."

"You're sober," Violet said.

"Fresh as a newly slaughtered lamb. Did I miss anything good?

"I'm so sorry," Violet said. "I had to act fast. My niece is here, and I can't let her see you. The kid's been through hell, and I'm trying to protect her as much as I can under the circumstances. This might be . . . traumatic. And also . . ." Violet pushed at her cuticles. How could she possibly tell her hero that she wanted her to behave herself? Who was she to admonish the great Dorothy Parker?

"Yes?"

"It's just . . . the drinking, the mess—"

"You think I've behaved badly."

"Um . . ."

Mrs. Parker waved off Violet's concerns. "Fine. I'll try to be as proper as a virgin when the child's around. You know what a virgin is, don't you? It's a mythical creature created in Hollywood and played by actresses who sleep with the casting director. But if you don't trust me, just shut the book and I'll be gone."

Violet took the chair opposite her guest. "Actually," she said, "I need your help. I'm sorry to do this, but I don't have much time. I need to call Carl and tell him he can't move in tomorrow. If you could just . . . just tell me what to say if I freeze. Would you do that?"

"Sounds like more fun than I've had since Calvin Coolidge was president. I could even make the call, if you wish."

"No, no," Violet said, holding up the phone in her hand. "I need to do this myself. But just so you know, I'll have to shut the book abruptly if I hear Delaney coming."

Violet dialed Carl's number and was relieved when his answering machine picked up. It might be tacky to dump someone via voice mail, but she was desperate. Besides, she had tried to do it right, but he wouldn't listen. Now he would have to. Violet put her hand over the receiver and told Mrs. Parker she would be leaving a message.

"It's Violet," she began.

"You can't move in tomorrow," Mrs. Parker said.

"You can't move in tomorrow," Violet repeated.

"I never want to see you again," Mrs. Parker said.

Violet shook her head. "It's over between us."

There was a click, and Violet heard Carl's voice. "What's the matter?" he said. "I'm in the middle of packing."

"I'm sorry," Violet said. "I'm sorry to do this, but I don't want you moving in. Period. I'm breaking up with you. It's over between us."

There. She said it, and it couldn't be clearer. Dorothy Parker had given her the strength she needed.

"Why are you doing this?" he said. "What's wrong?"

"No apologizing," said Mrs. Parker, who had surmised that Carl picked up. "Just tell him you loathe him. Tell him he's a lousy lay."

"Us," Violet said. "*We're* wrong. I'm . . . I'm not in love with you."

"Violet, honey—"

"No," she said. "No more discussions. It's over." Violet sat up a little taller. Her hands were trembling, but she was proud of herself. She was doing it. She was standing up to Carl.

"But I rented the truck. I bought twenty cartons."

"I'm sorry," Violet said. "I'll reimburse you."

Mrs. Parker rose. "Don't you dare!"

"What's that?" Carl said. "Is someone there?"

"It's the radio," Violet said. "NPR."

"Listen," Carl said, "I'm going to finish packing a couple more boxes, and then I'll drive over there so we can talk about this in person."

"No, don't come over."

"If he does, you'll call the police," Mrs. Parker said.

Violet stood and started to pace. "Please, Carl. Don't come here."

Mrs. Parker took a step toward her. "Don't plead with him. Just tell him if he shows up here the police will be waiting with handcuffs."

"I already told my parents I'm moving out," he said.

"They'll understand," Violet said.

"C'mon, baby. This is such an important step for me. For us, I mean."

"You were right the first time," she said.

He lowered his register to what he clearly thought was a sexy baritone. "I love you," he said. "You've been under so much stress. I know this is a big change, and it probably brings up a lot of stuff about losing your sister. But I'm here for you."

"Don't bring Ivy into this," Violet said.

"I know you miss her," he said. "I know it's hard."

Goddamn him. Of course she missed her. Of course it was hard. After her parents passed, Ivy was all she had. Losing her was so incomprehensible that when Violet first moved into the house, she could feel Ivy's presence in every room. And lately, well, she still felt Ivy's presence, but she could sometimes go hours at a time without thinking about her.

Now Carl had to go and bring her up, and the knot of pain in her belly was unfurling and spreading through her. She didn't even have to close her eyes to see Ivy's smile. Ivy was everywhere. Everywhere but nowhere.

It was so goddamned unfair.

"You're crying," Carl said.

Violet sniffed. Of course she was crying.

"It's hard," she choked out.

"I know it is, baby. I'm on my way. You need a hug."

Violet lost her bearings. She sank back into the chair, weeping. Almost immediately she felt a strange tingling in her feet that quickly turned to burning. She looked up expecting to see Dorothy Parker, but she was gone. And yet Violet could sense her very close. In fact, oh, dear God, she was entering her! Violet was seized with the same soul-sick nausea she had felt in the Algonquin, only this time it moved from her toes upward. She curled into a ball and moaned.

"You sound terrible," Carl said.

Within seconds, the nausea compressed itself into a tiny physical presence, like a marble lodged behind her navel. Violet uncurled and opened her eyes. Everything in the dimly lit room seemed to have sharper corners and higher contrast, like the world had switched to high-def. She craved a cigarette. She felt . . . alive.

"Are you still there?" Carl asked.

"I am," she said. "And if you set foot within fifty yards of this place I will have you shot and stuffed."

"That's not funny," he said.

"That's one thing we can agree on."

"I'm coming over."

"You most certainly are not," she said.

"You need me."

"Like I need arsenic."

"I'll be right there," he said.

"I'm locking the door."

"I have a key."

"I changed the lock."

"I'll use the window if I have to."

She crossed her legs, examined her nails. "That's breaking and entering."

"You need a *hug*."

Violet suppressed a yawn. "That's assault."

"What's the matter, baby? I thought you loved me."

"Not only do I not love you," she said, "but I loathe the sound of your voice, abhor your appearance, and am not entirely thrilled with your sexual performance. Furthermore, your artwork is uninspired, and you have bad breath. Have I made myself clear?"

"I guess so."

"You *guess* so?" Violet could hear the strength in her own voice. She was powerful, intimidating. She was Meryl Streep in *The Devil Wears Prada*. She was Glenn Close in *Fatal Attraction*. She was Faye Dunaway as Joan Crawford. Or Joan Crawford as herself.

Hell, she was the Terminator.

"I mean . . . yes," Carl stammered.

"That's better. Now lose my number, forget my address, and run along like a good little boy. We will not speak again. Good-bye, Carl."

Violet hung up the phone and rose, feeling tall and tough. She knew she should close Dorothy Parker back into the book, but she wanted to enjoy the exhilaration of power for just a few more moments. Then she heard a tiny voice behind her.

"Aunt V?"

Violet turned and saw her niece at the door, a confused look in her eyes.

"How long have you been standing there?" Violet asked.

Delaney leaned over to unclip Woollcott's leash. Though Violet yearned to ride the crest of this heady feeling awhile longer, she knew she was treading dangerous waters, and she couldn't risk frightening her fragile niece. So while the girl was distracted, she quickly shut the Algonquin guest book, which was accompanied by a jolt that made her gasp—it felt as if the marble in her belly flew up her gullet and out her mouth. Immediately, the room got duller and she felt depleted.

"Was that really Carl?" Delaney asked, as she scratched Woollcott behind the ears.

"Yes."

Delaney lifted her head, smiling. "Wow."

" 'Wow'?"

"I didn't know you had it in you, Aunt V!"

Violet had to sit down. This wasn't the reaction she was expecting. She was sure the Jekyll-and-Hyde transformation would terrify her niece, but it hadn't.

The kid was proud of her.

Chapter 8

"Do you have your sheet music?" Violet asked, as she loaded the breakfast plates into the dishwasher. The girl was sitting on the floor, playing with Woollcott. The neon fish was a hit.

"It's in my binder," Delaney said, as she pulled the plastic toy from the dog's mouth. She tossed it to the corner of the kitchen, and he dashed for it.

It was Sunday morning, and they were getting ready to leave for Delaney's lesson. Earlier, the girl had told her aunt she was working on a piece she would play at the upcoming recital but wouldn't say which song it was. She wanted it to be a surprise.

Violet glanced over her shoulder and saw Delaney's binder on the kitchen table. She went back to doing the dishes. "Why were your lessons switched to Sundays?"

"Good boy," Delaney said to Woollcott. "I don't know. I think His Royal Orangeness was busy on Thursday nights or something. But all he ever does is stay in the basement on his computer. And Lady Munchausen doesn't drive if it's dark out. Or raining. Or if there's a cloud anywhere in the Western Hemisphere."

Violet smiled. Delaney reminded her so much of herself as a kid. Or, rather, the kid she would have been if she wasn't afraid to open her mouth.

The doorbell rang, and Violet stopped what she was doing. Who could be dropping by on a Sunday morning? Please, God, she thought, don't let it be Carl.

Delaney was watching her, so she tried to appear nonchalant as she shook the water off a plate and slipped it into the dishwasher. She dried her hands on a towel.

"I'll get it," Delaney said.

"Let me," Violet said.

The girl smiled, excited. "You think it's Vincent van Loser?" she said, following her aunt to the door. "I'd love to see you give it to him again!"

Violet took a deep breath. *I thought I made myself perfectly clear,* she rehearsed in her head. She wasn't going to let him in, and she wasn't going to back down. She swung open the door.

"Malcolm!" she said, letting out a long breath. "This is a—"

"Oh, no," Delaney said. "Not *him.*"

"Hello, ladies." He grinned, and in the morning light Violet noticed that his teeth were blue-white. His orange complexion was leathery but so well moisturized he looked sautéed.

"What are you doing here?" the girl asked.

"I came to pick you up for your piano lesson."

"But I was going to take her," Violet said, trying to make sense of Malcolm's sudden appearance. Why would he drive all the way from Smithtown when the piano teacher was so much closer to Violet's house? And with all that greasy lotion, how did he keep from sliding out of the driver's seat? "It's less than five miles from here," she said.

"I know," he said, "but I have an errand to run in the area, so I thought I'd help out."

Violet looked past him at the red car by the curb and figured it out. The poor guy was looking for any excuse to zip around in his new RAV4.

"I'm going with Aunt V," Delaney said.

"But I'm already here," he said.

Violet was torn. Delaney wanted her to send him away, but he looked so pathetic standing there, freshly combed and oiled, smelling of aftershave and other grooming products, and so eager to help.

"Please," Delaney said, tugging on Violet's sleeve. "I don't want to go with him. The last two times he was late picking me up and I was just standing there on the sidewalk like forever."

"I promise I won't be late this time," Malcolm said.

Violet got an idea. "I'll tell you what," she said to her niece, "you go with your grandfather, and then this afternoon I'll take you to a screening."

Delaney always wanted to come with her aunt to movie screenings. It was a perfectly acceptable thing to do, as critics were invited to bring a guest. But the scheduling seldom worked out, as Violet usually attended showings during school hours. Besides, so many of the films were rated R that bringing Delaney wasn't an option she would consider. Today, however, there was a scheduled screening of a new PG-13 film—a comedy with Steve Carell that the kid might actually like.

"Really?" Delaney said. "In the city?"

Violet smiled. "We'll leave right after lunch."

And that was it. Violet had made both grandfather and granddaughter happy. A perfect compromise. She kissed her niece good-bye and went back to finishing the breakfast dishes.

A few minutes later she noticed that Delaney's binder was still on the kitchen table. The kid would surely need it for her lesson, so Violet grabbed her car keys and went to deliver it.

Delaney's piano lessons were in her teacher's home in an old North Shore neighborhood where the streets were small and the houses packed tightly together. As Violet drove through the winding blocks, she noticed something odd—a brand-new salsa-red RAV4 in the driveway of an unfamiliar home a few blocks from the teacher's address. Violet slowed down. It was almost certainly Malcolm's car. What was he doing here? Did he have a friend in the neighborhood?

Violet shrugged it off. After all, the guy was entitled to have acquaintances in this town, right?

After delivering the binder, Violet went back into the car to wait for Delaney to finish her lesson, as there was no sense in going home. She called Malcolm's cell to tell him not to bother coming back for the girl, but he didn't pick up and his voice mailbox was full.

Violet toyed with the idea of driving back to where she saw his red car and knocking on the door to the house, but thought it might be intrusive. So she called Sandra.

She explained the situation with the piano book and Malcolm's cell phone, but left out the part about spotting his SUV in a neighbor's driveway, as she was curious to see if Sandra knew that Malcolm was paying a call on someone.

"Do you know where he might be?" Violet asked. "If he's visiting with a friend, maybe you could call him and tell him not to bother coming back?"

"There's no way for me to reach him. He usually just drives around after he drops Delaney at her lessons."

"He does?"

"Sometimes he goes up the beach, takes off his shoes, and walks around. One time he did that and came home with only one sock, the old coot."

Interesting, thought Violet. *Very* interesting.

Sandra sighed. "Sometimes I think he looks for any excuse to get out of the house."

There was a note of sadness in her voice, and Violet actually felt sorry for her. "I'm sorry," she said. "That's too—"

"Never mind," Sandra said, recovering her bristly composure. "I . . . I was just kidding."

Oh, no, you weren't, Violet thought, sensing, for the first time, that there was trouble in the marriage. And as hard as it was to imagine Malcolm with a girlfriend, the pieces were starting to create a picture that resembled what Delaney had been saying about her grandfather being on the make.

Of course, it was entirely possible someone else had a special-order RAV4 in salsa red. Not likely, but possible. Violet looked at her watch. There was still more than enough time to drive to the neighbor's house and peek inside the car to see if there were any clues to the owner's identity.

So she turned the ignition key and drove the short distance to where she had seen the vehicle. She parked and walked right up to the tinted windows so she could peer inside. And sure enough, there was a paper slipper on the floor—the kind they gave you at nail salons.

That night, after Delaney had gone, Violet sat in front of her laptop, trying to compose her review. She was having trouble concentrating, as her mind kept going back to seeing Malcolm's car in the driveway. The evidence pointed so strongly to an affair, and yet . . . it was Malcolm. Goofy, pathetic Malcolm. Surely there was another explanation.

Violet decided to kick it around with her new friend, and a few minutes later they were face-to-face in the wingback chairs. Violet had a cup of tea, and Mrs. Parker was making do with scotch from the not-yet-restocked bar.

"I disagree," said Mrs. Parker, as she sipped her drink. "I add two plus two, and I get Grandpa, who can't keep his pants on."

"You might not feel that way if you met Malcolm," Violet said. "He's so . . . guileless."

"He has a dick, hasn't he?"

A dick? Violet smiled, amused by Mrs. Parker's euphemism. The modern-sounding term must have been around for generations.

"I try not to think about that," she said.

"Trust me, the man is cheating."

Violet shuddered at the thought. "You know what? It doesn't even matter. It's none of my business."

"It may well be your business," Mrs. Parker said. "Don't you think it would help your custody case if it turned out the grandparents were of questionable moral character?"

Violet considered that. Certainly in Dorothy Parker's day an extramarital affair would be scandalous enough to make all the difference. Today, though, it would constitute only a single round of ammunition in a lawyer's arsenal.

"Maybe a little," Violet said.

"So what are you going to do about it?"

"Nothing."

"Nothing?"

"What am I supposed to do?" Violet asked. "Follow Malcolm around? Stake out the mysterious house?"

"For starters."

"Forget it."

"You could hire a private investigator," Mrs. Parker offered.

"This is my life, not a movie . . . or a Dashiell Hammett novel."

She thought her guest would appreciate the reference to one of her contemporaries, but Mrs. Parker practically growled. Then Violet remembered reading that they had been adversaries. Dashiell Hammett—famous for creating iconic detectives, such as Sam Spade—was attached to playwright Lillian Hellman, one of Dorothy Parker's closest friends, but he made himself scarce whenever she visited. They just never got along.

"I'm sorry," Violet said. "I forgot that you two—"

"Never mind," Mrs. Parker said, waving away the comment. She took a long sip from her drink. "I'd rather talk about this other horse's ass, Malcolm."

"There's nothing more to talk about," Violet said.

"Don't you want to win your case?"

"Of course I do. Just not . . . like this."

Mrs. Parker put her drink down on the side table and stared at Violet. "I see."

Her tone of voice implied that she saw more than she was letting on, but Violet wasn't sure she wanted to know what her guest was thinking. "I should get back to work," she said.

Mrs. Parker was undeterred. "You're far too gentle," she said. "You don't want to hurt Malcolm."

"You make it sound like 'gentle' is a character flaw."

"It's not," Mrs. Parker said, "if you're a poodle. But for a woman trying to make her way in the world, there is a lot to be said for acrimony."

Violet folded her arms. "I might not be as sweet as you think," she said. "You should see what they say about me on the Internet. People think I can be pretty brutal."

"But only in your reviews, my dear. That's not where it counts."

Violet sighed. She'd heard it all before. Mostly from her sister, ironically, who often told her she needed to apply the courage she used in her reviews to her personal life. Ivy never took any responsibility for the role she played in making Violet so tongue-tied. And she certainly didn't relate to her sister's anxiety. Gregarious types like Ivy and Dorothy Parker could never understand how paralyzing social phobia could be. They thought all she needed was a little guidance, a pep talk, a set of instructions. If only it were that easy.

Violet changed the subject. "Look, I'm on deadline. I really should write this review and get it submitted."

Mrs. Parker polished off the last drops of her drink. "I'd like to watch."

"Really?"

"I've seen people using these things in the Algonquin," she said, pointing to Violet's laptop. "But I've never really understood what it was all about."

Violet took a seat at the desk and opened her notebook computer. "I'll show you," she said, and clicked the document she had been working on.

"Is this the Internet?" Mrs. Parker asked, peering over her shoulder.

"This part is more or less a glorified typewriter. I type documents in here and can then use the Internet to send them."

"Edify me."

Violet opened her browser and showed Mrs. Parker her e-mail account. "These are all electronic messages. This one's from Buck Skelly, my editor," she said, opening an e-mail she had read earlier. "He's reminding me that he's going away for a few days and won't be able to edit my next review before the issue closes. He trusts me enough to self-edit but says his assistant will eyeball it for any glaring errors. And see here? This line that says 'cc'? That means his assistant got a copy of this e-mail, as well."

"In my day, *cc* stood for carbon copy."

"Now it stands for nothing."

"Like your politicians. Are you going to reply?"

"Sure," Violet said. "Watch." She clicked reply and typed her message: *We'll try to behave while you're gone. Have a great time in Dallas, Buck.* She hit send.

"That's *it*?"

"That's it."

"How long will it take him to get it?"

"It's usually instantaneous."

"Goodness."

"Here's another one," Violet said. "It's from a colleague asking me to be the guest reviewer for a TV segment. I always turn these down."

"You should accept."

Violet laughed. "Me? On television? You've got to be kidding." Violet typed her message, expressing polite regrets, and hit send. Start to finish, it took less than thirty seconds.

"Extraordinary," Mrs. Parker said. "Can I try one?"

"You want to respond to one of my e-mails?"

"I do!"

Violet grinned. "Be my guest," she said, and rose to give Mrs. Parker her seat.

"What should I do?"

Violet showed her how to use the mouse, and let her click on an e-mail to open it. "I take kung fu lessons at a local studio, and this is from my instructor to our whole class. He wants to know if everyone would like to go out for coffee after this week's lesson."

"How do I answer it?"

"See where it says 'reply all'? Click that, and then type a message saying I'd love to go but can't make it."

"Why can't you make it?"

"I have an editorial meeting at work the next morning, and I need to make it an early night. So just express my regrets and then click here to send."

Violet folded her arms and stood back, excited to watch the great Dorothy Parker actually compose a sentence. Her hero poised her fingers over the keyboard and quickly typed the letters D-e-l-i-g-h-t-e-d. Before Violet could let out a single choked syllable, her guest hit send.

"What did you do that for!" Violet said.

"You need to socialize more."

"That's the *last* thing I need."

"I beg to differ."

Violet began to pace back and forth, thinking about the people in her martial arts class. There wasn't a single person in there she could have a meaningful conversation with. She thought about Suzette, the twenty-two-year-old anorexic girl who always came straight from a kickboxing lesson. Violet had tried to make polite chitchat before class, but the girl was interested only in getting sympathy for the fact that people were always trying to get her to eat more. "I *do* eat," she had said to Violet, "but mostly apples." Another classmate was Jason, a hairdresser from Hicksville who had such a short attention span that Violet tended to lose him in the middle of "I'm fine, thanks." Then there were the *Linda* twins, who weren't actually twins, or even sisters, but a pair of middle-aged suburban friends who shared the same name and an obsession with real-estate prices. The most intimidating classmate was Mariana, a stunning Latina and aspiring Broadway actress who had appeared in several television commercials.

And then, of course, there was Michael Jessee, the instructor, a mocha-skinned ex-Marine who looked like Terrence Howard with a thick neck and muscles. But it wasn't his looks that made Violet swoon, it was his voice. Before she even met him in person she had called his studio, the Red Dragon Kung Fu Academy, and listened to him on the answering machine. If it weren't for a tiny but endearing speech impediment—a sibilant *s* that created a soft whistle in certain sounds— Violet would have thought he had hired a professional to record his message. But no, it was Michael. And now, thinking about the way he sounded, Violet remembered a line from a short story by Dorothy Parker: *His voice was as intimate as the rustle of sheets.*

But, of course, he was out of her league. And there was simply no way she could imagine fitting into this group.

"I have *nothing* in common with these people," Violet said.

"So much the better."

"I'm going to cancel."

"No, you're not. You're going to invite them here so I can coach you through it."

"Coach me?"

"Sure, I'll buzz around unseen, but I'll be able to whisper in your ear, give you advice on what to say."

"I don't know," Violet said. "This doesn't sound like such a great idea."

"It will be the first in a series of lessons to teach you to be more assertive."

"I don't think it will work," Violet said. "I . . . I don't have it in me."

"Of course you have it in you. You're just afraid to let it out unless you're writing a review."

Violet couldn't argue that point. Sometimes she felt like a cauldron of vitriol bubbling beneath a tight lid. Her reviews were the only safe way to let out some steam. Trying that in a social situation could be dangerous, volatile, terrifying.

"I'm sorry," she said. "I can't."

"Are you giving up on winning custody of your niece?"

"Of course not."

"Then you owe it to her, my dear. You owe her a sincere effort to bring your inner bitch into the light, where she belongs."

Chapter 9

Violet made a point of going into the office at least three days a week. Aside from her weekly meetings, she could have done all her work from home, but she thought it was important to show her face at the magazine more often. And so she usually wrote her reviews on her home computer but did everything else—researching filmographies, responding to publicists, brainstorming headlines, approving edits, and submitting final copy—on premises.

Violet switched on her computer. As she waited for it to boot up, she carefully poured her coffee from the paper container into her office cup—an oversized purple ceramic mug imprinted with the movie title AMERICAN VIOLET. It had been given to her by a studio publicist with a sense of humor, and it had become something of an office joke; no one would ever mistake her cup for theirs.

The light on her phone was flashing, indicating that she had voice mail. She picked up the handset and played the messages back. The first voice she heard made her cringe.

Ms. Epps? This is Barry Beeman from the Algonquin Hotel. Please call me back at your earliest convenience.

He left his direct-dial number, but Violet hung up before he finished saying it. She knew he was calling to ask about the guest book she had stolen, and she just couldn't handle the confrontation. Besides, she wasn't ready to give it back. One day, she would slip it in a padded envelope and have it delivered to the hotel. But not yet. She needed more time with Dorothy Parker.

Her colleague Travis Ornstein stuck his head in.

"You're here," he said.

"Morning, Travis."

He was the magazine's other movie critic, so they worked pretty closely together, dividing up the responsibilities every week, covering for each other when something came up, and trading off the lead review slot.

"I hope you're in a good mood," he said, as he lowered himself into the chair opposite her desk. He wore a black shirt and black pants with a purple tie. Violet was pretty sure there was a black jacket on the hanger in his office.

"Why?" she asked.

"Andi," he said, referring to their department's new editorial assistant—the one their boss had put in charge of proofreading their final copy for this week's issue. With Buck, the young woman was respectful, even obsequious. With everyone else she had an attitude. It was as if she thought that being the boss's assistant made her second in command. The kid had a lot to learn.

Violet found a napkin in her drawer and put it under her coffee. "What did she do?"

"Red-penciled my copy. Changed every 'that' to 'which,' expanded the contractions, excised every hint of voice until it read like a term paper."

"Are you serious?"

"As Sean Hannity with acid reflux." Travis was known for his colorful turns of phrase—both in real life and in reviews. That was the big difference between them. He was the same person on and off the page.

Violet sipped her coffee. "I thought she was just supposed to eye-ball it for typos."

"Little shit thinks she'll make a splash by teaching us wretched critics the rudiments of grammar."

"God help us. What did you do?"

"Nothing yet, but I'm trying to work up an appetite. I plan to eat her for lunch."

Violet's computer screen came to life and she jiggled her mouse, waiting for Windows to finish loading so she could see what damage the young assistant had inflicted on her copy.

"Did you submit yesterday?" Travis asked.

"Turned in my piece on *Man Oh Man.*"

"How was it?"

"Had its moments."

The movie was about a single mom who had such a frustrating day of encountering sexism at every turn that she goes to sleep wishing she were a man. When she wakes up, she is. Violet had decided to open the review with a literary reference: Abby Collins awoke one morning from restless dreams to find she had been transformed into . . . Steve Carell. Of course, Violet brought the allusion full circle, ending the review by talking about the concept of metamorphosis as a Hollywood staple that just wouldn't die, kind of like a giant cockroach.

"Okay," Violet said, opening her Internet browser. "Let's see if she butchered me, too."

She clicked into the magazine's internal server, which was set up to connect writers, editors, and production in one place. Everything in the magazine went through this portal.

She navigated to her page and clicked on her latest submission, which showed her copy in black and the editor's changes in red. Almost every word of the piece had been changed, including the first line, which now read: Abby Collins woke up as Steve Carell.

"Oh, sweet God of mercy," Violet said. "Little Miss Grammar Nazi never read Kafka."

"How do you know?"

She started to explain about her opening reference but stopped at the sound outside her office. She and Travis both heard it at the same time, and their heads turned toward the door. It was Andi, talking to the assistant they shared.

"I hope she's up for a fight," he said, rolling his sleeves.

"You're not going to hit her, are you?"

"Only metaphorically. And as hard as I can."

He walked out the door just beyond Violet's line of vision, but his voice reverberated. "I'd like to see you in my office, Andi."

"Five minutes," she said.

Travis got loud. Frighteningly loud, in Violet's opinion. "Excuse me?"

There was a pause and then Andi's exasperated, impatient voice. "What do you want?"

Violet was appalled by the girl's attitude. She didn't seem to think she needed to treat anyone besides Buck with respect. But Travis was a fifty-one-year-old movie critic revered around the world. Andi was a twenty-three-year-old who had graduated from college less than a year ago. Talk about hubris.

"I just told you what I want," he said. "I want to see you in my *office*."

"Can't it wait?"

"Absolutely not."

Violet leaned forward in her chair, listening hard. *Absolutely not*, she repeated in her head. One day she hoped to be bold enough to say that to someone with the kind of conviction Travis had.

"I'm talking to Dolores right now," Andi said. "What's this about?"

"What do you *think* it's about?"

"Your review?"

67

"Listen, you little shit. I'm going to say this once, and if I ever have to say it again, it won't be to your face, because you'll be fired so fast you'll be lucky to leave with your tattoos. *Do not mess with my copy.* If you find a typo, you may bring it to my attention. But beyond that, you're not to touch a word. Not a noun, a pronoun, an article, a verb, an adjective, an adverb, a preposition, or a conjunction. Nothing. Do I make myself clear?"

No response.

Travis got louder. "I said, 'Do I make myself clear?' "

"I'm not an idiot."

"Answer the question."

"Yes, Mr. Ornstein," Andi said, her tone oily with sarcasm. "Perfectly clear."

"And that goes for Violet's copy, too."

Violet stood. She needed to be part of this. She took one sip of her coffee for fortification and walked to the door of her office. Everyone in the outer office looked up at her, waiting for a comment. She knew she had to say something, something big and forceful, something to let Andi know she was behind every word Travis was saying.

They waited.

She folded her arms in an attempt to look resolute. "Right," she finally said.

"Right?" Andi said.

"Travis, I mean. Travis is right."

Okay, so it wasn't big and forceful. But it was clear where she stood. That was something, wasn't it?

Andi shook her goth black hair out of her face and rolled her eyes, then turned back to Travis, dismissing Violet completely.

"What*ever*," she said.

Chapter 10

Everyone from Violet's martial arts class was there.

"This is beautiful!" Mariana said, and gave Violet a hug.

After learning that the reason for the coffee get-together was to celebrate the commercial actress's birthday, Violet took pains to set up the dining room the way Ivy would have. And though she lacked her sister's Martha Stewart touch, she had to admit she did a pretty good job. The long, narrow room was quietly lit with dozens of candles. A panel of gold brocade ran the length of the old farmhouse table. In the center was a vase of hydrangeas cut from the garden out back. To the left of it sat a multi-tiered dish filled with tiny pastries. In deference to Suzette the anorexic, a large bowl of red apples sat to the right. The pretty cake, decorated with buttercream flowers and *Happy Birthday Mariana* in yellow script, remained in the kitchen, waiting to be carried in.

Violet returned Mariana's surprising hug and backed away, excusing herself for a hasty retreat to the kitchen to make the coffee.

The two Lindas waylaid her in the hallway.

"We love the crown molding," said the Linda with the long face. Violet thought of her as Linda One.

"The crown molding is to die for," said the other.

"Thanks," Violet said, glancing up at the ornate woodwork.

"Did it come with the house?"

"My sister did all this," Violet said. "She was an architect and restored the place herself."

"She did a beautiful job," said Linda Two.

Linda One agreed. "Do you know how much she paid for the place? Next to nothing, I'll bet. And it's worth a small fortune now."

"My parents bought the house," Violet said, begging the question. She didn't think the price was anyone's business.

The Lindas pressed Violet on the purchase date, and when they learned the year, Linda Two gasped and Linda One squealed.

"They must have paid next to nothing for it!" she said.

"Next to nothing!" said Linda Two.

Violet left the two Lindas gushing over real-estate values and went into the kitchen, where she had left the Algonquin guest book. She took a few deep breaths, listening to the rest of her guests talking and joking in the dining room. For now, Mariana was holding court, entertaining the group with inside stories about the crazy world of commercial shoots. But soon enough they would expect some witty repartee from their hostess and resident movie critic, and the very thought made Violet want to throw up.

She opened the guest book, hoping Mrs. Parker remembered her promise to float around without taking on a corporeal form. Sure enough, there was no ghostly appearance.

"Are you here?" Violet whispered.

Nothing.

She shrugged and went about making coffee, hoping Dorothy Parker would appear in time to help her navigate the social waters of this little party. As she carefully counted the scoops of coffee, she became aware of a whooshing sound by her right ear, as if an insect were flying by. After a few seconds it became clear the sound was actually a whisper, though she couldn't quite make out what it was saying. It sounded like *covey, covey.*

Violet lost count and had to pour the grounds back into the sack and start over. Then she realized the word was *coffee*.

"Mrs. Parker?" she said softly.

Why are you serving coffee? came the whisper.

"To go with dessert."

Drinks. A party needs drinks. Liquor. How do you expect everyone to loosen up when you're serving coffee?

"Shit, I lost count again."

A male voice startled her. "Do you always talk to yourself when you make coffee?"

It was Michael, her kung fu instructor, looking even more beautiful standing at the door of her kitchen than he did in class. His shirt was blue, his eyes were hazel, his skin a warm brown. In street clothes, his rigid posture was movie-star dramatic.

Violet had a tendency to shut down around good-looking men. They expected too much, appreciated too little, and were rarely interesting. But Michael was different. She sensed that there was an epic or two beneath those hazel eyes. And then there was that voice. It made her want to get close enough to smell his neck.

But no. This guy was so far out of her league she didn't have the right to even think about him.

Dear God, but he's stunning. Ms. Epps, you simply must find a way to get this creature in your bed.

Was Dorothy Parker losing her mind? This guy could get any woman he wanted. He wouldn't be interested in Violet if he had cataracts and the lights were off.

"I . . . I keep losing count," she said.

Flirt with him. Say it's hard to concentrate in his presence.

"Who's Count?" he asked.

"What? Oh, no one. I mean, I'm talking about coffee scoops."

He smiled. "That was supposed to be a joke."

Violet cringed in embarrassment. How could she be so stupid? "Sorry," she said. "I should have known."

He put a warm hand on her shoulder. "No, you shouldn't have. It was dumb."

"I like dumb jokes," she said, "especially puns."

"Good," he said, "'cause I'm the king of bad puns. In fact, I always have a pun in the oven."

Violet shook her head and laughed. "That's terrible!"

"But you laughed."

She went back to counting out scoops of coffee. "There's a certain charm to the puns that make you cringe."

Excellent! Keep flirting. You're doing great.

Was she really flirting? Violet got flustered. "I'm still losing count," she said.

"Try doing it by tens," he said.

"What?"

"Count by tens. That's what I do. Helps the focus."

There was that sibilant *s* again. Violet could turn herself off to the handsome face and strong body. She might even find a way to resist the honey-toned voice. But that speech impediment touched the tenderest part of her heart.

"I'll give it a shot," she said, and started scooping the coffee again.

Tell him you're lousy at domestic tasks. Tell him you're only good at two things, and then when he asks what they are—

"There!" Violet said, though she had lost count once again. "Done. Thanks for the tip." She turned on the electric coffeemaker—the one Ivy used for parties—and it started making familiar hissing noises as it heated the water.

"What can I help you with?" he asked.

Violet dusted her hands and surveyed the kitchen. Except for the birthday cake, all the desserts were already in the dining room. "I think I'm in pretty good shape here," she said.

Find something for him to do, you fool!

"Um, actually," Violet added, "can you pour some half and half into that little creamer?"

He opened the refrigerator and got out the container. "Which half?" he asked.

Violet smiled. "I never saw this side of you," she said. "In class you're always so serious."

"I leave the goofy home," he said. "Kung fu requires concentration."

She had to agree with that. It was a pretty rigorous discipline.

"Anyway," he continued, "it's really nice of you to do this for Mariana. You must entertain a lot."

"Me? God, no. This is . . . almost unprecedented."

"Then it's especially nice. It really means a lot to Mariana."

Mariana. Isn't that the birthday girl? What's his particular interest in her? Find out if they're an item.

"I'm glad," Violet said.

His expression was suddenly serious. "Poor thing's had a rough year," he said.

He feels sorry for her. You might have your work cut out for you.

"I didn't know," Violet said.

"Her mother died a few months ago."

Splendid! If this guy's got a soft spot for women with sad stories, you win. Tell him about your sister. You'll have him wrapped around your finger in no time.

"I'm so sorry to hear that," Violet said. "She never mentioned anything."

"She puts on a brave front."

Damn. He cares about her.

"She certainly seems very strong," Violet said.

"She does. Though when you get to know her you can see she's dealing with a lot of pain."

This is going from bad to worse. Your goose may be cooked, my dear.

There's no goose and nothing to cook, Violet thought. Couldn't Mrs. Parker see that this guy was beyond her reach? Besides, it was becoming increasingly obvious he had something going on with Mariana.

He continued, "And in the middle of dealing with all that, her girlfriend left her."

"Girlfriend?"

Girlfriend?

Violet turned to look at him. Mariana, gay? She had never suspected.

Michael frowned. "I guess I have a big mouth."

Ha! Trust me, that was no accident. He wants you to know there's nothing going on between the two of them.

"No, it's okay. I'm sure it's not a secret. In fact, I think she tried to tell me, but I was too thick to connect the dots."

He laughed. "I've read your reviews. The last thing anyone could call you is thick."

This darling man is flirting, my dear. Flirt back.

Violet put the creamer, the sugar, and the cups onto a large tray and asked Michael if he would mind carrying it into the dining room for her. When he left, she whispered to her invisible mentor, "You have to stop this. He's not interested in me."

I beg to differ.

"A man like that . . . he probably dates twenty-year-old fitness instructors."

Don't sell yourself short. There's a lot to be said for intelligence and maturity. Besides, you're a perfectly lovely woman. I'm quite sure he finds you appealing. You have a certain lithe grace, you know.

Violet didn't want to let Dorothy Parker talk her into thinking she had a chance with Michael. It could only lead to disappointment.

"Please," she said, "just help me get through this evening without embarrassing myself."

You need to set your goals a bit higher, my dear.

Later, after the group sang "Happy Birthday" to Mariana, Violet sliced the cake and passed pieces around the table.

Why doesn't that skinny girl take a slice of cake? Hell, she can take two or three.

The Algonquin guest book was now on the dining room sideboard, and Mrs. Parker was in all her glory, floating around the room unseen, making snide comments about the guests.

"Suzette," Violet said, "there's a bowl of apples if you'd like one."

Suzette stared at them and sucked air. "Do you have any Granny Smiths?"

"Sorry. But these are very good."

Suzette extracted an apple with two fingers, as if it was dripping with something toxic, and set it on her plate. She picked up her fork and knife and cut a slice.

Well, now she's just making a pig of herself.

"How about you, Jason?" Violet asked the short-attention-span hairdresser.

He peered at the slice she was offering. "That looks like . . . What do you call that kind of cake that has a lot of layers?"

"Layer cake?"

"Layer cake," Jason repeated. "Yes, I love layer cake. Thank you."

I once had a dachshund smarter than this one.

The two Lindas discussed sharing a piece and finally decided they would each have their own.

"I shouldn't, but I will," said one.

Story of my life.

"So how old are you?" the other Linda asked Mariana.

"I'm twenty-eight. But I'm an actress, so I'll always be twenty-eight."

Appreciative titters spread around the table.

"How come you're not in Los Angeles, trying to get into movies?" asked Jason.

"Yeah," said the other Linda. "I bet Violet has connections and could help you out."

Oh, no, Violet thought. Not that. Anything but that. People often assumed she could help them out with their movie careers, but the truth was that critics had no Hollywood connections. In fact, keeping a distance was part of the job.

It was okay, though, because she had a joke all ready. She kept it stored in her arsenal for just such an occasion. It was the perfect quip to deflect the situation—not terribly witty, but light and cute without a hint of hostility. Now that she was faced with actually saying it, she worried it would be misunderstood.

She practiced it in her head: I'm barely connected to the *Internet.*

Did it sound foolish? Smug? Would they roll their eyes at her, as Andi had done the day before? Would they turn on her, as her sister had done when they were children?

She knew she looked like she was about to say something, and they all stared at her expectantly. Well, except for Jason, who was distracted by the table surface.

Didn't you tell me you had a joke prepared? Don't just sit there. Spit it out.

God, even Dorothy Parker was waiting for her to say something. But she couldn't. And the longer she waited, the worse it got.

She repeated the words to herself: I'm barely connected to the *Internet.* Was it even remotely charming? Why did it seem like the perfect response when she thought of it? Because there was no one to hear it, no one to think she was an arrogant little bitch . . . or an idiot. Too bad it lacked the silly fun of Michael's bad puns.

He came to the rescue and broke the silence. "Mariana has no interest in Hollywood," he said.

"That's right," said the actress. "I'm in love with the *theatah, dahling*." She flipped her hair dramatically, and everyone laughed.

Why was it so easy for some people?

"Seriously," Mariana continued, "I really do love the stage. It's intoxicating."

Tell her that's the greasepaint.

Violet pushed her cake around with her fork.

"How many people get to do something they really love?" said one of the Lindas. "I think it's marvelous."

"Are you in anything now?" asked the other.

"I'm in rehearsals for an Off-Off-Broadway production called *Biting*. Opens next week."

Jason asked what it was about, and Mariana laughed. "It's kind of a weird show about vampires in Manhattan."

Just what the world needs. A play about agents.

Violet sipped her coffee.

Say it. It's funny. They'll laugh.

She shook her head.

What are you afraid of? That they won't find it amusing? That they won't like you? Why should you care? They already think you're a stiff, anyway.

"Is it any good?" Violet asked Mariana, mostly to get Dorothy Parker to shut up.

"Actually? Yeah, I think it's funny. You guys should come. All of you. I can get you in as my guests."

"That would be great," Michael said. "What do you folks think?"

"I'm in," Jason said.

Suzette used a napkin to wipe some imaginary food from the corner of her mouth. "Me, too."

"We love going downtown," said one of the Lindas.

"What about you?" Michael asked Violet.

Say yes. He's practically asking you for a date.

"I would love for you to come," Mariana added.

"As long as I don't have to write a review," Violet said to be funny, and immediately regretted it. She meant to be light, to imply that she wanted to have fun and not work, but the others might think she was copping an attitude about the show.

To her relief, they laughed.

That was good. Now tell your darling Michael there's nothing you like more than attending the theater on the arm of a handsome man.

Violet coughed in an effort to convey to Mrs. Parker that she needed to drop this line of discourse. She was *not* going to flirt with Michael and make a fool of herself.

"Can I get anyone more coffee?" she asked.

"Love some," said one of the Lindas.

Michael rose. "Relax," he said to Violet. "I'll get it."

"I don't know if there's enough," Violet said. "I could make more."

This is perfect. Ask him to come into the kitchen and help you.

I will *not*, Violet thought.

"I think we're fine," Michael said.

"I don't want you to go to any more trouble," Mariana said to Violet. "It was so nice of you to do this."

"Everything looks so beautiful," Linda One added. "We love the house. It's so . . . North Shore."

"So Gold Coast," said Linda Two.

This is when you're supposed to tell your guests they're welcome any time. But look straight at Michael when you say it.

"Thank you," Violet said, embarrassed by the praise. She loved the house, but thought the key to its charm was its lack of pretension. It was the opposite of the McMansions that had been springing up in the neighboring towns. Because the original structure was three hundred years old, the ceilings were low and the rooms fairly modest. It was, Violet thought, the perfect home, neatly proportioned and quietly nestled on wooded property between gently rolling hills.

"Thank you"? Is that all you have to say? Ms. Epps, it's time you broke free of your timidity. It's most unattractive. You need to—

The whispering abruptly stopped, as Violet had walked over to the side table and discreetly closed the Algonquin guest book. She had had enough.

"Did you know it was her sister's house?" Linda One announced to the group, looking proud that she had the inside information to share. "She's an architect."

"*Was,*" Violet corrected, taking her seat. "She passed away." It was more information than she wanted to give, and she hoped the group would respect her privacy and move on.

Linda One gasped. "I had no idea!"

"No idea at all," added Linda Two. "How did she die?"

"Car accident, but I don't really want to—"

"When did it happen?" Linda One asked.

"Last year," Violet said. "Would anyone like another piece of cake?"

"So it's still fresh," Mariana said. "God, I'm so sorry. Were you very close?"

Violet meant to push on, to quickly change the subject so the group would know it was off-limits. But the question pierced right through her center, and Ivy's presence was as fresh as the pretty hydrangeas that sat in a vase her sister had bought at a local yard sale.

Violet remembered a day not long before the accident. She had just started seeing Carl, and Ivy had invited the two of them for brunch so she could meet him. It was a day that turned quickly sour, and Violet wished she could snip the scene from her memory, like a dispassionate film editor. But it was beyond her control. Why, she wondered, were so many negative memories floating to the surface lately? She and Ivy had been so close. Sure, they fought when they were young—they were sisters, after all—but Ivy had outgrown her childhood cruelty, and Violet had long since forgiven her. As adults, they were best friends and loved each other fiercely.

In this memory, Ivy was standing by the sink, washing lettuce. Violet was cutting bagels and placing them in a large basket Ivy had lined with a cloth napkin. They were alone in the kitchen, talking about Carl.

"He reminds me of Andrew," Ivy said, referring to Violet's ex-husband.

"*Andrew?* He's nothing like Andrew. Carl is the *anti*-Andrew."

Ivy shrugged. "If you say so."

This infuriated Violet. It was so smug, so filled with the implication that Ivy had seen and assessed all in one brief conversation, and that she possessed powers of observation that had completely eluded her sister.

Violet put down the knife and turned to Ivy. "What," she demanded, almost daring her sister to find a common thread between these two men. Andrew Epps was an engineer who worked in quality control for a large manufacturer. He was logical and businesslike. On weekends he wore khakis. Carl was an artist with dirty fingernails and wild hair. He talked about feelings and wore a pendant with a crystal.

"You sound angry," Ivy said.

"What could you possibly see in common between these two men? They're night and day . . . fire and ice."

"Sure, sure," Ivy said. "You're right. Should I put onions in the salad?"

"Don't condescend to me. Tell me what you think."

Ivy sighed and wiped her hands on a dish towel. She blew a strand of hair out of her eyes and looked straight at her sister. "He strikes me as kind of selfish," she said. "That's all."

"Selfish!" Violet said, thinking about Andrew's almost pathological stinginess. "That's ridiculous. Carl would give a stranger the shirt off his back."

"Maybe *selfish* is the wrong word," Ivy said. "What do you call it when a person is overly impressed with himself and needs everyone around him to feel the same way?"

Narcissism, Violet thought. The word is *narcissism*. But she wouldn't give Ivy the satisfaction of filling in the blank. She just told her sister to go to hell and spent the rest of the day brooding, furious that Ivy refused to embrace her happiness.

Now she wished she could tell her sister she had been right.

"Please excuse me," Violet said to her guests, and went into the kitchen, where she turned on the faucet so no one could hear her crying. Struggling to get herself under control, she put her face in the sink and splashed cold water on it.

She felt a hand on her back.

"You okay?" It was Michael. He pulled a paper towel off the roll and handed it to her.

Violet dried her face. "I guess. I'm sorry. I didn't mean to fall apart."

"Do you want to talk about it?"

She shook her head.

"I can tell everyone to leave, if you want."

"No, it's all right. I'm . . . I'm better."

"You sure?"

She wasn't, but she said yes and followed him back into the dining room. Mariana held out a chair for her, and she sat.

"I'm sorry we upset you," Mariana said.

Violet kept her head down and swallowed. She told herself she was done crying. After all, these people were practically strangers. It was ridiculous for her to be breaking down in front of them. Michael crouched beside her, taking her hands, and it was such a tender gesture her eyes welled and tears spilled down her cheeks. As she struggled to find some way to get past it, to find words she could choke out in order to move on, she noticed a strange tingling in her feet. It almost felt like her spirit guest was entering her again, but that was impossible, as she had closed the book.

Violet lifted her head and looked at the sideboard, where she had left it, and there stood the two Lindas, hunched over the open volume. She was horrified.

"Please!" she cried. "Close that book!"

One of the Lindas turned to her. "This?" she said. "We're being very careful, I promise."

"We have a lot of respect for antiques," said the other.

"I recognize some of these names," said Linda One. "What a fascinating relic."

Violet doubled over, stricken. "Oh, God."

Everyone turned to look at her.

"Are you sick?" Michael asked.

"Yes."

As the nausea mounted and pummeled her, body and soul, Violet was only vaguely aware of movement and voices surrounding her. People were shuffling about, saying good-byes, leaving. A cool breeze from the front door reached her just as the sickness compressed itself into a tight ball in her gut. The nausea was gone, replaced by a feeling of giddy anticipation.

She was transformed.

Violet smelled something heavenly. It could have been the flowers or the bakery cookies, or some divine combination of both. She lifted her head. It was Michael.

"Are you feeling better?" he asked.

She did indeed. Better. Stronger. Bolder.

She looked around. They were alone. She looked back at him. Was it possible for any man to be that exquisitely desirable? She wanted so badly to kiss him she didn't care what the consequences were. Nothing else mattered. It was as if everything that had ever happened in her life—everything that had ever happened in all of human history—had led to this point.

A kiss. A kiss. A kiss.

"Definitely feeling better," she said, and smiled. She put her hand on his strong arm and looked deep into his eyes. His heat was electrifying.

He hesitated for a moment, looking confused. He stood and took a step back. "Can I get you anything? A glass of water?"

She smirked. "Why don't we have a drink?"

"A drink?"

"Sure. We're two consenting adults. We can have a drink together, can't we?" She smiled broadly so he would catch her drift.

He felt her forehead with the back of his hand. "Are you sure you're okay? You sound kind of funny."

"I'm better than okay. I'm four stars." She stood and got as close to him as possible. "How about you? Are you four stars, Michael?"

"That's a . . . 'general' question," he said.

She threw her head back and laughed heartily.

"I don't mean to be rude," he said, "but are you on some kind of medication?"

"There's only one kind of medicine *I* need," she said, putting her hand on his magnificent chest.

He took a step back. "Violet, I don't know what's going on here, but I think I'd better be leaving. Is there someone I can call for you before I go? I just . . . I don't think I should leave you here alone."

She pouted. "I don't think you should leave me alone, either."

"I'm really sorry," he said, "but it's late, and—"

"Suit yourself," she said, glancing coquettishly over her shoulder as she headed toward the doorway. "But I'm going to fix myself a nightcap. You can join me or not."

As soon as she put one foot over the threshold she felt a strange force press against her middle. At the same time, another force tried to pull her forward. She stood there, holding on to the door frame, as the two forces pushed and pulled.

But the battle inside her wasn't just physical. With one foot over the threshold, the real Violet was almost fully conscious, and she fought to rid herself of Mrs. Parker's spirit. She knew that if she could take one more step outside the room she would be free, but the force that held her back was just too strong.

Her other option was closing the Algonquin guest book. The last time Mrs. Parker took up residence within her, Violet had been able to do it quite easily. But this time felt different. Her consciousness was weaker, and the inhabiting spirit was stronger. Violet feared that if she took a step toward the sideboard where it lay she would disappear again and lose her resolve.

She tried to speak, hoping Michael could help her.

"Tha—" she said, pointing.

He turned to follow the line of her finger. "What is it?" he asked. "You need something from the sideboard?"

She nodded.

"This?" he asked, picking up the open book. She tried to tell him to close it, but nothing came out. He put the book down again and moved toward her. "Let me help you," he said. "You need to sit down."

No, she thought. No! He was going to pull her back into the room, and then Mrs. Parker's possession would be impossible to fight. The results would be disastrous, as she would continue to throw herself at this man with shameless abandon. Oh, the humiliation! She couldn't let that happen. She wouldn't.

With Michael just inches from grabbing her, Violet summoned all the strength she could, and with one massive effort that felt like she was hurling herself against a brick wall, she crossed the threshold and hit the floor, blacking out.

Chapter 11

Violet awoke in bed to the sound of Michael's voice.

"Are you okay?"

"What happened?" she asked, still dazed.

"You passed out."

Oh, no, she thought. Not this. She was in her bed, under the covers, with Michael hovering over her. She lifted the blanket for a peek. Still dressed, thank God.

Michael pulled the side chair close to the bed and sat. "You look better," he said, "like your old self. Do you remember what happened?"

"Unfortunately," she said, sitting up. "This is so embarrassing."

"Don't be silly," he said. "Medication affects everyone differently. What are you taking, if you don't mind my asking?"

"Um, all kinds," she lied. "Cold medicine. And antibiotics. And, uh, something for an inner-ear thing. Guess I shouldn't have mixed all that. But it's passed. I'm good as new."

"Still, you should probably call your doctor in the morning."

"I will. I definitely will. Thank you for taking care of me."

"I'm just glad you're okay. Do you need anything else? Can I call someone for you? A relative? Your friend who picked you up a few weeks ago—what was his name? Carl?"

"No. I mean, yes, his name is Carl. But we're not . . . I broke up with him."

Michael paused as he considered that, and Violet felt sure her declaration had embarrassed him somehow. He had probably thought that as long as she was unavailable it was okay to be alone in the bedroom with her. But now that he knew she was unattached, it changed everything.

She waited for him to speak, and all he managed to utter was a single syllable.

"Ah."

Ah? What on earth did that mean? Violet pulled her legs out from under the covers and swung them around the side of the bed. Now it was her turn to say something.

"Thank you," she said. "Thank you for taking care of me like this. You've been so helpful, but I don't want to keep you."

Violet rose slowly to be sure she had regained her strength. Then she walked him to the front door, thanked him again, and told him she would see him next week at class.

"And at Mariana's opening?" he asked.

"I'll try."

He smiled and took one step out the door but paused, turning back to her. "And Violet?" he said. "I'm glad you're not seeing Carl anymore."

Then he was gone, shutting the door behind him.

Now Violet really did feel feverish. She stood in the middle of the foyer and replayed his parting words. What did he mean? Was he saying he was interested in her? Or was he simply observing, in a paternal way, that Carl wasn't good for her?

That had to be it. It had to be.

And if it wasn't? Surely, any interest on his part could be tied to those few moments Dorothy Parker was steering the ship. Now that she thought about that, an indignation took root. Why had her mentor done such a thing? The longer Violet stood there considering it, the angrier she got. The nerve of her!

The Algonquin guest book, which Michael had apparently closed, was still in the dining room. Violet brought it into the study, opened it, and stood back. She was too agitated to even sit.

"I could use a drink," Mrs. Parker said, when she materialized.

"Is that all you have to say? After what you did?"

"Didn't work, eh?"

"Excuse me?" Violet said.

"We didn't succeed in getting that luscious creature into your bedroom?"

"As a matter of fact, he did wind up in my bedroom. But no, we didn't sleep together."

"Pity."

"You humiliated me!" Violet said.

"Oh, come, now," Mrs. Parker said. "All I did was offer the dear boy some encouragement."

"Don't ever do that again," Violet said. "Don't ever enter me again without my permission. That was terrible, awful. Just completely out of bounds."

"Fine. But may I remind you that you were making a spectacle of yourself *before* I entered you? You were blubbering like a child . . . and you weren't even drunk."

"I know," Violet said. "But all you did was pile one humiliation on top of another."

"Did it work at all? Did he express an interest?"

Violet looked away. "I don't know."

"What did he say?"

Violet didn't want to talk about it. She asked Mrs. Parker if she still wanted that drink.

"You can assume, my dear, that the answer to that question is always yes."

Violet left to make the cocktail, and Mrs. Parker called out after her, "You may wind up thanking me!"

"Unlikely!" Violet shouted back.

When she returned with her guest's drink, Mrs. Parker asked what she knew about Michael.

"Not a lot," Violet confessed. "I know he's an ex-Marine. I think he served in the Gulf War, but he doesn't like to talk about it. He loves martial arts, and always wanted to run his own studio, so when he got out of the service he got a job teaching kung fu and eventually bought out the owner."

"The man knows what he wants. I like that. What else?"

"He has a kid—a daughter. I'm not sure if he was ever married to the mom. But he's head over heels in love with the girl. She comes to the studio sometimes. Her name's Kara—about a year older than Delaney."

"That could be good or bad."

"What do you mean?" Violet asked.

"Depends if the girls get along."

"You're already planning my life with this guy? I think you're getting a little carried away. A *lot* carried away."

"This is what women do, Ms. Epps. We meet a man, we develop a crush, we get carried away. It's perfectly ghastly, but we never learn."

"Who said I have a crush on Michael?"

"Please. I know a crush when I see one. Hell, I *invented* crushes. As to your Michael, well, he is exactly the kind of man I would have been all over in my day."

"Really? I thought you had a weakness for blond-haired, blue-eyed leading-man types."

"I like martinis," Mrs. Parker said. "It doesn't mean I wouldn't adore a whisky sour every now and then."

Violet's interest was piqued; interracial dating was almost unheard of in Dorothy Parker's day. "So you would date a black man?"

"Would and have."

Violet's eyes widened. "Are you serious?"

"My dear, I hope you don't take me for a racist. I devoted much of my life to the civil rights movement."

"No, no. Not a racist at all," Violet said, worried she had offended her guest. "I know how passionately you fought bigotry and injustice. You even got yourself arrested—"

"Sacco and Vanzetti," Mrs. Parker said.

"Yes." Violet had read that Dorothy Parker protested the unjust murder trial of two Italian immigrants in the 1920s. "They took you away in handcuffs."

"A lot of good that did."

Violet nodded. She knew the men had been executed. She also knew that, guilty or innocent, the prejudice against them for being foreigners and anarchists had sealed their fate. Violet wished she could say something supportive, like, 'You fought the good fight,' but it sounded too facile for something so tragic. It had to have been an excruciating injustice to witness. "I'm sorry," she simply said.

"It just about ruined me."

"But you didn't give up."

"Never. And that's the cold, hard truth about me. I'm the greatest little hoper that ever lived."

Yes, Violet thought. It was why she left her entire estate to Dr. Martin Luther King Jr. and the NAACP—her abiding hope that the world could change.

"I'm sorry if you thought I was accusing you of being prejudiced," Violet said. "I know how hard you fought."

Mrs. Parker waved away the comment. "I've been called worse."

"You must have been bursting when you heard about our 2008 election . . . I mean, you know about President Obama, right?"

"I do . . ." Mrs. Parker said, and stopped. She was literally choked up.

Violet waited while her guest tried to collect herself, but Mrs. Parker seemed unable to speak.

"I guess you didn't think we'd ever get this far," Violet offered.

"But I did. And isn't that the damnedest thing? I suppose inside every cynic beats the heart of an idealist."

Chapter 12

Delaney started taking piano lessons when she was eight years old, and Violet had been to almost every recital. But last year's performance was only two months after the accident, and the girl wasn't emotionally ready for it, so they skipped it. That meant this year's recital would be the first time Delaney would play without her parents in the audience. Violet was almost sick with worry. How on earth would the kid get through this?

The event was in a cavernous subterranean space beneath the showroom of a large piano store, and the mood, as always, was exuberant. The parents were nervous and excited about their children's impending performances. The kids, dressed in crisp clothes reserved for special events, were proud and anxious.

Sandra and Malcolm sat on one side of Delaney, and Violet sat on the other. The piano teacher, Mr. Lawrence, introduced the children, and one by one they rose from their seats and stepped up onto the platform to take their place in front of the Steinway grand. There was a mix of students, from beginner to advanced. Some made mistakes as they went along; all got enthusiastic applause.

Now and then Violet glanced at Delaney's face to see how she was handling the event. The girl seemed cool and composed, but her aunt could sense a layer of tension beneath.

Please, Violet thought. Please let her play a happy song.

At last it was her turn. Mr. Lawrence announced, "Our next student is someone I take extra-special pride in, and I'm thrilled she's playing for us this year. Please welcome Delaney Weber, who will be performing Ludwig von Beethoven's 'Moonlight Sonata.' "

Oh, no, Violet thought. Not the "Moonlight Sonata." She knew, of course, that it was a beautiful song, but the tune was so heart-wrenchingly poignant she couldn't imagine Delaney playing it. Not today. Not for her first recital performance as an orphan.

As Delaney rose, Violet saw people throughout the room leaning in to one another, whispering. She sensed what they were saying: *That's her. That's the poor girl who lost her parents.* Violet reached into her handbag for a tissue.

Delaney parked herself on the piano bench and smoothed her skirt. Violet had been in this room so many times over the years with Ivy and Neil that it was impossible not to feel their presence. It was as if Ivy were sitting in the row behind her, beaming, while Neil was grinning behind his camcorder. She was sure Delaney felt it, too.

Hands still on her lap, Delaney turned to the audience. "This is dedicated to my parents," she said.

The whispering stopped, and a hush fell over the room. A hard lump formed in Violet's throat. Delaney had said "my parents," not "parental units" or some other jokey designation. To anyone else it might seem insignificant, but Violet knew it was an important step in the healing process. She looked over at Malcolm and Sandra to see if they caught it, but their eyes were trained on their granddaughter in rapt concentration.

Delaney opened her sheet music and poised her fingers over the keyboard. The crowd waited as the girl seemed to focus. She closed her eyes, hands still hovering. A few moments passed, and Delaney seemed frozen in place. Someone coughed. A chair leg scraped. People began clearing their throats.

Still more time passed. What is she waiting for? Violet wondered.

She glanced over at Mr. Lawrence. He had his hand over his mouth as he stared at Delaney. Clearly, he was getting worried, too.

Violet considered approaching him to say that he should step in and tell Delaney it was okay, she didn't have to play.

She looked back at Delaney. The girl still had her eyes closed, only now her lips were moving the tiniest bit, as if she was talking to herself. Violet waited.

Nothing.

I have to get up and say something, she thought. I have to.

But just as she was about to rise, Violet noticed that her niece took a deep breath. And then, with a single nod, she began.

Delaney's slim fingers landed on the keys, and Beethoven's sad, soft, slow, lovely lament began to fill the room. And Violet felt it. The sorrow was exquisite. The melancholy as delicate as a remembered scent. It drove home what it means to be human, to feel and be moved, to have a hole in your heart because someone you loved—a mother, a father, a son, a sister—is no longer part of your life. It joined her with Delaney and the Webers and Beethoven and everyone in this basement listening to one tender, damaged orphan playing for her dead parents.

And when she was done, when that last sustained minor chord went quiet, there was a moment when the song still hung in the silence . . . a moment that dissipated in grateful applause and audible sniffs. Violet looked around. Indeed, everyone was crying.

She looked back at her niece, who stood, wet-faced and somber. Delaney took a deep bow. When her head came up, she was smiling.

"Chocolate-chip cookie dough," Delaney said. "With hot fudge, please."

"Whipped cream?" Sandra asked.

Delaney smiled and nodded. "Thank you, Grannygran," she said, and gave Sandra a hug.

In a spirit of temporary détente, the four of them—Sandra, Malcolm, Delaney, and Violet—had decided to go out for ice cream together after the recital.

"You're in a good mood," Violet said to her niece after Sandra and Malcolm had gone up to the counter. She hadn't seen the girl being this sweet to her grandmother in years.

"Don't get used to it," Delaney said, smiling. There was no edge to her humor today. The kid was glowing.

"I guess Beethoven hath charms to soothe the savage breast," Violet said. "And even the occasional teenager." She pulled a napkin from the dispenser and wiped some stickiness from the table.

"It's not Beethoven," Delaney said. "It's you."

"Me?" Violet was surprised. The girl seemed serious.

"It's just . . ." Delaney leaned in to be sure the conversation was private. "I've been thinking about that phone conversation you had with Vincent van Loser. You were *fierce*."

Violet swallowed. That wasn't me, she thought. That was Dorothy Parker. "Thank you," she said, "but what does that have to do with—"

Delaney glanced over her shoulder to be sure her grandparents weren't within hearing distance. "I know you're fighting for me, Aunt V," she said. "And I know you'll win. You're like a superhero, with special secret powers."

"Oh, Delaney," Violet began, "I don't know if—"

Her niece cut her off. "I'm coming home soon," she said. "I just know it."

Malcolm and Sandra came back to the table with a tray full of ice-cream sundaes.

"They didn't have chocolate-chip cookie dough," Sandra said, as she placed a sundae in front of Delaney. "So I got you plain choco-late chip."

"Plain chocolate chip?" Delaney said.

"See? I told you we should have asked her," Malcolm said.

Sandra looked pained. "I guess I'm the bad guy *again*."

"It's fine," Delaney said, digging her spoon into the ice cream.

"Are you sure?" Malcolm asked.

"I'm sure," she said, and to prove her point she stuck a spoonful in her mouth and smiled, never taking her eyes off Violet.

Chapter 13

Violet got off the elevator, leaning to the left so that the giant tote bag hanging from a shoulder strap wouldn't knock the cup of coffee she held in one hand or the brown bag containing a toasted whole-wheat bagel in the other. She walked through the open door to Enjoy's reception area, where a stack of freshly printed magazines sat on the desk for staff members to grab on their way in.

"Morning, Lisa," she said to the receptionist as she balanced the paper bag on top of the coffee cup so that she had a free hand to grab a magazine and stick it under her arm.

"Andi asked me twice if you were in yet," the receptionist said.

"Andi? Why?"

"Didn't say."

Violet shrugged and continued to her office, where she settled herself in so she could perform her Wednesday morning routine of thumbing through the new issue while having her breakfast.

She ignored the flashing light on her phone, as she knew there would be another message from Barry Beeman about the guest book, and just hearing his voice made her nervous. Sooner or later he would probably call the authorities, and she didn't even want to think about it.

Easing into her day, Violet opened the wrapping on her bagel and poured her coffee from the paper container into her ceramic mug. The magazine's cover story was about a TV actress who had made the

ELLEN MEISTER

crossover to movies and was quickly becoming the darling of romantic comedies.

Early in her career, Violet left an unhappy job to work as an editorial assistant at a local weekly covering events and entertainment in New York City. The pay was low and the offices cramped, but she had the opportunity to move up the ladder pretty quickly, and in less than two years she had a byline and was covering local events. A year later she started reviewing movies, which was a dream come true, as she had a lifelong passion for film. The real world, with its paralyzing social challenges, had been such a struggle for her. But movies were where magic lived and anything was possible. The only thing Violet loved more than losing herself in a book was losing herself in a darkened theater.

So when she got the assignment to review movies, she was ecstatic, especially since it was such a small local publication. The limited circulation felt intimate and familiar, and Violet was relaxed enough to be honest with her opinions. And God knows she had a lot of them just bursting to get out.

Of course, it took a while to find her voice. In the beginning, it was almost like a game, where she could pretend to be Dorothy Parker working at *Vanity Fair* or *The New Yorker* in the early days. But slowly, a metamorphosis took place. Violet went from feeling like she was playing a role in someone else's hat and shoes to shedding the layers that had been wearing her down. Her inner critic had found an outlet, and it was the most exhilarating experience of her life. In person, she was still as timid as she had ever been. But on paper she was liberated. All those opinions she had been holding in for fear of offending someone had found a release, and it was intoxicating.

Perhaps she wouldn't have felt so uncensored if she had considered who might be reading her reviews. But it so happened that someone pretty influential was paying close attention. It was Travis Ornstein at *Enjoy*, the country's leading entertainment weekly. And when the slot opened up for a second reviewer, he recommended her to the editor. It was an enormous step up for Violet. And though it was a dream job for her, she was so overwhelmed by the idea she almost didn't take it. Ivy convinced her she would be crazy to pass it up.

"Trust me," her big sister had said. "You let this opportunity go and you'll regret it for the rest of your life."

And that was all it took. The fear of regret outweighed the fear of being read by millions.

That was more than six years ago. And while she still wasn't the least bit jaded about the job, she no longer opened the magazine and turned straight to her reviews to see her words in print. Now she lingered over the article about the new star, scanned the full-page memorial feature on a movie actor who had recently passed away, and read the gossipy highlights of the week, before thumbing past several ads and reaching the section of the magazine devoted to movie reviews.

Travis's lead review—the one Andi had tried to cut to shreds—was an appreciative nod to a high-budget action movie, complete with megastar and dazzling CGI effects. In Violet's opinion, one of the things that made him a great critic was his lack of pretense. He was a true movie lover, and never shunned a film for being lowbrow. Even his most scathing reviews demonstrated his love for the medium. His expectations were high; Travis knew and adored what movies were capable of.

Violet turned to the next page, where her review of *Man Oh Man* was featured. She glanced at the first line and froze.

Abby Collins woke up as Steve Carell.

No, she thought. No, no, no! It can't be. Andi wouldn't have done that. She wouldn't have submitted the altered review that Violet had rejected.

She read on. Dear God, it was true. It was the ghastly, butchered version.

Violet stood, holding on to her desk as she hyperventilated. This wasn't just unacceptable. This was unfathomable. How could that little smartass have dared to cross the line like this?

But Violet knew. She was being alpha-dogged. Andi did this to her because she thought she could get away with it.

It wasn't the first time something like this had happened in Violet's career. People like Andi always sniffed her out. She was the weakling in the office pack, the one who could be easily taken down.

Violet closed her eyes. Not this time, she thought. Her voice would not be quieted. She was going to stand up for herself. She had to. She had to prove to herself she could do it.

With the rolled-up issue in her hand, she marched across the office to Andi's desk, which was in a cubicle outside the office of the managing editor, Buck Skelly.

"We need to talk," Violet said.

Andi didn't look up from her computer. "I'm a little busy."

Violet stood there for a moment while the young woman continued to type, her stubby black-painted fingernails quickly tapping away. She was completely unfazed by Violet's presence.

What would Dorothy Parker do? Violet thought. Certainly, she wouldn't just stand there waiting for the girl to look up.

"Andi," she said loudly.

Nothing.

"*Ms. Cole*," Violet said, using the young woman's last name.

That got her attention, but only for a second. "*I'm busy*," she repeated, without looking up.

Violet uncurled the magazine and slapped it in front of Andi's computer screen. "My review," she said.

Andi folded her arms and sighed. She finally looked up. "What about it?"

"I did not approve these edits."

"You should be thanking me. That review was for shit."

Violet took a long, deep breath. "No, your edits were for shit."

"That's a matter of opinion."

Fury was a powerful generator. Violet felt unstoppable. "And the opinion that counts," she said, "is mine. You had no right to go behind my back and put this through."

Andi picked up a paper clip and seemed to be studying it. She smirked and glanced back at Violet. "What are you going to do about it?"

"Excuse me?"

"What . . . are . . . you . . . going . . . to . . . do . . . about . . . it?" she said slowly, enunciating each word as if she were talking to an imbecile.

Violet choked. This wasn't the reaction she was expecting. She thought that once she stood up to Andi the girl would be contrite. Her plan was to make the girl suffer a bit while she waited for Violet's forgiveness, which she would give only after Andi promised never to let it happen again.

But this? This was shocking. Andi was out for blood. Violet had to take it all the way or be defeated. She tried to summon the fury-fueled strength she had started with, but it was as if all her resources had been siphoned.

As Violet struggled to find her voice, she became aware of how quiet the office had become. People were listening from behind their cubicles. Everyone wanted to know how this would play out.

Violet closed her eyes for a moment, composing an answer to Andi's question. She formed a perfect response. The *only* response. But would she be able to get it out?

She took a deep breath and replayed Andi's challenge in her head: *What are you going to do about it?*

Violet looked straight into the young woman's kohl-lined eyes. "I'm going to get you fired," she said.

Without waiting for Andi's reply, Violet turned and walked away, heading straight for Buck Skelly's office. Her hands were still trembling, but she was as proud as she had ever been. Best of all, she was able to compose another perfect line of dialogue: *Delaney, I did it.*

Chapter 14

"A laudatory first step," said Dorothy Parker. "Congratulations, Ms. Epps. I think this calls for a toast."

Violet laughed. "You think everything calls for a toast."

"Nevertheless," her friend said, holding up her glass. "Cheers." She took a long sip. "So what happened when you spoke to the boss? Did he kick the little shit to the curb?"

"Not yet. He said he could either fire her right away or put her on probation, under whatever terms I dictate. I told him I'd consider it."

"Probation. That has a certain music to it. We'll come up with a set of demands to teach the child a lesson. Good for her, and good for you. Submission and dominance. Get something to write with."

Violet retrieved the laptop from the desk and rested it on her knees.

"I suppose pencil and paper have gone out of style," Mrs. Parker said. "Do they even bother teaching penmanship in school?"

"Not with the same emphasis. And we call it *script*. The word *penmanship* sounds almost romantically old-fashioned."

"God help me," Mrs. Parker said. "I've skipped right over obsolete and gone straight to *quaint*." She sighed. "Let's get started. Number one, your young lady will bring you coffee every morning that you are in the office."

Violet looked pained. "Oh, I don't know if Buck will even go for that."

"Why not?"

"It's considered . . . demeaning."

"My dear, the whole *object* is to demean her."

"Okay, coffee," Violet said, tapping her keyboard. "What else?"

"I know you people all use first names now in business, but she will call you Ms. Epps. And you will call her Andi."

Violet grinned. "I have to admit I like that."

"Of course you do. It puts you in the powerful position. And I think you'll find that power is exactly as intoxicating as they say. We may make a monster out of you yet. Now, let's see. Who opens your mail?"

"You mean actual letters? I don't get many of those. Almost everything is electronic."

"Pity," Mrs. Parker said. "How about filing?"

"Filing?"

"Surely, you have some papers to file."

"Again, not very much."

"Is there anything you can find for her to do on a daily basis?"

"I suppose I could have her respond to some of my less important e-mails. Maybe do some Internet research for me on filmographies."

"That will work. And when she answers your e-mails, she will list her title as 'secretary to Violet Epps.'"

Violet tapped that into her computer. "That's good, only I'm changing it to 'assistant.' We don't use the word *secretary* anymore."

"Why not?"

Violet shrugged. "I guess someone decided it was too degrading."

"For heaven's sake. Why don't they just call everyone 'vice president'? No work will get done, but everybody will just feel so damned important. No wonder a new employee acts insubordinate. Young people aren't taught their place."

"Like you, Benchley, and Sherwood at *Vanity Fair*?" Violet said, remembering what she read about the behavior of the young trio. Their boss didn't know what to do with them.

"Excellent," Mrs. Parker said. "I almost feel dressed down."

Violet felt close to panic. The last thing she wanted to do was alienate her mentor. "I . . . I didn't mean it that way," she said.

"Don't apologize. It was an apt observation. We behaved very badly."

Violet sighed, relieved. She made a mental note to try to remember that Dorothy Parker wasn't easily offended.

And yes, Mrs. Parker and her friends *had* behaved badly. Violet remembered reading about the practical joke the famous wit liked to play on a pompous *Vanity Fair* editor who, during the Great War, followed the position of the American Army in France by pinning little flags to a large map on the wall. Before he came in to work, Mrs. Parker liked to rearrange the flags to show the kaiser winning.

"You were mischievous," Violet said.

"Maybe even obnoxious," her guest agreed. "But our motivation was quite different from that of your young nemesis. We were fun, coltish, pushing the boundaries of taste, humor, and, God help us, creativity. It's what young people do. And though you describe your Andi as edgy, she is anything but. She is smug and punctilious, trying to rein in her older colleagues. Insubordination in the form of priggishness is simply *intolerable.*"

Violet smiled. She loved that Dorothy Parker was so heated about Andi's misbehavior, and so clear on the difference between the girl's conduct and the defiance that had gotten the famous wit fired from *Vanity Fair.*

For all her playfulness, Mrs. Parker took her role as a theater critic seriously. So when the actress Billie Burke gave what Dorothy Parker considered a terrible performance in a play, she wrote a scathing review, despite the fact that the actress was married to Florenz Ziegfeld, a prominent producer and one of *Vanity Fair*'s biggest advertisers.

Dorothy Parker was promptly dismissed.

Violet was glad the world didn't work that way anymore. Critics were encouraged to be honest. For most editors, it was a matter of principle. Though, of course, Violet wasn't naive enough to believe there was no commercial interest behind it; negative reviews sold more magazines than positive ones.

Dorothy Parker went back to Andi. "After your *assistant* brings you coffee, you'll dictate a list of tasks for her to accomplish. Make sure you give her tight deadlines, and be strict about it."

"Tight deadlines," Violet repeated, as she typed.

"And no insubordination," Mrs. Parker said. "She'll do everything you ask, and be pleasant and professional about it."

"What else?"

"That will do for now, I think."

Violet had a few other ideas, like making Andi pick up lunch for her and straighten her office shelves. She started adding them to the list.

"I could use another drink," Mrs. Parker said.

"Just a minute," Violet said, as she continued typing.

"Now, please. Don't forget I'm at your mercy."

"Hold *on*," Violet said. She read through the list one last time and made a few corrections. When she looked up, Mrs. Parker was smiling.

"What is it?" Violet asked.

"One of these days you'll tell me to go fuck myself, and then we'll really be onto something."

Violet laughed. There was that language again. She had read in several biographies that Dorothy Parker loved the shock value of the f-word, but she never understood how much impact it could have until hearing it in Mrs. Parker's genteel accent.

And sometimes the famous wit needed only to allude to the word to get a rise out of people. There was an anecdote about Mrs. Parker arriving at a party where people were playing a new game involving fruit in a bucket of water. When someone explained that the guests were *ducking for apples*, Dorothy Parker said, *That, with the exception of one consonant, is the story of my life.*

"I guess I'm becoming inured to your desperation about drinking," Violet said.

Mrs. Parker held up her empty glass. "If you were left with only one physical pleasure, you'd be desperate, too."

Violet paused to take that in. She was becoming more and more attuned to the pain behind Dorothy Parker's glib jokes.

"Do you miss the other physical pleasures?" she asked.

"You mean sex? Of course. Wouldn't you?"

"I guess, but . . . it's hard to say." Violet put her computer back on the desk and turned to face her guest. "I've never been dead."

"Exactly," Mrs. Parker said. "Sex very nearly defines what it means to be alive." She handed her empty glass to Violet. "I miss it like hell."

Inspired, perhaps, by the end of her conversation with Mrs. Parker, Violet was in the midst of a lovely sex dream when the phone rang. She didn't want to answer it. She wanted to go back into Michael's arms. His touch was exquisite. The pull of desire, merciless. Nothing mattered but reaching the summit she was climbing toward. Please, she thought. *Please.*

The phone rang again. Damn it. Violet looked at the clock. It was two-thirty in the morning.

"Hello?" She barely croaked it out.

"You sound so sexy."

It was Carl, drunk.

"Do you know what time it is?" she asked.

"Did I wake you?"

"Of course you woke me," she said. "What do you want?"

"I want *you*, baby."

"I told you—it's over. Don't call here again." It came out easily. She was still half asleep, and her filter was off.

"Don't you miss me at all? Even a little bit?"

Violet sat up to get a firmer grip on consciousness. He was trying to manipulate her—use her sense of guilt to get her to say something she would later regret. She wasn't going to do it.

"It's time to move on, Carl."

"I did. I did move on. I fucked another girl last night."

She hated his stupid drunken confessions, even when they were benign. But this was intolerable.

"You're sloshed, and it's the middle of the night, and I'm going back to sleep. Good-bye."

"I fucked another girl, but I pretended it was you."

"That's disgusting."

"I know, baby. But it's because I need you. I need you so bad. You take care of me. You make me a better man."

"That's not my job. You need to make yourself a better man."

"You're right. I don't deserve you."

That was her cue to argue with him and insist he was worthy, but she wasn't going to bite. "Get yourself to AA or something. Get a life."

"If I go to AA, will you take me back?"

"I'm hanging up now," she said. "Don't call here again."

Violet shut off the phone and dug herself back under the covers, looking for the dream she had lost. It was gone. But had she found something else?

Violet adjusted her pillow and asked herself why she had been able to remain firm with Carl this time. Was it simply because she was too tired to be fearful, or was something else going on?

Finally, she drifted off, and dreamed she was watching small stones dancing in a line. Or perhaps they were tiny bones, balancing on a wire. No, not a wire, but a cord—something organic that gave them strength. It fortified her.

When she awoke the next morning, Violet had to laugh at the obvious imagery of her subconscious. If the dream were a movie, the word *banal* would have found its way into her review. But trite or not, the message made her happy. Violet was growing a spine.

Chapter 15

"You okay?" Travis said, when Violet got on the elevator. "You look a little tense."

"A *little*?" It was the day she would be meeting with Andi to lay down the law. And though she had discovered her inner alpha dog when she spoke to Carl, this was a different animal entirely. Andi wasn't a drunk calling her in the middle of the night. She was a fierce little beast, intent on taking Violet down.

"What time's your meeting?" Travis asked.

"First thing," she said, her heart racing. She didn't want to do this, but she had to. It was important in every possible way. She needed to save face in the office and show that she couldn't be pushed around. But perhaps even more important, it was a chance to step up her game. If she could do this, maybe she really could get through the custody hearing without crumbling. It could make all the difference for Delaney . . . for both of them.

"Want me to be there?" Travis asked.

The elevator dinged, and the doors opened on their floor. "Thanks, but I need to do this on my own."

On the way to her office, Violet passed Andi chatting with two other assistants. They stopped talking when they saw her. One of them elbowed Andi, who looked up.

Violet pointed to her watch, affecting what she hoped was a stern expression. "Nine o'clock," she said, reminding Andi of their meeting time.

"Might be closer to nine-thirty," Andi said. "I'm pretty busy today."

It was, Violet knew, the first test. If she let this pass, she was sunk. The three young women stared at her, waiting for a response.

"Nine o'clock," Violet repeated. "If you're a single minute late, you might as well pack your things." It was a rehearsed line, and her voice sounded a little shaky when she said it, but she did it. And the impact was evident. Andi looked stricken.

Violet kept walking. "And bring something to write with."

She didn't look back but listened carefully. Silence. No laughter. No giggles. No snorts. Maybe she really *could* pull this off.

Sure enough, at five minutes to nine Andi poked her head into Violet's office. "You ready for me?"

"Give me one minute," Violet said.

It was pure posturing. Dorothy Parker had suggested it as an effective power ploy—a way to set the tone from the onset. She had said it was a trick she learned from the movie studio heads, who always kept her waiting.

Andi stood at the door as Violet stared at her computer screen. She opened and closed her e-mail a few times to make it look like she was busy, and then she clicked on the list of demands she had created with Dorothy Parker. She stared at it for several moments and then looked up.

"Okay, have a seat."

Andi took the chair facing Violet's desk. "Look," she said, "I want to apologize. I know I can be an asshole sometimes. I shouldn't have submitted that altered review. I'm really, really sorry."

Sorry my ass, Violet thought. If the girl wasn't worried about her job she would still be in the hallway, snickering with her friends.

Still, on an ordinary day, Violet would have accepted the apology. It was the way she had been self-programmed—make peace, move on. But not today. Today she was playing a role. She was the monster boss. Donald Trump meets Samuel Goldwyn meets *The Devil Wears Prada*.

"From now on you'll call me *Ms. Epps*," she said.

"What?"

"Write it down." Violet folded her arms to show that she wouldn't move on until Andi did as she was told.

The young woman opened the notebook on her lap and started writing.

"It's a six-month probation," Violet said. "And I'm giving you the terms. This is very serious. A single violation is cause for immediate dismissal. Understand?"

Andi didn't respond.

"Do you *understand*?" Violet repeated.

"Yes," Andi said, with a slight edge to her voice. It was just enough to show she was holding on to her contempt.

"*Yes, Ms. Epps*," Violet corrected. As she heard herself say it, she wanted to cringe. Surely, she had gone too far. But when she looked at Andi's face she saw a changed demeanor. The smartass attitude might not have vanished, but at least it was tamped down beneath a layer of discomfort and apprehension. Violet sat up a little straighter.

"So here's how it's going to work," Violet said. "We'll have a standing nine-o'clock meeting every time I'm in the office. You'll come with a pad, pencil, and a cup of coffee for me."

Andi looked horrified. "You . . . you want me to bring you *coffee*?"

"Milk, no sugar," she said, handing her the AMERICAN VIOLET mug that everyone in the office knew so well.

"Seriously?"

Violet knew the coffee demand would be the tipping point. To someone like Andi, it wasn't just demeaning, it was humiliating. She would have to walk past all the other assistants, carrying Violet's mug. More than anything else, this would put Andi in her place. Violet simply could not back down. She hid her trembling hands under the desk.

"Do you want to keep this job or not?"

"I do, but—"

"Write it down," Violet said.

"Vi—I mean, Ms. Epps. Please. I'll do anything else."

Violet folded her arms again and shook her head, maintaining eye contact. This was the moment that would make all the difference, and they both knew it. Andi had a decision to make, and it was a big one. She could roll over and acquiesce. Or she could tell Violet she was being a bitch, and face the very real possibility that she would be immediately dismissed.

Violet sensed that Andi was calculating the risk, wondering if Violet would really follow through and get her fired.

I'll do it, Violet tried to transmit. *I'll march right into Buck's office and you'll be unemployed in time to watch today's edition of* The View.

Andi broke eye contact and looked down at her black-painted bitten nails. She let out a long breath, and her whole being seemed to deflate. She clicked her pen and wrote it down.

I did it, Violet thought. I won.

With that out of the way, she launched into phase two of her plan. The Incentive. It was Violet's insurance, as her gut told her that without dangling a carrot, Andi's resentment would quickly fester and things would get ugly fast. And if this probation ended quickly with Andi's dismissal, neither of them would have learned very much. So Violet came up with a strategy and cleared it with Buck. She leaned across her desk.

"What do you want from this job?" she asked.

Andi shrugged. "I don't know."

"Sure you do."

"I guess . . . I want a chance to write for the magazine."

"Movie reviews?"

"Um . . ."

"It's okay," Violet said. "It's natural for you to want to move up."

"I could write book reviews, television—"

Violet held up her hand as a stop signal. She got it. The girl was trying to assure Violet she wasn't after her job. It was heartening to see
that Andi was concerned with appeasing her new master, even if she
didn't mean it.

"Here's the thing," Violet said. "If you can show me that you can follow these new rules without complaint or insubordination, I might be
able to give you a movie review assignment every now and then. And
who knows? If it works out, Buck might just be able to find a place for
you in books or television or some other department. How does that
sound?"

"Oh, my God. I . . . I don't know what to say. I thought you were going
to fire me or something and now. Shit, I can't believe this. You mean I
could really be promoted? That's . . . that's amazing."

"Let's take it one step at a time," Violet said.

"I can do this," Andi said. "I swear. I can toe the line. And I'm a
really, really good writer. Honestly."

"Hubris, Andi. You might have some talent, but at this point it's
important to remember that you're still pretty raw."

"Of course. I didn't mean to get cocky. I'm just excited, and, well, I
think I have potential. I really do. I'll prove it to you. I'll make you
proud."

Violet smiled. This kid knew when to suck up.

Chapter 16

Mrs. Parker held up her empty glass. "Another drink, if you don't mind."

"Can you hang in there for a few minutes?" Violet said. "I have to take Woollcott for a walk. He seems pretty desperate."

"And I don't?"

Violet looked at Mrs. Parker, whose languid repose seemed to border on sleepiness. "Frankly?" she said. "You seem . . . bored."

"Boredom is the ultimate desperation, my dear."

"How about if I close the guest book and make a drink when I get back?" Violet said, clipping the leash to Woollcott's collar.

"Here's a better idea: I'll take Cliché, and we'll both go for a walk."

Violet stared at her guest. "Seriously?"

"I could use a change of scenery."

"But how?"

"You can carry the guest book."

Even the thought made Violet nervous. "But we'll be out in public," she said. "What if someone asks who you are? I can't very well—"

"We'll tell them I'm your friend from East Egg or something. I'll use a pseudonym."

"East Egg is not a real town. Fitzgerald made that up."

"Fine, you decide where I'm from. Just be sure it's someplace with old money and mansions. I've never been rich, but I'm sure I'd be darling at it."

Violet grinned at the quip and considered Mrs. Parker's request. Now that she thought about it, there was indeed a kind of desperation about her—Violet could see it in her eyes. And, of course, it made perfect sense—it had been decades since the legendary wit had seen anything but the inside of the Algonquin Hotel or the rooms of this suburban house.

Violet took a deep breath and tried to imagine the worst that could happen. She supposed they could run into a neighbor who might find her companion odd, but that wasn't a big deal, was it?

She pulled an extra leash from the drawer and handed it to her guest. "Just don't do anything outrageous if we meet someone. I don't want my neighbors saying I have a houseguest who claims to be Zelda Fitzgerald."

"Wouldn't dream of it," Mrs. Parker said. "Take your purse. We'll stop someplace for cigarettes."

Violet made a face. "Has anyone ever told you what kind of poison is in those things?"

"You'll excuse me if I'm not overly concerned with my *health* at present," said Mrs. Parker.

Fair enough, thought Violet. But the problem was that she needed to maintain a healthy environment for a thirteen-year-old girl. Between the gin and the cigarettes, Dorothy Parker could turn the place into a speakeasy.

"Promise you'll only smoke outside?" she said.

"Outside?" Mrs. Parker seemed incredulous.

"Indoor smoking is prohibited just about everyplace nowadays."

"God help me, Western civilization is over. This country has turned into a nation of barbarians."

"Promise?" Violet repeated.

"I swear on my life," Dorothy Parker said. She didn't crack a smile, but Violet could read the joke in her eyes.

"Very funny," she said, "but I'll hold you to that."

Violet put her wallet and the open guest book into a large tote bag and stepped outside, expecting Mrs. Parker to follow. But when she turned around she saw her guest frozen in fear, clinging to the door frame.

"Are you okay?"

"It's been—" Mrs. Parker seemed to choke, unable to speak.

"So long?" Violet offered.

"Yes, so very long."

Poor Woollcott strained at the leash as Violet waited for her mentor to move, but the woman stood, stricken, her eyes wide in terror. Violet's heart broke for her new friend. While she couldn't imagine what it felt like to hover around this earthly plane in a strange limbo, she could come close to understanding how overwhelming it might be to experience the outdoors after decades in musty rooms. Mrs. Parker looked like she might collapse.

"Do you want to go back inside?" Violet asked.

Dorothy Parker took a long, slow breath and closed her eyes. When she opened them, her expression was transformed. The fear was gone, and Violet was in awe. Where had her friend gone to find such courage? It seemed to come from someplace too deep to mine with nothing but the force of one's will.

"Let's go," Mrs. Parker said in a strong, clear voice. Then she stepped from the shadows into the sunlight and looked toward the sky. She gasped, as if she were seeing it for the first time.

"We can take this slowly," Violet said.

"No need. I'm fine."

"Do you want to talk about it?"

Mrs. Parker pulled a handkerchief from her sleeve and wiped her nose. "Nothing to talk about, my dear. Which way is the closest smoke shop?"

Violet pointed to the right. "There's a 7-Eleven if we head south."

"South, then," Mrs. Parker said, and they set off.

Violet glanced at Dorothy Parker's face as they walked. It occurred to her that beneath the courage, beneath the rapture at seeing the sky, beneath everything, there was a sadness that never went away. She didn't know if she should probe. Clearly, Mrs. Parker didn't like to talk about her feelings, especially if they revealed any weakness. Still, Violet wanted her friend to know she cared.

"I'm sorry for you," she finally said. "I'm sorry you're stuck in this in-between place."

"Who said I'm stuck?"

"You're not?"

"Heavens, no."

"But I thought—"

"Every time the book is open there's that damned white light again."

Violet stopped walking and turned to her friend. "You mean you could cross over to the other side if you wanted to?"

"Of course."

Violet was stunned. She had assumed Mrs. Parker was trapped at this point midway between life and death, with no exit. "Why don't you, then?"

"Would you?"

"Of course. I mean, if the choice was between spending eternity trapped in an old book and going toward the light, I'd choose the light. They say it feels like a destination, like the place where it all makes sense. And most of all, where you get to see all the people you've lost." Violet could feel the hole in her heart where her mother and sister had been. She simply had to believe they would be reunited one day.

"Yes, well, most of the people I've lost can *stay* lost," Mrs. Parker said, and continued walking.

Violet stood for a moment, taking in this information. The sadness in her friend's eyes took on a new meaning. Something was keeping Dorothy Parker from heading toward the light.

She caught up with her mentor and walked along in silence. Mrs. Parker looked left and right as they strolled, and Violet followed her gaze, trying to see the surroundings from her friend's perspective. It was late spring, and the neighborhood was in full bloom.

"This place is lovely," Mrs. Parker said. "So verdant. And the flowers!"

"I thought you hated spring," Violet said, remembering one of Dorothy Parker's famous poems: *Summer makes me drowsy, Autumn makes me sing, Winter's pretty lousy, but I hate Spring.*

"Another lie," Mrs. Parker said. "I love this tender season. But if you tell anyone I'll break your pretty neck."

A short while later, Violet noticed a woman jogging on the other side of the road, her golden retriever trotting alongside her. It was inevitable that they would run into a neighbor on this long walk, and Violet was relieved it was the relatively benign Candy Baker, a sweetly named dental hygienist whose daughter had been Delaney's friend since they were small. Violet knew the kids were still close, as Delaney had recently received an invitation to the girl's bat mitzvah, and was eager to attend.

Violet glanced at Dorothy Parker, worried Candy might be able to pick up on something not quite earthly about her. She hoped that Candy was just neurotic and self-conscious enough to overlook any strangeness in others.

Candy waved to Violet and slowed down.

"What is that woman *wearing*?" Mrs. Parker asked.

"Spandex," Violet said. "It's for exercising."

"It's perfectly vulgar."

"Good thing Emily Post didn't live to see this," Violet said. "Right?"

"I wish she had," Mrs. Parker said. "It would have killed her."

While Candy stopped to catch her breath, her big retriever pulled on the leash toward Woollcott and Cliché. The woman and her dog approached.

"Hi, Violet! Hello! Hi," Candy said. She had a habit of compulsively repeating herself, as if you couldn't possibly understand what she was saying until she found two or more ways to phrase it.

"Hi, Candy."

"How are you? How's everything? How's Delaney? Everything okay? How *are* you?" Her dog sniffed Woollcott's behind and then moved on to Cliché. Almost immediately, the retriever leapt back and started barking. Clearly, the ghost dog had spooked her.

"What's gotten into you, Missy?" Candy said. "What's wrong, girl? Is something the matter? What is it? What's going on?" The dog strained against the leash, trying to get away. "What is it, Missy? What's wrong?" She looked up at Dorothy Parker.

"Don't stop on my account," Mrs. Parker said. "I'm keen to see if she answers."

"You're a hoot!" the neighbor said. "I'm Candy Baker, by the way."

"Surely, that's a stage name?"

Candy petted the retriever, who was now whimpering. "Ridiculous, isn't it? Baker is my married name, my husband's name. So I wasn't originally Candy Baker. But it's my real name. And you are?"

"Daisy Buchanan," Dorothy Parker said.

Violet shot her a warning look. The last thing she wanted was a buzz of neighborhood gossip about Violet Epps's crazy friend who thought she was a character from *The Great Gatsby*.

"Why do I know that name?" Candy asked. "It sounds so familiar. Are you famous or something? What do you do?"

"I'm an authoress," Dorothy Parker said.

"That must be it," Candy said. "I've probably seen your name on a book."

"Quite impossible, my dear."

"Impossible? Why? Why is it impossible? I know lots of writers."

"Not writers like me."

"Why? What kind of writer are you?"

Mrs. Parker's expression remained stoic, but Violet noticed a subtle change. It was in her eyes. Yes, there was a mischievous sparkle, and it made Violet panic. She knew exactly what was going on. The famous wit had manipulated Candy Baker into setting her up with a straight line.

Please, Violet tried to convey. Don't say it.

"I beg your pardon?" Dorothy Parker said to the neighbor, even though it was clear she had heard the question.

"What kind of writer are you?" Candy repeated.

There was a pause, and Violet held her breath. *Let it go, Mrs. Parker.*

Dorothy Parker waved away the question and looped her arm through Violet's. "Would love to stay and chat," she said, "but we're on our way to the smoke shop, and if I don't get a cigarette soon I'll pass out right here on the street. I'm sure you understand."

Violet sighed, relieved.

"Smoke shop?" Candy said. She was still glistening from her healthy run and looked confused.

"Great to see you," Violet said quickly. "Send my love to Alexandra."

Candy blinked. "Smoke shop?" she said again.

Mrs. Parker shrugged. "Vile habit. I used to say, 'I'll quit when I die,' but it turns out even *that* was harder than I thought."

"Wha—"

Violet nearly choked. "We'd better be going."

"Yes," Mrs. Parker said. "It was lovely meeting you."

Violet began to walk away, pulling on Mrs. Parker's arm. But the famous wit took one step with her and hesitated. She turned back to the neighbor.

"Didn't mean to be rude before," she said.

"Rude?"

"You had asked what kind of writer I am, and I didn't respond."

"Well, what kind are you?" Candy said.

"A ghostwriter," Violet answered, and steered her mentor away.

"How unkind," Mrs. Parker said, after they'd walked away. "You stepped on my punch line."

"You deserved it."

"I know. I'm awful—always trying to be so damned clever."

Violet softened. She didn't want Dorothy Parker to feel bad about her gift for witticisms. "It's okay," she said.

"It's not. I'm nothing but a wisecracker."

"You're much more than that," Violet said. "Besides, your wise-cracks are legendary."

"Exactly," Dorothy Parker said. "All I'm remembered for are my dreadful jokes."

They turned onto the commercial street and approached the con-venience store.

"Your jokes aren't dreadful," Violet said. "And anyway, your short stories and poems are still being read. How many writers have that kind of longevity?"

"My longevity is the sort I wouldn't wish on my worst enemy. Wit-ness this," she said, and waylaid a disheveled elderly man on his way out of the store. "Sir," she said, "have you ever heard of Dorothy Parker?"

"Sure. She was the broad who said, 'Men never make passes at girls who wear glasses.'"

"See what I mean?" Mrs. Parker said to Violet. "It's all anyone will ever remember—one smartass little poem."

"You got a couple bucks you can spare for a sandwich?" asked the old man.

"Certainly not," Mrs. Parker said. "And it's *seldom*. Men *seldom* make passes at girls who wear glasses."

The man rubbed the stubble on his face. "Seldom. Never. Who gives a damn?"

"Precisely," said Mrs. Parker.

The man stood looking at the two women, his eyes cloudy and sad, and it occurred to Violet that he might really need money for a sandwich. She considering giving him those few bucks he requested, but she was torn, like she always was with desperate drunks, as she knew the odds were pretty good that he would use the money to buy another bottle of whatever was in the paper bag he held.

Mrs. Parker seemed oblivious to the man's plight, and so he shrugged and walked off to find a place to sit against the side of the building.

"Shall we go in?" Mrs. Parker said, and Violet explained that they couldn't take the dogs into the store, so one of them would have to wait outside and hold the leashes.

"If you don't mind," said Mrs. Parker, "I'll go in so I can see what brands they offer. It'll be a regular adventure for me." She held out her hand. "A dollar, please."

Violet laughed.

"What's so funny?" Mrs. Parker asked.

Violet pointed to the sign in the window that said CIGARETTES: $9.99.

"For one pack? Heavens! It really is the end of the world."

Violet handed her mentor a twenty and watched as she went into the store carrying the tote bag containing the guest book. She wondered if it had ever before occurred to Mrs. Parker that she could move about in the world if the open book was placed in something she could carry.

After a few minutes, Violet sat on the curb with the two dogs.

Woollcott nosed his snout under her hand for a pet, while Cliché licked her arm. It made Violet laugh even more, and she petted them both.

Thank God for dogs.

She remembered the day she had gone to the North Shore Animal League with Delaney to find a dog to bring home. Every pooch they saw was lovable, but there was something special about the bond between Delaney and this little guy. She gave Woollcott a scratch behind the ears.

The trip to the animal shelter had been a present for Delaney's ninth birthday from her Aunt Violet. Of course, she had cleared it with Ivy and Neil beforehand, but she didn't tell the girl where they were going until they were in the car and on their way.

"A dog? Really? This is the best day of my *life*."

But her joy quickly turned to tears as the child had a meltdown trying to decide which dog she wanted. Aunt and niece were together in a private outdoor pen, where they got acquainted with the dogs one by one as the handlers brought them out. There were three that seemed particularly sweet, and Delaney wanted them all.

"How do I choose, Aunt Violet?" she cried.

Violet knew which dog was right—it was the funny-looking little guy with the bug eyes. He and Delaney had clicked immediately. But the handlers had also introduced them to a pretty little whitish dog with long, soft fur, and a frisky pup that appeared to be part beagle.

"They're all so cute," Delaney had said, after all the dogs had gone back inside. "What should I do?"

"What is your heart telling you?" Violet said.

"I don't know."

"There's no rush," Violet said. "We can ask the handler to bring them back outside. Which one do you want to see first?"

"The tan one with the funny eyes, I guess," Delaney said.

Violet sat on a bench and watched while the girl played with the little dog. After about ten minutes, Delaney picked up the animal and sat on her aunt's lap.

"I still don't know what to do," she said. "I really like this one, but I like the others, too."

"Let me tell you a story," Violet said. "When you were born, your mother called me to come to the hospital and meet you for the very first time. I didn't have a lot of experience with babies, and I was nervous to hold you. You were so tiny, like a fragile little doll. But your mother insisted. I sat in a big chair next to the bed, and she placed you in my arms. I thought, Okay, this won't be so bad. I'll just hold her for a second and give her right back."

"But you didn't?"

"I couldn't. I looked at your small, sweet face and something in me changed. I was washed in this warm feeling and the sense that I had known you all my life and that I was meant to love you. I wanted to hold you and hold you and hold you."

Delaney looked down at the dog cradled in her lap. She rubbed his belly, held his little paw, scratched his head.

"That's how I feel about this guy, Aunt Violet."

And that was it. When they got in the car with the dog, Violet called her sister to tell her about the animal they were bringing home.

"What does he look like?" Ivy had asked.

Violet thought for a moment. "Kind of like Alexander Woollcott."

"Woollcott," Delaney repeated from the backseat. "I'll love him forever."

Now, sitting in the parking lot of the 7-Eleven, it seemed like nothing in the world could be more important than getting the girl home and reuniting her with this little dog . . . and the aunt who was meant to love *her* forever.

Violet noticed a shadow over her and looked up to see Dorothy Parker standing beside her, smoking a cigarette.

"Ready to go?" Violet said.

"Just one minute," Mrs. Parker said, and pulled a wrapped package from the paper bag. It wasn't until she walked over to the disheveled old man and handed it to him that Violet realized what it was. A sandwich.

Chapter 17

"Close your eyes," Michael Jessee said. "Relax. Take a slow breath in. Let a slow breath out."

It was the beginning of kung fu class, and he was leading the group through a meditation before starting their exercises. His voice, commanding yet soothing, enabled Violet to let go and float into a deep relaxation. When it ended, she was focused and ready to begin.

First, Michael led them through floor exercises, including push-ups, which Violet hated. Her upper body just wasn't strong enough to go all the way down and get back up again. She normally did modified push-ups, with her knees on the floor. And even those were nearly impossible to complete. Today, though, she was determined to do one full regular push-up. Mind over matter, she told herself. God knows she had heard enough stories about people who had accomplished Herculean tasks by sheer force of will. Surely she could coax one damned push-up out of her skinny arms and narrow shoulders.

Give it everything, she commanded herself, as she bent her elbows and lowered her body toward the mat. Her slender arms trembled, threatening to collapse under her own weight, but she refused to give in. She hovered, feeling the strain of blood rushing to her head. No, she thought, I am not going *down*. I am going *up*. Up! Just one . . . damned . . . push. Violet harnessed all the power she could and pressed her body upward until at last her elbows straightened. She did it! One perfect push-up.

She felt proud and pleased as they moved on to the basic drilling of kicks and punches. Michael broke the group down into pairs for each routine. Violet noticed immediately that there was an odd number of students in tonight's class, which meant that he would be participating in the exercises. For the first one, he paired himself with Jason, and Violet got one of the Lindas. She chided herself for feeling rejected. It was stupid and immature. There was absolutely nothing personal about it.

She tried to stay focused as they went through their punches, using a thick pad that Linda held as Violet jabbed. Then they switched places. When it came time for the kicking drills, Michael reassigned the pairs. *Me*, Violet thought, as she waited for Michael to make his choice. *Pick me.* But this time, Violet got Mariana, and Michael paired himself with Suzette.

Each time they finished an exercise, Violet thought it was her turn to be paired with Michael. But he went through every member of the class until she was the only one who hadn't been matched with him.

And then he ended the pairing exercises.

Was it her imagination, or was Michael purposely avoiding her? Perhaps he was embarrassed by what he had said when he left her house the other night. *I'm glad you're not seeing Carl anymore.* He must have meant it in a paternal way, after all. It made perfect sense. How could she have thought for a second he would have been interested in her?

At the end of class, everyone bowed to Michael and said, *"Dohr-che Sifu,"* Cantonese for *Thank you, teacher*, before exiting the training room.

Violet was in the reception area, stooping to put on her shoes, when she heard Michael's voice.

"Can I see you for a minute?"

She looked up. "Me?"

He nodded and pointed to his office. She followed him inside.

She had never been back there before. It was a small room, with red industrial carpet and a wood desk, neatly arranged. She expected the walls to be adorned with Chinese watercolor prints, or perhaps with Asian weapons and trophy cases, like the reception area. Instead, there were Marx Brothers movie posters—*A Night at the Opera, Duck Soup, Animal Crackers, Horse Feathers.*

"You're . . . you're a Marx Brothers fan," she stammered. It was the last thing she expected from a martial artist and ex-Marine. But his attraction to puns was suddenly making a lot of sense.

"That's the most ridiculous thing I ever heard," Michael said, pretending he was holding a cigar.

Violet laughed. "*I'm* a Marx Brothers fan," she said, thumping her chest for emphasis.

"I know."

"You do?"

"Well, I figured it out. You've made a couple of oblique references in your reviews, and I thought, 'Ah, she's one of us!' "

Violet smiled. He'd been reading her reviews pretty closely. "It's like we belong to a club, except . . ."

"Except we refuse to belong to any club that would have us as members," he said, finishing her thought by paraphrasing Groucho.

She laughed. "I didn't even think you knew who Groucho *was!*"

"I didn't," he said, "until I saw my first Marx Brothers movie. I was fourteen and had been home with a sore throat and slept all day. So at two in the morning I was wide awake, watching TV, and this crazy black-and-white movie came on. I laughed so hard I woke up the whole house. The next day my parents insisted it was the fever that made it seem that funny. I knew they were wrong, so as soon as I could, I borrowed every Marx Brothers video from the library, and that was it. I've been a fanatic ever since."

She watched his mouth as he talked. Now I'm really in trouble, she thought. Dorothy was right. This was a crush. And it was getting worse by the minute. She put her hand to her throat. "You're full of surprises," she said.

"So are you."

Violet was sure he was referring to her strange, aggressive behavior when she was possessed by Dorothy Parker, and she felt herself flush. Did he expect her to respond? To defend herself? She struggled to find the right words, but he jumped in and took her off the hook.

"You did a push-up," he said, smiling.

So *that's* what he meant. Violet let out a breath. "I didn't think anyone noticed."

"It's my job to notice."

Violet knew a single push-up was a small thing, but the thought that Michael noticed pricked at her heart. "I was determined."

"I could see that. And you know, if you can do a push-up, you can do anything."

He looked so serious and intense—so genuinely impressed with her—that Violet actually believed him. She *could* do anything. In fact, she could even say exactly what was on her mind. The trick, she told herself, was to do it without hesitation. Don't overthink it—just say it.

"Is there," she said, and paused. Damn it, she told herself, don't chicken out now. Just do it. Do it like you did the push-up. "Is there a reason you didn't pair up with me for any of the drills?"

There, she said it. And Michael didn't even flinch. He didn't roll his eyes. He didn't look at her like she was being ridiculously childish. He just stared her straight in the eyes and nodded.

"Yes," he said, his delicate speech impediment making it sound almost like *yesh*. She realized that it wasn't just the idea of a tender imperfection that made her heart constrict. It was that he was so unselfconscious about it. How could she possibly not admire this man?

"After the other night," he continued, "I thought it was important for us to talk so you wouldn't feel awkward in class. And I hope this isn't embarrassing for you, but I need to be frank. I'd really like to . . ." He paused to find the right word, and Violet thought she might pass out waiting to hear what came next.

What? she thought. You'd really like to what? Kiss me? Fuck me? Beat me with a stick? Sell me life insurance?

"Go out with you sometime. On a . . . *date.*" He smiled when he said the word, as if it was in quotes. Like it was a word that was so charmingly old-fashioned it deserved special reverence. "I know you were medicated the other night," he continued, "so I don't want to just assume you like me, too, though I hope you do. But if not, just say so and I'll drop it. No weirdness, no hard feelings."

"Of course I like you," she blurted, and then grabbed a chair for balance. Had she really just said that?

Michael grinned, and looked like he was about to say something, but got distracted by the sound of students in the reception area.

"I wasn't even supposed to teach the next class," he said, apologetically, "but one of my instructors didn't show up."

"It's okay," she said, though she didn't quite mean it. She wanted to hold this moment as long as she could. The feeling of standing there, facing him, and knowing how he felt was just too sublime.

"You sure?" he said.

She took a breath and let it out, releasing him. "I'm sure. Go teach."

"How about Mariana's show—Friday, right?" he asked. "Can I pick you up?"

She grinned at the thought of making that group outing an official date. Sure, they were meeting the whole class at the theater, but if he was picking her up and dropping her off, they would get a chance to be alone together. And at the end of the evening he would walk her to the door, kiss her good night with that lovely mouth.

He stared at her, waiting for a response. This is no time to freeze, she told herself. He's waiting. Just say it. Just say yes.

The fear was sneaking in from all sides, trying to get her to doubt herself, to worry that he wasn't being genuine, to convince her he was interested only in the woman she could never be. She imagined the fear as a noxious gas seeping in under the door, depriving her of oxygen and threatening to consume her.

But it wasn't a gas, damn it. It was a habit—an insecurity she had control over. And she *could* control it. Then, just as she had done on the exercise floor, Violet harnessed all her strength. Only this time, she forced herself to look Michael straight in the eye and utter one powerful syllable.

"Yes."

Chapter 18

Even as Violet said it, she realized there was a complication. Friday was her day in the office, and she had planned to go straight from work to Mariana's show. If she wanted Michael to pick her up at home, she would need to rush through work and leave early enough to catch the train home and then change for her date, only to go *back* into the city.

"This is not the way a grown woman behaves," she said to Dorothy Parker, as she went through her closet trying to find the right clothes for Friday night. They were in her bedroom, and her guest was sitting in the side chair. Violet was in her underwear, and had already rejected three different outfits.

"Alas, this is *exactly* the way a grown woman behaves," Mrs. Parker said, as she absently petted Cliché. "Let me see that blue thing you passed."

"This?" Violet said, pulling out a sleeveless silk charmeuse dress in cornflower blue. "Too fancy."

"Nonsense."

"This is Off-Off-Broadway," Violet explained. "People will be wearing jeans. Or black."

"Then it's perfect. Try it on."

Violet made a face.

"Humor me," Mrs. Parker said.

Violet stepped into it. "Okay," she said, "but I'm not wearing it. I'll look ridiculous." She zipped it up and stood back from the mirror.

"Good heavens," Mrs. Parker said. "That's a dress that will get you laid."

"Then I'm definitely not wearing it."

"Don't you *want* to get laid?"

"Not on a first date."

"Of course not," Mrs. Parker said. "But if you want him to court you, to want you, to burn for you, wear that damned dress."

"I just don't think it's appropriate," Violet said. The way it hugged her slender contours made her feel like she was wearing her sexuality on the outside, and that frightened her. What would people think if they knew how desirable she felt in this slinky satin sheath?

"Attractiveness is nothing to be ashamed of," Mrs. Parker said. "Besides, it's not even that revealing. You should have seen some of the numbers we wore in the twenties."

Violet knew all about the skimpy flapper dresses of Dorothy Parker's youth. At the time, they were positively scandalous. Mrs. Parker came of age in an era of sexual liberation more revolutionary than the 1960s. When the roaring twenties hit, many people in the younger generation rejected their parents' Victorianism by embracing sex and alcohol with wild abandon. They were the original party animals. Was it any wonder, then, that Dorothy Parker was responsible for popularizing the phrase "one-night stand"?

Still, much of her wit targeted promiscuity, like the time she said, "If all the girls at the Yale Prom were laid end to end, I wouldn't be at all surprised." Or when she was looking for a new apartment and told the real estate agent, "All I need is room enough to lay a hat and a few friends."

Violet stared at herself in the mirror. She did look hot in the dress.

She remembered the first time she'd tried it on. Ivy was with her, and they were shopping for a cocktail dress Violet could wear to an Oscar-night party for journalists.

"I'm not letting you walk out of this store without that dress," Ivy had said.

"I feel like I'm in a costume," Violet protested.

"What's wrong with that? Everyone feels like they're in a costume when they get dressed up."

There was something almost magically beautiful about the garment. It was sexy but not slutty, with a neckline that reached her collarbone in front but plunged into a deep V in the back. And the fabric was exquisite.

But it was so flattering to her lanky figure it made Violet nervous; there was only so much attention she could handle.

"What will people *say*?" she had asked her sister.

"They'll say, 'That Violet Epps is *smokin'*!'"

"You don't know these people. They'll say, 'Violet Epps thinks she's all that.'"

"But you *are* all that."

"I wish it came with a jacket."

Violet turned from the mirror to Dorothy Parker. "I have an idea," she said, and pulled a black cardigan from her closet. She put it on over the dress and looked back to the mirror. Yes, it was just the thing to dress it down . . . and cover it up.

"What do you think?" she asked.

Mrs. Parker stared and thought. "There's something to be said for the wrap," she finally said. "He'll spend the entire night wondering what's underneath. Just be sure you take it off at the end of the evening, as he walks you to the door."

"Great advice," Violet said, though she had no intention of doing so.

The next day, Violet arrived at the office bright, happy, and counting the hours till her date with Michael.

She stopped at the door of Travis's office and saw his head down on his desk.

"What's the matter?" she asked.

"Toothache," he said, without looking up. "Goddamned toothache."

"Is there anything I can do?"

Say no, she thought. Please say no. Violet was trying to rush through her day so she could leave early enough to get home in time to shower and change before Michael came to pick her up.

"Waiting to hear back from the dentist," Travis said. "If I can't get an immediate appointment, please shoot me."

"Did you take anything?"

Travis picked up his head. He looked awful. "With all due respect?" he began.

"Leave you the hell alone?" Violet offered.

His eyes were glazed in pain. "Yuh," he said, and let his head drop again.

She went to her office and got to work, which was a breathless blur of returning phone calls, proofreading copy, meeting Buck about next week's schedule, and writing up proposals for two feature articles—one on a former ingenue who was making an impressive comeback, and the other on two Brat Pack actors who had teamed up to start a production company. She was slowed down a bit by passing some of the work on to Andi, as it took longer to explain how to respond to a particular e-mail than it would to answer it herself. But she knew it was important to keep a flow of demands going.

Late in the morning, Andi came in to relay a message from Buck about a special issue they would be publishing in the summer, and Violet told her to have a seat.

"I need to ask a little favor," Violet said, handing Andi a slip of paper with Barry Beeman's name and number on it.

"Who's this?" she asked, looking at it.

"He's the general manager of the Algonquin Hotel, and he wants to talk to me, but I need to stall him for a while. Could you—"

"Easy," she said. "Anything else?"

"Easy?" Violet repeated, surprised. Wasn't Andi even going to ask why?

"Sure," the young woman said. "You're out of town, but you're eager to meet with him in person, so after exchanging several phone calls and e-mails we finally settle on a mutually convenient date three weeks from now. Unfortunately, you'll have to cancel at the last minute due to a medical emergency."

Violet's mouth opened and nothing came out.

"I'm scaring you, aren't I?" Andi said.

Violet nodded. "Just a bit."

After Andi left her office, Violet got back to work, alternately rushing through tasks and checking the clock. She was making good time and was almost ready to leave when Travis appeared at her door.

"How are you feeling?" she asked.

He stepped inside. "Like shit. But my dentist said he can squeeze me in. I'm leaving."

"Thank goodness."

"One problem," he said. "I was supposed to see a screening of that new Matt Damon today. Can you cover for me?"

"I have tickets to a show tonight," she said.

"When's the curtain?"

"Eight, but—"

"Then it won't be a problem," he said. "The film will be over by six-thirty. That should leave you plenty of time."

"I was supposed to go home first."

"Do you *have to* go home first? This is the last screening."

"Are you sure?" she said.

He frowned. "Sorry. I'll make it up to you."

"It's not that, it's . . ." She trailed off, knowing how frivolous it would sound if she said she wanted to shirk this responsibility for a date. Still, she couldn't remember the last time she had looked forward to anything this much, and it seemed so unfair. Disappointment pressed so hard on her heart that she wanted to cry.

Be a grown-up, she coached herself. It's just a date. Just one stupid date. Still, she felt herself sinking. She'd have to get rid of Travis quickly if she didn't want him to see her start sniveling.

Andi appeared at her door behind Travis.

Oh, no, Violet thought. Not her, not now.

"Sorry to interrupt," Andi said, in her most polite voice. "I just finished researching those filmographies. Want me to e-mail them to you?"

"Sure," Violet said absently.

"Is there anything else?"

"No . . . wait, maybe." Violet had an idea that lightened her heavy heart with a giddy rush. She looked at Travis, who raised an eyebrow.

"I don't know," he said.

"It'll be okay," Violet said. Then she addressed Andi. "How would you like your first review assignment?"

Chapter 19

Violet tried to keep her hand steady as she applied a thin sweep of black-brown eyeliner. "I just hope Buck isn't angry that I gave the review to Andi."

"Why would he be?" asked Mrs. Parker, who was sitting on the bed, watching Violet get ready for her date.

"Because it's my job to cover for Travis. It's a bit irresponsible of me to pass the assignment to an assistant just because I have a date. If Buck gets mad, I have no defense." She finished with the eyeliner and opened her mascara.

"To hell with it," Mrs. Parker said. "Bosses always get angry. It's what they do. Think of it as a privilege of rank."

Violet applied the makeup to her lashes. "So I'm doing him a favor by giving him something legitimate to sound off about?" she said.

"Precisely."

The doorbell rang, and Violet panicked. "Shit. He's early."

"So what?" asked Mrs. Parker.

"I'm not ready!"

"He'll wait. Finish what you're doing."

Violet took a deep breath. "You're right," she said, smoothing out her dress. She slipped on her sweater and took one last look in the mirror. Dorothy Parker was right about the outfit. It was perfect. She put on her earrings and brushed her hair.

"All done?" Mrs. Parker asked.

"Except for one thing," Violet said, as she approached the guest book on her dresser.

"Oh, come, now," said her guest.

Violet shrugged. "Sorry," she said, and slammed the book. Then she dashed downstairs, where Woollcott was already stationed by the door, barking and yipping and running around in quick circles. He wasn't usually this hyper when guests arrived, and it made her laugh.

"I know exactly how you feel," Violet said, and gave him a pet.

She took a deep breath and told herself there was nothing to be nervous about. She was just going to a play with a group of friends, and Michael happened to be taking her. It wasn't even a real date, was it?

Okay, so maybe it was. And maybe it was all right to let the giddiness dancing around her belly come right to the surface. It was real. She was going out with Michael Jessee.

Violet opened the door, trying to temper her ridiculous smile into an even sort of expression. But almost instantly the effort became moot.

Confused, Violet blinked . . . and blinked again.

"Delaney?"

Violet looked past her niece and saw Malcolm's salsa-red RAV4 at the curb. Sandra was next to him in the passenger seat. They waved, smiling. Violet struggled to get her bearings.

"What are you doing here?" she asked her niece.

"Can I stay here tonight, Aunt V?" Delaney said. "Please? The old farts are going to a fiftieth-anniversary party for some cousins of Sir Tansalot and won't let me stay home alone. I've been begging and pleading for the past two hours, and they finally agreed that I could stay here if it was okay. Please say yes, Aunt V. *Please.* I can't do this. I can't go to a party with a bunch of creepy old people trying to be cool."

"How come no one told me about this?"

"They just sprang it on me. They thought I'd *want* to go. Seriously. The grandfather unit said, 'There will be dancing, Del,' like that would convince me. Dancing, Aunt V! Old people *dancing*. I think I'd rather die."

"I wish I'd known."

"Please say yes. You have to. Don't make me go to this thing."

Violet almost choked on her own disappointment, but she tried to resign herself. After all, maybe this was meant to be. Maybe this was the universe's way of telling her she was aiming too high. She put her arms around her niece.

"Of course you can stay with me," she said.

"Thank you!" Delaney said, and waved to her grandparents. "I'm staying here!" she shouted, and the Webers drove off.

Delaney bent to pick up Woollcott, who was frantic with delight. "You look hot," she said to her aunt when she rose. "Did you have a date or something?"

"Or something," Violet said. "But it's okay. I'll call his cell phone and cancel." She swallowed against a lump in her throat and smiled. Mentally, she was already taking off her lovely dress and hanging it in the closet, changing to sweats, and curling up on the sofa with Delaney. This is exactly what it means to be a parent, she thought. The child comes first. The child always comes first. She put her arm around her niece.

"Is that him?" Delaney said, pointing to a shiny white SUV pulling up by the curb.

Violet sighed. "It is."

Michael got out of the car and slammed the door.

"Holy shit," Delaney said, taking him in. "No wonder you broke up with Vincent van Loser." She put the dog down. "You should keep your date with him. I'll stay here with Woollcott. I'm old enough. I really am. All my friends stay home alone."

All your friends didn't lose their parents a year ago and then get ripped from their home, Violet thought.

"Don't be silly," Violet said. "I'd rather stay here with you. I can go out with him another night."

When Michael approached, Violet introduced him to Delaney and explained what had happened.

"I hope you understand," she said.

"Of course," he said. "I would have done the same thing."

"Sorry I didn't call you to cancel, but this only happened moments ago."

"Did you see that red RAV4 pulling away?" Delaney said. "That was them. It's my grandfather's midlife crisis car. He actually thinks it's sexy."

"Well, I only saw the rear," Michael said. "But it sure was smokin'."

Violet laughed. "Michael likes corny jokes," she explained to her niece.

"That's only because I have an *ear* for them," he said.

Delaney groaned, and Michael smiled at the reaction.

"Now I bet you're sorry you didn't go to that party with your grandparents," he said.

"No way!" Delaney said. "A hundred bad jokes are still better than watching old people shake their booties." She shuddered.

"In that case," he said to the girl, "I have an idea. How do you feel about edgy Off-Off-Broadway shows?"

"You want to take me with you?"

"What do you think?" he said to Violet.

"I think . . . I think it's great, but what about tickets?"

"Mariana told me they're not even close to sold out. In fact, I can think of another person who might want to join us."

And that's how Violet, Delaney, Michael, and his lively daughter, Kara, wound up settling into seats at the Little Harlequin Theater on the West Side of Manhattan. It was a compromise that Violet thought was the best of all worlds. She got to spend time with her niece doing something that was a real treat, while getting to know Michael and his chatty daughter, who brought quite a bit of energy to their small group. Violet was delighted by how well the girls hit it off. Then something happened that changed Violet's mood entirely.

The curtain rose.

Mariana, as the main character, Laci Harper, was in a bed, stage right, sleeping. The lighting was dim, to indicate that it was nighttime. There was a loud noise that woke her, and she sat up, holding a blanket over her body. A spotlight shone on her as the noise happened again. This time, she jumped out of bed.

Naked.

Facing the audience.

Bathed in light.

Violet looked at Michael. "I'm sorry," he whispered. "I had no idea." He looked back at the stage. "Oh, God."

The audience gasped as the source of the noise revealed itself. There was a man hiding in the shadows of Laci's bedroom.

He, too, was naked.

Violet looked over at the girls, whose faces went from shock to uncontrollable giggles. They collapsed into each other.

"Maybe we should go," Michael whispered to Violet.

"Right now?" she said. "One minute into the show?" Violet cringed at the thought of making a scene and pushing their way past everyone to leave the theater. But how on earth could Delaney handle this when she was horrified at the thought of fully dressed old people on a dance floor? She tapped her niece.

"Are you okay?" Violet whispered. "Do you want to leave?"

"Are you kidding? This is the best thing that ever happened to me *in my life.*"

Violet sighed. "I guess we'll wait until intermission," she said to Michael.

But at intermission the girls begged to stay, making a very good argument that they had already seen everything there was to see, so what point was there to leaving?

And so they went back inside. Afterward, while the rest of the kung fu class went out for drinks with Mariana and some of the other cast members, Michael and Violet took the girls out for ice cream. The youngsters huddled together as they texted their friends about the adventure, and laughed as they showed each other the responses. In between, they scraped at their ice-cream scoops—chocolate-chip cookie dough for Delaney and mint chocolate chip for Kara—with tiny plastic spoons. Violet didn't think it was possible for any two kids to be happier than those girls were at that moment, and it filled her up.

"They're certainly bonding," she said to Michael.

It continued throughout the car ride home, with lots of whispering and giggles. Violet and Michael talked about the play and parenting and how he came to own the kung fu studio. It was clear there were topics they both skirted because of the backseat passengers, as "We'll talk about that another time" became a familiar refrain whenever they came close to discussing Violet's custody of Delaney or Michael's relationship with Kara's mother.

But there was another issue Violet knew wouldn't be addressed that evening—the good-night kiss. With the girls in tow, they would have to shake hands like business acquaintances, or perhaps steal a chaste peck on the cheek.

Violet tried to convince herself it was for the best, but sitting that close to Michael—smelling his aftershave and watching his strong hands as he drove—made her ache for contact.

As they turned into Violet's neighborhood and got close to the house, the whispering in the backseat intensified and then stopped. Delaney cleared her throat.

"We're going to walk the dog together," she announced. "Me and Kara-bon."

Violet knew just what they were up to. Clearly, the girls were conspiring to give the grown-ups some time alone.

"'Kara-bon'?" she asked. Violet didn't always understand how her niece came up with her nicknames.

"She's practically a Kara-bon copy of her father," Delaney explained.

Michael laughed, delighted. The pun was right up his alley. "I might need to steal that," he said.

"Be my guest, Groucho."

"Groucho?" he said.

Violet blushed. "I might have said something to her about your Marx Brothers posters."

When they got to the house, Violet and Michael stayed by the door as the girls went inside to fetch the dog. They watched as the youngsters walked off, being pulled along by the leash.

"See you later," Delaney said.

"Just around the block!" Violet called. "It's late."

"They'll be okay," Michael assured her.

"Aren't kids amazing?" she said. "It's like they've been best friends forever."

"Delaney really took me by surprise," he said. "I didn't expect her to be so . . . together."

"She's come a long way."

"That must have been a hard road for both of you."

"There were times," she began, and stopped, remembering those early months when it seemed impossible that Delaney would ever be pulled from her grief. In the hospital, she had been catatonic. At home, she didn't want to do anything but stay in her room and cry. And then there were the days when she decided she needed to break everything in sight. Just getting her into the car to visit her therapist sometimes took hours. Violet had wanted to break a few things herself.

She shook her head. It was too much to even talk about.

"Yes," she simply said. "It was hard."

"You moved mountains," he said, and she felt her throat constrict. It was true—she *had* moved mountains.

"Thanks," she choked out, and wanted to change the subject. She didn't want to talk about death or grief or anything else that pushed them from the romantic mood they had been approaching just moments ago.

She wanted him to kiss her.

"I guess we should talk about something else," he said.

She laughed. "You read my mind."

He moved a piece of hair from her face. Yes, she thought. Now. Kiss me now.

"What should we talk about?" he asked.

"I think I might be out of words." It was the perfect thing to say. Surely he'd take the hint and move in for contact.

He smiled. "I think we should do this again."

Violet was getting dizzy waiting for that kiss. Why was he still talking?

"Only next time," he continued, "just the two of us."

"I'd like that."

"I think those smart little girls are conspirators," he said, taking a step closer.

"Partners in crime," she agreed. "They wanted to be sure we had some time alone together."

He smirked. "I wonder why."

She got it. He was teasing her, prolonging the moment, making the tension mount. And it was working. *If you don't kiss me now,* she tried to transmit, *I'm going to collapse into a quivering heap.*

"They'll be back any second," she said, "so you can ask them yourself."

He looked amused. She had just shown him her hand, revealing her impatience. Damn it, she thought. Now I'm as naked as Mariana was on that stage.

Violet heard the girls' voices and knew they were on their way back. A few more seconds and it would be too late.

"I hear them," he said.

Defeat. He had stalled too long. There would be no kiss after all. Now there was nothing left but to wait for him to leave so she could go up to her room and wallow in self-pity.

Then he did it. And the surprise worked. Violet turned into liquid in his arms, lips to lips, body to body, locked in a kiss that could have gone on forever if it weren't for a couple of young teenagers making more than enough noise to announce their arrival.

Chapter 20

"Of course," Dorothy Parker said, when Violet explained what had happened at the end of the date. "I knew he'd be a sublime kisser."

Delaney was upstairs sleeping, and they were trying to keep their voices down.

"Why were you so sure?" Violet asked.

"Please. That man is as sensual as a ripe peach."

Violet hugged herself. His scent was on her clothes, and it made her shiver. She closed her eyes and inhaled. When she opened them, Dorothy Parker was staring at her, amused.

"I must look ridiculous," Violet said.

"Indeed."

"I can't believe how giddy I feel about this. I feel like . . . listening to love ballads, reading poetry. Maybe yours." She blushed at the confession.

"Good heavens, don't read mine," Mrs. Parker said. "It's cynical tripe. Enjoy this feeling."

"It's not tripe. And anyway, maybe I need a little cynicism right now. I feel like some silly little girl with a terrible crush."

"Of course you do. Most women would push their best friend overboard to sleep with a guy like that."

"It's not just about sex," Violet said.

"But you *do* plan on sleeping with him?"

"I hadn't thought that far ahead."

"Liar."

Violet laughed. Was she that transparent? "Right now I'm just hoping he asks me for a second date."

"You didn't make plans?"

"Not exactly," Violet said, and heard her cell phone vibrate. "Wait a second—maybe that's him." She picked up her phone, and, sure enough, there was a text message from Michael. "He says Kara fell asleep less than two blocks from here."

"What else?"

"He had a great time, and doesn't think the girls are traumatized from the nudity."

"And?"

"And he wants to know if I'm free this Wednesday."

Violet looked up, smiling, and Mrs. Parker brought her small hands together in a clap of delight. "There you have it! Your happily ever after."

Violet pressed reply and began typing a message.

Mrs. Parker frowned. "What on earth are you doing?"

"I'm saying yes."

"Are you mad? Put down that damned contraption. Worst thing you can do is respond immediately."

"You think?"

"If you never trust me again on a single thing, trust me on this. He can wait until tomorrow for your reply."

Violet nodded. Dorothy Parker was right. She had already tipped her hand on her impatience to be kissed. No sense in showing him just how insanely eager she truly was. That could scare him off for sure.

She shut off her phone. "You're right," she said, and leaned back in her chair. When she realized she was jiggling her foot with nervous energy, she decided to change the subject to get her mind off the urge to text Michael back. And anyway, there was something she had been meaning to discuss with her mentor, and this seemed like a good opportunity. "As long as we're talking about happily ever afters," she began, "can I ask you a question?"

"It's still a free country, I believe."

"One day I'm going to have to return this guest book to the Algonquin. The general manager is breathing down my neck. And even if he wasn't, I can't keep what isn't mine."

"Yes, of course. But I'm in no hurry. Time isn't exactly in short supply with me."

"That's really what I wanted to ask you about."

"We're not going to have a conversation about eternity, are we?"

"Well, yes," Violet said.

"How dreadfully dull."

"Don't you think about it?"

"I spent my whole life thinking about death. I even tried to hasten it a few times with the help of pills and razor blades. But now that I'm dead I can see it's just as boring as a cocktail party when the bar runs dry."

Her mentor was deflecting, but Violet was determined to stay on point. "You have a choice to make," she said. "Either you plan on staying in the book forever or will one day go into the light."

Mrs. Parker took a sip of her drink. "You put too much tonic water in this."

"I know you don't want to talk about this."

"I just don't see what the rush is," Mrs. Parker said.

"I didn't say there was a rush, it's just that you're all alone in there. Wouldn't you be better off on the other side? I don't mean now, or even anytime soon, but—"

"My dear child, what do you think is waiting for me on the other side?"

"You had a sister, too, didn't you?"

"Helen."

"Don't you miss her?" Violet asked.

Mrs. Parker ignored the question and petted Cliché, studying his fur as if his dander held the answer. Violet waited and waited. Just when she decided her guest was not going to answer, Mrs. Parker looked up.

"Every single day," she said.

"And what about your mother?" Violet asked.

"What about her?"

"Don't you think about her, too?"

Mrs. Parker's expression hardened. "My mother had the gall to up and die when I was five years old."

"So you feel like she abandoned you?"

"Dear God, we're not really going to discuss my childhood, are we?"

"But you do want to see her," Violet said, "don't you?"

The famous wit stared into her drink. "I don't even remember her," she said quietly.

"Deep down I'm sure you do. I mean, when you reunite . . ."

"This conversation is getting tiresome," Mrs. Parker said, and drained the last few sips of her drink. "Fetch me another, will you, dear? Not so much tonic this time."

Chapter 21

Violet knew better than to press Dorothy Parker on a subject she refused to discuss, so she let it go, and hoped that eventually her mentor would feel comfortable enough to open up.

In the meantime, Mrs. Parker had made a special request. She wanted to see Violet's former nemesis, Andi, in action. And so Violet agreed to bring the guest book to the office, as long as Mrs. Parker promised to keep herself invisible.

"Someone's birthday?" Travis asked, as she passed his office carrying a Macy's box large enough to hold a folded winter jacket . . . or an open guest book stolen from the Algonquin Hotel.

"No, just . . . uh, something for a friend."

Quite the riposte. You must be some kind of genius.

Sarcasm from a ghost, Violet thought. This could be a long day.

She laid the box on her credenza and got to work, hoping Dorothy Parker would behave herself and stay quiet. After scanning her e-mails to see if there was anything urgent, Violet's first order of business was to read Andi's review of the Matt Damon movie. She clicked into the document and ignored the distinct sound of buzzing as she tried to concentrate.

Is that the little shit's review?

"Mm-hm," Violet said quietly.

Any good?

"It needs work," Violet whispered. "But stop asking me questions. If anyone hears me talking to you, they'll think I'm crazy."

Someone coughed, and Violet looked up. It was Andi. standing at the door of her office holding a big, steaming cup of coffee—Violet's coffee.

"Everything okay?" Andi asked.

"I was just . . . uh . . . reading something aloud. Why don't you come in. We can talk about your review."

Andi handed over the coffee and took the chair opposite Violet's desk. "What do you think?" she said. "Do you like it?"

"There's a lot of excellent stuff here," Violet said, conscious of the fact that the best way to critique someone's writing was to start with a positive. "I especially liked the line about the actors finding a chemistry that seemed to surprise them as much as it surprised the audience."

Andi grinned. "That was my favorite part, too."

"The trickiest thing about writing a review," Violet continued, "is finding your own voice. It takes a bit of practice and a leap of faith. You have to acknowledge that your opinion has value and that the reader wants to know what *you*, Andi L. Cole, think of this movie."

"You don't think I found my voice?"

"It reads a little formally, like a book report."

"I was trying to make it perfect."

"I know," Violet said, "but remember that you're not trying to impress an English teacher."

"I don't understand."

"You've got a big personality, Andi. God knows I've seen it. If you can capture some of that on paper, your review will sing." Violet paused to let that sink in, but as she studied Andi's face, it occurred to her that they were two sides of the same coin. Andi needed to bring her real-life courage to the page, and Violet needed to bring her writer courage to real life.

Still, Andi looked skeptical.

"Trust me on this," Violet said. "Take another crack at it. Write it like you're talking to a friend."

"Do you mind if I show it to Travis first?"

Violet sighed. Her protégée had a classic case of amateur's hubris. She was so enamored of her own words she didn't think a single one needed to be changed.

Don't let her step on you, Mrs. Parker buzzed.

I hadn't intended to, Violet thought. She laced her fingers and leaned toward Andi.

"Actually," she said, "I do mind. But I'll make you a deal. You rewrite this, and if I find your revision acceptable, we'll show both versions to Travis and get his opinion on which is best."

God, that's good. She'll not only do the revision, but will start to understand just how much she really has to learn. You may be a genius after all.

Andi smiled. "That sounds great."

Violet could tell the girl was sure her original version would be deemed brilliant by Travis. She really did have a lot to learn.

"Do you need me to do anything else this morning?" Andi asked.

"I forwarded you an e-mail from someone at ABC inviting me to appear in an upcoming *Good Morning America* segment about romantic comedies. Tell them thanks, but I can't make it. Say I have a previous commitment."

Andi opened her pad and wrote it down. "You always seem to be busy when these TV things come up."

The girl has a point, Mrs. Parker whispered. Violet ignored her.

"That's no coincidence," she said to Andi. "I don't do television."

"Why not?"

"I get too stressed. I do better in a dark theater than under the bright light of a camera."

"Man, if I ever become a famous critic . . ."

"Something to strive for," Violet said with a smile, and dismissed her apprentice, as she needed to go see Buck and Travis to discuss the upcoming issue.

Later, as the day was drawing toward an end and Violet was rushing through the final things she wanted to complete before heading home, the receptionist buzzed in to tell her Sandra Weber was on the line.

Violet couldn't imagine why Delaney's grandmother would be phoning her at work, so she closed her office door and took the call.

"Are you crazy?" Sandra said. It was more of an accusation than a question.

"What's the matter?" Violet asked. "Is Delaney okay?"

"A nudie show? You took her to a *nudie* show?"

"Oh, that. Listen, Sandra—"

"The child is thirteen years old! Are you insane or just perverted?"

"Calm down."

"I will *not* calm down! This is my grandchild. After all this girl has been through, how could you!"

"If you give me a second to explain—"

"A naked man!" Sandra said. "With his *penis* showing!"

"I didn't know there was going to be nudity," Violet said, and noticed that Dorothy Parker's form began to appear in the chair opposite her desk.

"That's pretty darned irresponsible, don't you think? I mean, you take a child to a show and you don't even know that it's pornographic?"

"It wasn't pornographic, I promise you."

"A penis!" Sandra shrieked.

Her voice was loud enough to carry, and Dorothy Parker's eyebrows raised.

"I know. Yes, a penis. But it was actually a comedy."

"So you think this is funny?" Sandra said, still shouting.

"It's amusing the hell out of *me*," Mrs. Parker said.

Violet shook her head at Dorothy Parker and put her finger to her lips. She hoped her mentor would get the message that she needed to keep her mouth shut.

"I wanted to leave the second I realized there was nudity," Violet said, "but she seemed fine with it. It was a judgment call."

"That's the kind of judgment this child doesn't need. And if you think you've got a chance of getting custody now, you're even crazier than I thought."

"You're overreacting," Violet said.

"Am I? You're lucky I'm still letting you have visitation!"

"Honestly, Sandra, Delaney is fine. This is a big nothing."

"I doubt the man whose penis was dangling in her face thinks it's a big nothing!"

Dorothy Parker opened her mouth to speak, and Violet waved her hands frantically. This was no time for a wisecrack.

"I know you think she's traumatized by this," Violet said, "but I guarantee it wasn't the first time she saw a penis." As soon as she said it, she realized it was a mistake.

"What do you mean!" Sandra said. "Is there something I should know? Have you taken her to other pornographic shows? Oh, this poor child!"

"That's not what I meant," Violet said. "But, you know, they do sex education in school. I'm sure they've discussed both male and female anatomy."

"So you think it's your place to further her education with this smut?"

"No, that's not what this was about. I just thought she would enjoy going to the theater. I honestly had no idea—"

"That's the problem with someone who's never been a parent. You have no real sense of responsibility."

No real sense of responsibility? How dare she! Violet rose, her fury turning her blood white hot. Did Sandra conveniently forget everything Violet had done? Did she need to be reminded that after the accident, while Sandra and Malcolm were indulging in grief, Violet put her emotions on hold so she could pack up everything from her Manhattan apartment and move into her sister's house to care for Delaney? She had given up everything for this child . . . and she would do it again in a heartbeat.

She wished she could reach across the phone line and throttle the woman.

"Sandra," she said calmly, "you know I would do *anything* for Delaney."

"I'll bet the judge agrees with me at the custody hearing. And you can be darn sure we're going to tell him about this."

The judge. Damn it. Violet's palms started to sweat. Would he actually take these accusations seriously? God, what had she done!

She swallowed hard. "I'm sure the judge will understand—"

"He will! He'll understand that he can choose the responsible, law-abiding grandparents or an irresponsible single woman of questionable moral character."

" 'Questionable moral character'!"

"And I promise that if you ever do anything like this again, you'll not only lose custody but lose visitation!"

Violet slammed her desk. "If you really loved Delaney, you wouldn't even say such a thing."

Silence.

"Sandra?" Violet said. "Sandra!"

"What happened?" Mrs. Parker asked.

Violet returned the phone to the receiver and sat down. "She hung up on me."

"Are you in trouble?"

"Deep trouble," Violet said, and put her head in her hands. "I have to call my lawyer."

"She accused you of having questionable moral character?"

Violet grunted her assent.

"Ironically," Mrs. Parker said, "her own husband is the one whose morals are in question."

Violet looked up. "We don't know that," she said. "The mysterious friend he visits during Delaney's piano lessons could be just that—a friend."

"Weren't you planning to hire a private investigator?"

"I was thinking about it, but my attorney said it won't do any good. All a private investigator can do is get pictures of Malcolm walking in and out of a private house. It proves nothing. And if the investigator is sneaky enough to go further—say, actually spy on the lovers inside the house—it would be illegal and inadmissible."

"Submitting evidence in court is not the point," said Mrs. Parker.

"It's not?"

"My dear, you only need enough proof to present to Malcolm so that he knows you know. He doesn't even need to be told how you obtained the information."

"What good would that do me?"

"You simply explain to him that if he and his darling, long-suffering wife don't drop the case, you will have no choice but to tell her about the affair."

"That's almost blackmail," Violet said.

"No, my dear. That *is* blackmail."

"Whatever it is, it's crazy. I'd have to find a private investigator willing to break the law, and that's not the kind of character I want to get involved with."

"Nonsense," Mrs. Parker said. "You wouldn't even *need* a private investigator."

"I don't understand."

"There's something on your shirt, dear."

Violet looked down. "Where?" she asked, but when she looked up, Mrs. Parker was gone. "Very funny," she said.

I'm trying to make a point.

"A point?"

My dear Ms. Epps, I can be less visible than a fly on a wall.

Violet considered that for a moment. "*You* want to spy on Malcolm?"

Why not?

"For one thing, we'd have to find a way to get the guest book into his alleged mistress's house."

Not an insurmountable problem.

"I disagree."

Have a little faith, my dear. I'm fairly skilled in the art of lies and manipulation. I can counsel you on this.

"It sounds like you've already worked out a plan."

It's fairly foolproof.

Spying . . . blackmailing . . . it was all such nasty business that even the thought of it made Violet wish *she* could disappear. "I don't know," she said. "I just don't feel comfortable with this."

Dust particles appeared in the chair opposite her desk and quickly took on Mrs. Parker's shape and substance again.

"When you change your mind," she said, "I'm here."

Chapter 22

Delaney had been talking about the bat mitzvah for months. It was her friend Alexandra's special day, and it promised to be a big, splashy party where Delaney would get to reconnect with old friends. So when that weekend finally rolled around, Violet expected her niece to be in a happy mood.

"Let's go," Delaney said, throwing her backpack into the car. She flopped into the passenger seat as if she couldn't bother to fight gravity.

"Everything okay?" Violet asked.

"Of course," she said bitterly. "Of course. I'm the luckiest girl in the world. Let's just get out of here."

"What's wrong?"

"Nothing."

"Delaney . . ."

"I said nothing's wrong, okay? My life is perfect."

"Don't be sarcastic."

"Sarcastic? Moi? What could possibly make you think my life isn't perfect? Except maybe that my parents are dead and that I have to take heart medicine every day for the rest of my stupid life. Or maybe that I'm living with two old farts who won't even let me keep my own *dog* in the house, and that I hardly ever get to see my friends. And, oh, let's not forget that my clueless grandmother throws a fit if I don't wear the fugly sneakers she bought for me at Payless." She pulled off her shoes and threw them into the backseat.

"You want me to talk to her?"

"God. Let's just *go*."

Delaney's therapist had warned Violet not to get alarmed every time the kid was in a bad mood. *Teenagers can be mercurial*, she had said. *Don't assume she's in a crisis every time she throws a hissy fit. Just wait it out.*

Violet took a deep breath and pulled away from the curb, assuming that surely by Sunday—the day of the big bat mitzvah party—Delaney would come around.

By that morning, however, even her favorite breakfast didn't lighten Delaney's mood.

"I don't *want* French toast!" the girl yelled, when Violet set her plate in front of her.

"But you love French toast."

"I'm not in the mood, okay? You never ask me if I'm in the mood. You always just *assume*."

"Delaney, please tell me what's wrong."

"Can't I just not be in the mood for French toast? Why does every-thing have to be such a big deal?"

Violet pulled out a chair and sat. This wasn't the simple moodiness the therapist had warned Violet about. In fact, she hadn't seen her niece act out like this since the dark months after the accident. Her stomach lurched at the thought of losing the valuable ground they had gained.

"What *are* you in the mood for, Del?"

The girl pushed her plate away and folded her arms. "Nothing."

"You need to eat something."

"I'm not hungry."

"It's almost time for your piano lesson," Violet reminded her.

"If the prince of orangeness is coming to pick me up again, I'll vomit."

"He won't. I specifically told him I would drive you today, since you're going to this party and we have limited time together."

"When do I have to go to the bat mitzvah?"

Have to? Violet was getting more and more concerned. Delaney had been bubbling with excitement about this party.

"Right after your lesson," she said. "We'll come back here, you'll change, and we'll scoot right out. Are you sure you don't want to eat something?"

Delaney shrugged.

Violet took that as a sign of softening, but understood the girl's need to save face by holding fast to her petulance. So the loving aunt simply slid the plate of French toast back in place.

"In case you change your mind," she said, and left the room with her fingers crossed.

When Violet picked up Delaney after her lesson, the girl continued to brood. She didn't even notice Malcolm's salsa-red RAV4 pass them on the road, right around the corner from her piano teacher's house. But Violet sure did. Clearly, something besides his granddaughter's musical education was bringing him to this neighborhood every week.

Later, when Delaney was dressed in a short black shift she had begged her aunt to buy for her ("I swear, *everybody* wears black to these things!"), Violet drove her to a pretty country club where the party was being held.

"I changed my mind," Delaney said, when Violet parked the car. "I'm not going."

"What do you mean?"

"I don't want to go. Let's just leave."

"But we're already here. And all your friends are inside. Don't you want to see Alexandra? And Ashley? And look, isn't that your friend Caroline walking in?"

"I don't care." She folded her arms.

"It'll be great, Del. You'll dance and play games. And I bet your friends will do that loud girl-squeal thing when they see you."

Silence.

"I don't understand," Violet said. "I thought you were dying to connect with all your old BFFs."

"What difference does it make now? I'm never going to see them again, anyway."

"What are you talking about?"

Delaney folded her arms and Violet stared at her profile, waiting for a response. Her heart ached for this child's suffering. She would do anything to make the girl feel whole.

"Delaney . . ."

The girl huffed and rolled her eyes. "You think I'm *stupid*?"

"Sweetheart, what is it?"

"I heard them talking. My grandparents . . ."

"About what?"

"About me and that dumb show. They found out about the naked people, and now they're not going to let me come back home because they think you're a bad influence." She put her head down and started to cry. "I'm stuck there for*ever*!" She buried her face in her hands.

"Oh, honey . . ."

"I just want to die!" she said into her palms.

"Delaney, look at me," Violet said, taking her niece's hands. She felt a surge of righteousness as she steeled herself to do what was right. She was going to break the law by defying the court order. The judge had been very clear on this—neither Violet nor the Webers were allowed to discuss the custody case with Delaney. But sometimes, justice is blind to the pain of a troubled girl who needs to know the truth.

"Listen," Violet said, "your grandparents might think they've got custody sewn up, but they don't. I spoke to my lawyer about this, and she really doesn't think it's a big deal. She said we can fight this. And I will, Delaney. I can't make any promises about the outcome, but I can promise you it's not over, and that I won't stop at *anything*. I'm still fighting for custody, and I'll continue to fight."

Delaney was silent.

"You understand?" Violet asked.

The girl nodded.

Violet released her hands so she could retrieve a tissue from her purse. She gave it to her niece.

"Thanks," Delaney said, as she wiped her nose.

"You don't have to go to this party if you don't want to."

"I know."

Violet waited for her niece to say something, but she kept folding and unfolding the tissue and wiping her nose.

"Do you want to talk about it some more?" Violet asked.

A shrug.

"Do you want to go home?"

"I don't know."

Violet started the car.

"Wait a second," Delaney said, looking out the window.

Violet peered out to see what she was looking at. It was a boy with exceedingly curly hair.

"Is that Brian?" Violet asked. "The kid who plays first violin?"

"No and yes."

"No he's not Brian, but yes he plays violin?"

"Right."

This was where things got dicey. Delaney simply would not utter the kid's name, and if Violet didn't get it right she would take it as a personal affront—as if her aunt were trying to trick her into saying it.

Violet closed her eyes to think. She remembered that Delaney had spoken about him, insisting they were "just friends," which Violet thought was so damned adorable she wanted to burst. But had she ever said his name?

"Ryan?" she guessed.

Delaney's expression softened as she nodded. "The lion," she said, touching her hair to show Violet where the nickname came from.

"He's cute," Violet said.

Delaney handed her aunt the balled-up, mucus-filled tissue. "Pick me up at six?"

"I'll be here at five."

"I'll keep you waiting."

Violet smiled. She had made the right decision to tell her the truth about the custody battle. "I'll bring a book," she said, and kissed her niece good-bye.

Chapter 23

"Is tonight the night?" Mrs. Parker asked.

Violet was getting ready for her third date with Michael. And though the second date had been as romantic as she had hoped, she didn't think she was ready to take the next step and invite him into her bed. After all, she had jumped into her relationship with Carl too soon after her divorce from Andrew. Maybe it was wise to take things slowly this time around, especially since she was in a state of near constant anxiety over the custody case, despite her assurances to Delaney.

"I think it might be best to wait," she said.

"Didn't you enjoy your last date with him?"

Violet looked at herself in the mirror. She was wearing a silky green tank top and lean black jeans. Their last date had been at a fancy waterside restaurant on the Long Island Sound, and tonight they would be going to a local pub, where a friend of Michael's was playing in a band. She held a pair of dangly earrings against her face and decided they were too glittery. She put them back and pulled out her favorite hoops.

"It was wonderful," she said. And it was. Violet hadn't meant to compare him to her exes, but she couldn't help it, especially since he came out so far ahead. Unlike Carl, who expected her to be the mommy and take care of all the details, Michael had gone ahead and made reservations. And unlike Andrew, who was so cheap he never wanted to eat anyplace more expensive than Applebee's, Michael had selected an elegant spot.

It had been a mild evening, so they dined on the deck overlooking the water. She hadn't meant to spend so much of the evening talking about Delaney, but Michael was deeply moved by all the girl had been through.

"Was she able to go to her parents' funeral?" he had asked.

Violet shook her head, "She was still in the hospital. When she recovered, I asked if she wanted to visit the cemetery, but she just rolled her eyes. The therapist said I shouldn't push it, so I didn't."

"She'll let you know when she's ready," he said.

"I think she's moving in that direction," Violet said. "She brought it up the other day—wanted to know if they were buried side by side, and if someone was taking care of the graves. That was the first time she ever asked about it."

"Every step must feel so significant."

Later, she opened up to him about the phone call from Sandra and her custody worries, and he tried to quell her fears.

"Judges aren't stupid," he had said. "I bet yours will see the incident for what it was—one isolated event that wasn't even especially traumatic."

Violet shook her head. "The Webers' lawyer is an animal," she said. "He's going to sink his teeth into this and not let go."

"Even so," Michael said, "the judge will be able to see the whole picture once your own lawyer has a chance to weigh in. You need to have a little faith."

"I know," she said. "But I'm petrified. There's so much at stake."

He reached out and took her hand. "I'm so glad she has you."

It was the single moment from the date she replayed most in her head. This guy had a real heart, and the way it made Violet feel was as exhilarating as it was frightening. She was falling too hard too fast. Tonight she would try to keep a level head and slow this train down.

Dorothy Parker rose from the side chair and sat on Violet's bed as if testing it out. "I think you should invite him up here."

"Forget it," Violet said. "I'm not ready."

"Of course you are. Just tell yourself you deserve some fun."

"I appreciate the thought."

"Won't you even consider sleeping with him tonight?" Mrs. Parker asked.

"I told you. I've decided to wait."

"Well, don't wait too long. Playing hard to get only works to a point. Men enjoy a challenge, but they look at dating as an investment. If it's not going to pay off, they take their business elsewhere."

"And I thought you were a romantic," Violet said.

"The space between romance and pragmatism is exactly where a girl can get herself in trouble," Mrs. Parker said.

Violet sighed. She knew Michael wouldn't cut and run if she didn't put out tonight. Still, he was a man, and he wasn't going to wait forever. If his patience was running out, would she sense it? Or would he just stop calling and move on to someone more ready for a relationship?

Her nervousness seemed to have a direct line to her bladder, and she excused herself to the bathroom. Almost immediately the doorbell rang. Violet cursed her timing, rushed through her business, washed her hands, and ran down the stairs.

"You look beautiful," Michael said, when she opened the door.

He did, too, in a light green oxford shirt and jeans. Violet smiled.

"People will assume we're intentionally coordinated," she said, indicating their almost-matching outfits.

"Do we care?" he asked.

"We do not," she answered.

"Then let's go."

Violet hesitated. There was something she was forgetting, wasn't there? Something she absolutely had to do before she left.

She went through a mental checklist. Perfume, cell phone, earrings. . . Then she remembered. Dorothy Parker was still loose on the second floor. That was a disaster waiting to happen.

"Just give me one second," she said to Michael, and dashed up the stairs.

"I'm sorry," she whispered, when she walked into her bedroom, "but I have to close the book now." She looked around. "Mrs. Parker? Where are you?"

Her mentor had gone invisible.

"Are you hiding from me? Don't be childish."

No response.

"Fine," Violet said. "Be that way. But I don't have time for this now. I'm going to close the book."

She took a step toward the dresser, where the Algonquin guest book lay open, and stopped. There was a hot tingling in her feet so severe she couldn't move another inch.

Oh no, she thought. No!

Violet looked around. There had to be something she could do to prevent Dorothy Parker from taking over her body.

The heat moved up her legs. "I know why you're doing this," she said out loud. "But I'm not ready. Please, Mrs. Parker!"

The sensation continued to rise, and Violet called on all her strength. She *had* to close the book! But it was no use. The tingly feeling spread throughout her torso. When it hit her soul, the nausea overwhelmed her and Violet collapsed on the bed. The misery was so intense she would have done anything to end it.

Stop, she thought. I can't take this. Oh, dear God.

But the sickness kept mounting until it seized Violet's consciousness and the room went dark.

And then, just like that, she felt fine. Better than fine. The nausea had compressed itself into a small tangible mass in her belly that fed her strength. Violet rose feeling powerful and determined, pulsing with animal sexuality. Why had she even bothered to fight it? This feeling was better than any drug she had experienced or could even imagine.

And she wasn't going to let the opportunity pass.

She looked in the mirror. Usually, Violet fought hard to deny her own beauty, but there it was. Her skin was soft and glowing. Her hair shone like satin. And her eyes had a sensual fire no man could possibly resist.

She took her time straightening the bedroom and shutting off all the lights except for one small lamp, which she dimmed by throwing a sheer blouse over it. Then she stepped out of her clothes and opened her lingerie drawer. She dug to the bottom for the red lace teddy she had received as a gift for her bridal shower. She wore it on her honeymoon and never took it out again, as she found it simply too embarrasing.

She slipped it on and admired herself in the mirror again. That beautiful man would be helpless. She fluffed her hair and called out to him, "Michael! Can you come up here?"

"Everything okay?" he yelled.

"I need you."

She heard him bound up the stairs.

"In here!" she called.

When he reached the door of her room, she was at the dressing table putting on perfume, acting as if she hadn't expected him. She turned to face him, arching her back.

"Why, hello there," she said, and could barely believe how sultry she sounded. She rose so he could get a full view.

His eyes went wide and his jaw went slack. He looked her up and down.

"You," he said, "are full of surprises."

"Come a little closer," she said. "I won't bite. Not too hard, anyway."

He moved in and took her in his arms. They kissed, and the sensation was beyond anything she had ever felt. It wasn't just heat, it was fire—hungry fire. She wanted him with everything she had—her mouth, her flesh, her center, her soul.

His erection pressed against her, and she knew she had him. Not that there was ever any doubt.

"Are you sure you're ready for this?" he asked.

"I don't think I've ever been surer of anything," she said.

They rolled onto the bed, panting as they yanked at fabric and pulled off clothes. This wasn't just sex. It was every god of love and desire. It was Eros and Aphrodite. It was life and breath, earth and fire, flesh and blood, and the ending of all great stories. He touched her. She touched him. They joined. They panted. They held on to each other as if they might otherwise die. Was sex really supposed to be this good? It had never been before.

But it was. It was. It truly was. Hallelujah.

And then it was morning.

Violet awoke foggy and confused. When she opened her eyes, she felt as disoriented as she did when the lights came on after a particularly intense movie, and the world created by the film director abruptly ended. By comparison, real life always looked soiled, squalid, and too brightly lit. Indeed, on this morning her room was practically repulsive to her, with a beige water stain on the ceiling, smudges on the windows, clothes thrown in unaesthetic heaps, and a distinct wet spot on the sheet.

Then she noticed Dorothy Parker in the side chair reading a book, and it all came back to her. God, what had she done?

Violet felt the other side of the bed. Empty. She sat up and looked around.

"What the hell?" she said.

"He's downstairs, making you breakfast," Mrs. Parker said, without looking up. She turned a page in her book.

Violet fell back onto the pillow. "I could kill you."

"Not likely."

"That was—"

"Sublime," Mrs. Parker said dreamily.

"Horrible."

"Oh, come, now. Surely you enjoyed that."

"How could you!"

"My dear, it was time. If you hadn't slept with him last night, who knows what would have happened with this relationship."

"It wasn't your call!"

"A Freudian would insist you wanted it to happen," said Mrs. Parker.

"That's ridiculous."

"Is it? You left the book open . . . in your *bedroom.*"

"Don't twist this around," said Violet.

"I don't see why you're so displeased. I did you a favor."

Violet got out of bed and grabbed her robe, which she put on furiously. "You did *yourself* a favor!" she said, her finger in Dorothy Parker's face.

"Don't point, my dear. It's impolite."

"Impolite! You want to talk about impolite? How about taking over your host's body and fucking her boyfriend? How's that for impolite?"

"I didn't fuck him, Ms. Epps. You did."

"With you orchestrating the whole thing!"

"Don't raise your voice," Mrs. Parker said. "He's right downstairs."

Violet sat on the edge of her bed. "I can't even face him."

"Don't be silly. He had a marvelous time. He'll want to see you again. And again and again."

Violet covered her eyes with her hands. "What am I going to do?"

"Go downstairs and have breakfast. Then maybe fuck him again if he's up for it. I promise I'll stay out of it this time."

Violet looked up. "You'll stay out of it forever."

"Don't get dramatic."

"Dramatic? Try furious."

"Have a heart, my dear. I've been dead for decades. Do you have any idea what it's like to go that long without sex? And when would I ever get another chance?"

"So you admit it was selfish! You didn't do it for *me*. You did it for *you*."

"I did it for both of us."

"One thing is for certain. You'll never do it again. I'm going to close the book and return it to the Algonquin!"

"Don't be so hasty, my dear."

"I should have done it sooner. Then I wouldn't be in this mess."

"Mess? There is no mess, silly child. Change the sheets and you'll be as good as new."

Violet started to pace. Mrs. Parker had ruined everything. This relationship had been so promising, and now . . . now it was destroyed. Instead of moving forward in comfortable steps, it had leapt forward to a place she wasn't nearly ready for. Not only that, but the woman he slept with last night—the woman he would want to see again—was someone else entirely.

"I have to go downstairs now and tell Michael I can never see him again," Violet said.

"Don't be absurd."

"I'm humiliated!"

"You have nothing to be ashamed of. I'm sure he thinks you're one of the best lovers he's ever had."

"He thinks I'm a wild woman who puts on a slutty red teddy and throws herself at him!"

"My point exactly."

"Mrs. Parker, I am not fooling around. I'm going to close the book and get rid of you. I simply can't have you in my life anymore." She was crying now.

"But you need me."

"Not anymore."

"What about Malcolm?"

"I don't need your help with Malcolm."

"Who else can spy on him for you?"

"I don't give a damn about spying on him," Violet said.

"But it could be your only hope of winning custody."

Violet rose and approached the dresser, where the Algonquin guest book lay open. She picked it up with two hands, closed it, and tucked the book under her arm.

"I'll find another way," she said to no one.

Chapter 24

Violet followed the scent of bacon and coffee into the kitchen, where Michael was standing at the stove, flipping pancakes. She cleared her throat.

He turned and smiled. "Good morning."

"You're making breakfast," she said, tightening her robe. She didn't know what else to say.

"Figured it was the least I could do. I have a class this morning, and I have to scoot out early. I didn't want you to think I was one of those guys who took off with the sunrise."

"You didn't have to do this," she said.

"I wanted to."

She crossed her arms and looked around, searching for something to say. "I'm sorry you missed your friend's gig last night."

He laughed. "I'm not."

Michael was happy. Of course, she thought. The aggressive hellcat who had summoned him to her bedroom last night was probably the woman of his dreams. How disappointed he would be to discover Violet was nothing like her.

"Sorry I can't give you a good-morning hug right now," he said, holding up a spatula and a measuring cup filled with pancake batter to show her his hands were full. "But I'll take a kiss."

She stood, frozen.

"Something wrong?" he asked.

Violet tucked her hair behind her ears. "We need to talk," she said, pushing herself to get this over with. If she had learned anything from her breakup with Carl, it was that a quick end was best.

"What is it?"

"This is . . . uh, moving a little fast for me."

"I don't understand," he said.

"Last night," she said. "I'm sorry. It was a mistake."

He put down the cooking implements and wiped his hands on a dish towel. "What did I do wrong?"

"Nothing. It's not you. It's—"

"Was I too fast? Too slow? Was there something—"

"Honestly, no. You were . . . Last night was wonderful. Perfect. But I'm just not ready."

"Violet, I never would have pushed myself on you. But you called me upstairs, and you were dressed in that—"

She felt herself flush. This was excruciating. "I'm sorry. I can't do this. You have to go."

"You want me to leave?"

She nodded.

"But Violet, why? Don't you think we should talk about this?"

Be strong, she told herself. Don't cave, or you'll just wind up dragging this on like you did with Carl. Only it will be worse, because the day he discovers you're not the woman he thought you were, he'll walk out on you. And that would just be too much to bear.

"I'm sorry," she said, then turned and left the room. She went upstairs to her bedroom and didn't come out again until she heard the click of the front door closing behind him.

Chapter 25

Violet sat in the study in front of her laptop, trying to compose a review of the movie she had just seen. The guest book was in the corner of her desk, shut tight and tied with a string, even though she had placed it well out of Woollcott's reach. She just wasn't taking any chances. And one of these days, when she had the gumption, she would return it to the Algonquin with an apology.

The little dog trotted into the room and put his paws on the desk, as if trying to scramble onto the surface. She picked him up and held him on her lap. He whimpered as he tried to escape her grasp and reach the book.

"Sorry, boy," she said, as she stroked him. "I know you miss our friends. I do, too. But we can't open that terrible thing. Not anymore."

She soothed him with a few scratches in his favorite spots. Then she put him down and tried to focus on her work. Dorothy Parker had nothing to do with the movie she was reviewing. Neither did Woollcott nor Michael nor Delaney nor anything else in her life.

Compartmentalize, she told herself.

Compartmentalize. For Violet, it was practically a mantra. Indeed, it had to be for anyone who considered herself a fair movie critic. She simply could not let the emotional turmoil of her life affect her work.

With this particular film review, that was going to be a challenge. It was, God help her, about an orphan involved in a custody battle. Okay, so it wasn't about a smart, funny, maddening thirteen-year-old girl, but a baby boy found in the most banal of places, a trash can. And the foundling was being fought over by the homeless woman who had discovered him and a powerful couple with more money than heart. Violet was in such a weakened emotional state that she wept from beginning to end.

Objectively, she knew the film wasn't any good. It was maudlin and manipulative, and some of the performances were so over the top she cringed just thinking of them. Plus, the swelling, corny soundtrack was almost embarrassing. Even the title, *A Foundling's Story*, was sappy.

But how could she slam a movie that had touched her heart so deeply?

If she wasn't so furious with Mrs. Parker, she would be discussing it with her right now. But what was the point? She knew Mrs. Parker would say: *Don't get too caught up in being cute. Or mean. Just give an honest review about what made it so terrible. And if it touched you? Well, for God's sake, say so.*

Violet's fingers hovered over the keyboard for a few moments, and then she began:

> *There's nothing I like better than a cheesy story done well. Then, when it's over, I can cheer for the triumphant protagonist free of embarrassment, and carry my tissues to the trash with pride.*
>
> *So I was rooting for* A Foundling's Story. *I truly was. But from the opening shot, depicting a clichéd homeless woman pushing a shopping cart down an alleyway, I knew we were in trouble. I said a little prayer I save for these moments:* Please, surprise me.
>
> *In fact, I wound up saying that prayer about a dozen times during this movie. It was never answered.*

From there, Violet summarized the plot, identifying the key moments in which the director could have made unexpected choices but never did. She ended it by writing:

Movie critics can be a jaded bunch, yet there were more than a few audible sniffles in the theater during the screening of this film. One seat, in particular, seemed to shake with sobs as the damp tissues piled up. Some hard-hearted soul had cracked.

Clearly, it's possible for even the most hackneyed direction to elicit tears. So if you're eager for a good cry despite obvious manipulation and single-note characters, go see A Foundling's Story. *You might not feel proud of yourself for losing control when the violins swell (yes, violins—I meant it when I said there were no surprises), but you'll have handfuls of tissues to hide your embarrassment. And as you throw them in the trash receptacle on your way out, you may feel one last pang as you listen for the muffled cry of a baby.*

As for that reviewer who was shaking with sobs? I carried my tissues home.

There. It was just right. She wasn't telling anyone to stay away. In fact, she encouraged a certain type of viewer to see it while warning them about the movie's shortcomings. Was it a more positive review than the movie deserved? No doubt other critics would think so. But it was a fair review, and she would stand behind it.

As she started to proofread it, the phone rang. It was probably Michael, who had called again and again, leaving impassioned messages. But she didn't call back, and wouldn't. She didn't even go to her next kung fu class, as she simply couldn't face him again. She knew she wouldn't be able to avoid him forever, as Delaney and Kara had become friends and were eager to see each other again. But she just wasn't ready.

She picked up the handset next to her and glanced at the caller ID. It was Delaney, which surprised her. Violet looked at the clock. It was almost ten p.m.

"Everything okay?" Violet asked.

The response came in sobs.

"Del? What's the matter?"

"It's my fault," the girl choked out.

"Take a deep breath, sweetie. Tell me what's going on."

"She was being such an asshole."

"Who?" Violet said, though she already had a pretty good idea.

"I had a big fight with . . . *her.*"

Sandra, Violet thought, holding on to the phone with two hands. Please, God, let this just be some overblown adolescent drama.

"Start from the beginning," Violet said.

"She enrolled me in Wildwood this summer, without even asking if I wanted to go," Delaney said. Violet understood that her niece was talking about the day camp she had attended when she was younger.

"Wildwood!" the girl continued. "It's for little kids!"

"I know," her aunt said, sympathetically.

"So I told her, 'No way, I'm not going.' And she said that I have to because she already gave them a deposit. So I said, 'That's not my problem; you should have checked with me first.' Then she got really pissed off and called me ungrateful. So I said if she thinks I'm such a little piece of shit, she should just send me back to Aunt V."

Violet swallowed hard. She could see where this might be going. But she pressed on. "Then what happened?" she asked.

"She got even madder and said that I could just cross that off my list because she knows what kind of person you are. So I said, 'Oh, yeah? Well, Aunt V told me she'll never stop fighting for custody. And she's going to win, too.' " The girl started to sob.

It was just what she had feared. Now Sandra knew Violet was in contempt of court for discussing the case with Delaney.

"It's okay, Del," she lied. "It's going to be fine."

"No, it's not! It's *not* going to be fine! Cruella De Vil turned all red and started screaming to the tan one, 'She defied the judge! She's in contempt! Open the champagne, because we just won custody!' "

"God," Violet said.

"Then she told me I was going to Wildwood whether I liked it or not."

Violet put her head in her hands. This custody battle was crumbling before her eyes. Delaney's weeping grew louder, and with each choking sob, Violet's heart broke a little more. Poor Del. It was all so hopeless now.

I've let her down, Violet thought. I opened my mouth and destroyed the girl's world.

Still, she couldn't let Delaney know the fight was all but lost. She would find out soon enough. Right now, the girl needed a bit of hope or she would wind up blaming herself.

"Delaney," she said, "let me ask you something. Do you think that I would ever give up on you?"

The sobbing stopped as the kid took a jagged breath. "No," she said.

"Okay, then. Let's make a pact to be strong."

"You don't think it's over?"

The note of hope in Delaney's voice sharpened Violet's focus. There had to be something she could do.

She glanced up at the Algonquin guest book. Of course—her secret weapon. She leaned forward and untied the string.

"I still have a few tricks up my sleeve," she said.

Chapter 26

"Does this mean you forgive me?" Dorothy Parker asked, as she sipped her drink.

Violet remained standing. "It means I need you."

"I suppose that's roughly the same thing."

"It's not even *close* to being the same thing."

"For someone asking a favor," said Mrs. Parker, "you're being awfully snippy."

Violet was incredulous. "'Snippy'?" she said. "You took over my body without asking. You made me have wild sex with Michael . . . and you knew I wasn't nearly ready to sleep with him."

"You needed it."

"Stop acting like you did it for *me*. You wanted to get laid, plain and simple."

"Well, it *has* given me a certain glow," Mrs. Parker said, "don't you agree?"

Violet lowered herself into the other wingback chair and put her head in her hands, picturing the word *incorrigible* tapped out on an old-fashioned manual typewriter. She wasn't amused. "You don't think you owe me an apology?"

"My dear, you knew I was desperate for sex. And you knew I could be a selfish little shit. So stop acting like a wronged innocent. You're a bright woman. You simply had to know this was a possibility."

Violet sat back in her chair. Was Dorothy Parker right? Had her subconscious played a role in this, letting Mrs. Parker take over so she could act out her basest desires?

No, it simply wasn't true. Dorothy Parker had pulled a sneaky trick on her with little regard for the consequences. It was obnoxious. It was reckless. And sure, Violet knew not to trust the infamous provocateur, but she never expected her to do something like this.

"At least you'll never have the opportunity again," Violet said. "I broke it off—told him I won't see him anymore. I even stopped going to his martial arts class."

"Stupid girl."

"You traumatized me!"

"Rubbish, my dear."

"Think what you like, but the truth is that it's over between Michael and me, and that's all your fault."

"Ms. Epps, if you choose to use this incident as an excuse to stop seeing a luscious man who's not only crazy about you but glorious in bed, that's your problem, not mine."

"You don't understand."

"Oh, I believe I do. You think you're punishing me, but you're punishing yourself."

"That's ridiculous," Violet said.

"I disagree," said Mrs. Parker. "I believe you're angry at yourself for making such a terrible mess of your custody case."

"Spare me the analysis."

"I thought people of your generation loved that sort of thing—grand revelations of heartbreaking self-pity when you recognize your pattern of avoiding that which would give you the most pleasure."

"Talk about projection," Violet mumbled.

"I beg your pardon?"

"Projection," she repeated. "But I guess that's a modern term—the kind of Freudian jargon hijacked by my generation, navel-gazers that we are. Your contemporaries would just say it's the pot calling the kettle black."

Dorothy Parker took a sip of her drink. "My contemporaries avoided clichés," she said.

"Like you're avoiding the truth?"

"How darling," Mrs. Parker said. "You're learning to parry."

Violet was irritated, exasperated, and out of patience. No more waiting for Dorothy Parker to be ready for the truth. It was time to lay it all out.

"I'm talking about the white light," Violet said. "*That's* what you're avoiding. People who have come back from the brink describe it as even beyond pleasure. They say it's . . . rapture. And yet you resist. Why, Mrs. Parker? What's in there that you can't handle?"

"We were discussing you and that gorgeous man."

Violet stared at Dorothy Parker, who gazed into her glass and wouldn't look up.

"Is it your family?" Violet asked.

"I'm sure I have no idea what you're talking about," she said, still staring into her drink.

"What are you afraid of?"

Mrs. Parker drained her drink. "A dry glass," she said, holding it up. "Fetch me another, will you, dear?"

"No."

"No?"

"I want you to tell me why you won't go into the light," Violet said. "Isn't your father there? Your sister, Helen? Your *mother*?"

"I suppose."

"Then why are you avoiding it? They say it feels like love, like pure love. Can't you sense that?"

A dark flash of anger crossed Mrs. Parker's face. "Now, why on earth would my mother love me?" she said.

Violet was taken back. The line didn't sound like a wisecrack. Not with that hard expression. "Excuse me?" she said.

"Never mind," said Mrs. Parker. "Get me another drink. I'm parched."

Violet folded her arms. "Why do you think your mother didn't love you?"

Dorothy Parker waved away the comment. "Please," she said. "I've never been an analysand, and I don't plan to start now."

"Just tell me what you meant. Do you really think you're so unlovable that—"

"Let's not get carried away."

"I just want you to clarify," Violet said. "Explain yourself, and I'll be happy to get you that drink. I'll get you as many drinks as you want."

Mrs. Parker put down her glass. "You really want to know?"

"Yes."

Dorothy Parker paused, as if considering whether or not she would answer. Then she straightened up, in what Violet recognized as her courageous posture.

"My dear," said Mrs. Parker, "I *killed* my mother. Now, another drink, if you please. And make it strong."

"What do you mean you killed your mother?"

Dorothy Parker said nothing.

"Come on," Violet said. "You can't drop a bomb like that and not explain yourself."

"You want an explanation? Fine. I was an accident, born when my mother was forty-two years old—a terribly dangerous situation in those days. She managed to survive my birth but was never well after that. Certainly not well enough to chase after an obnoxious and demanding toddler. So five years later it was all too much for her and she died, leaving her children motherless. There were four of us, you know.

So, as you can imagine, I was quite popular in the family. Everyone loves a mother killer."

Violet was dumbstruck. This wasn't a glib joke. Mrs. Parker honestly believed she had taken her mother's life.

"And just like your niece," Mrs. Parker continued, "I was excluded from the funeral. But unlike her, I got to visit dear mother's grave every Sunday. Father believed fresh air and the stench of death built character. Also, what better way to prove the depth of one's grief to strangers? We put on a grand show for anyone who happened to be walking by—the four poor children and the unfortunate widower."

"You don't think your father mourned your mother's death?"

"He probably did, but the real truth is that he didn't want to waste it by grieving in private. Better to trot us out for a good show. We were the Von Trapps of misery."

God, Violet thought. No wonder she's so unhinged about her mother. She was raised to see grief as hypocritical. She never got to mourn her mother in any very real sense.

"Have you ever gone back to the cemetery?" Violet asked.

"Why would I?"

"I think you need to visit your mother's grave for the same reason Delaney needs to visit hers."

"You think I would get some message of motherly love from her bones? My dear, you are sorely mistaken."

Here, Violet felt she knew something about grief that Dorothy Parker didn't. It wasn't that she thought spirits communicated from their final resting place, but it was a way to find peace by paying your respects. Violet had visited her own mother's grave many times, and always, she left feeling like she had had the chance to express her gratitude that her mother had lived to be part of her life. It didn't make her any happier, but it made the pain more understandable, and it helped her remember that she would always be connected to her mother.

Perhaps one day she would put the guest book in her car and drive to the burial ground of Eliza Annie Rothschild so that the former Dorothy Rothschild could experience that opening of the heart.

"You need to do it," Violet said. "You need to visit your mother." Then she rose, took her friend's glass, and went into the other room to fix her a cocktail. As she took the cap off the gin, she considered what else she could say to Mrs. Parker. Was there anything in her arsenal that might be able to break through so many decades of distortion?

There was. Of course there was. But was she ready to reveal it?

After making Mrs. Parker's cocktail, Violet took out another glass, poured a slug of gin, and gulped it down. She made the decision. She was going to tell her secret.

"You did not kill your mother," Violet said, as she entered the study and handed Mrs. Parker her drink.

"I most certainly did."

Violet shook her head. "First of all, it's not your fault that you were born when she was forty-two or that you made your appearance on this earth before certain medical advances that could have saved her. But beyond that, there's something you need to understand. She loved you."

"A ridiculous assumption. You weren't there."

"No, but I understand a thing or two about motherhood."

"That's aunthood, my dear. No matter how much you love your niece, you are *not* her mother."

"I know what a mother's love feels like."

"Because your own dear mother loved you?" Mrs. Parker said.

Violet ignored the acid tone in her friend's voice and took a deep breath. "Because I had a child."

"I beg your pardon?"

"Andrew and I had a stillborn," Violet said. "A baby boy. I held him in my arms."

"Dear God."

"His name was Nathan. We were going to call him Nate. He would have been five years old now."

"I had no idea."

"I don't talk about it," Violet said. "It was . . ." *Excruciating*, she thought, but couldn't even utter the word. "It ended my marriage and practically ruined me. But it did teach me how powerful a mother's love is. Even though I never got to know him, the way I felt about that baby changed me forever. So that's how I know. That's how I know your mother loved you."

"I'm very sorry for your loss," Mrs. Parker said. "Very sorry. I had three miscarriages, you know."

Violet nodded.

Dorothy Parker sipped her drink. "I wanted a baby."

"I understand," Violet said.

"Still," Mrs. Parker said, shaking her head. "I know you believe with all your heart that my happy ending resides in that white light. But I disagree. And I ask you to respect my wishes and close the subject."

"But, Mrs. Parker—"

"Please," the older woman said. "I request so few favors. Besides money and alcohol, that is."

Violet let out a long breath. This was so tragic. But what could she do? It was clear she couldn't change her friend's mind. Not yet, anyway.

"Okay," she said softly.

"Wonderful," said Mrs. Parker. "I'm delighted that's settled. Now, would you like to hear how I propose to solve your problem with the custody case?"

Chapter 27

The next night, Violet brought the guest book into the kitchen so Dorothy Parker could keep her company as she made herself dinner. Mrs. Parker sat at the table, pouring herself gin from a bottle, while Violet opened the refrigerator and scanned the shelves for ingredients.

"You know," said Mrs. Parker, indicating the guest book, "I don't even remember signing the damned thing. But then, everything from those Algonquin years is so vague."

Violet pulled a head of romaine lettuce from the fridge and brought it to the counter. "Not to me," she said. "I've read so much about that decade I feel like I was there."

Violet knew that Dorothy Parker's long and illustrious connection to the Algonquin Hotel began early in her career. She was twenty-five years old, working at *Vanity Fair*, when her friend and fellow theater critic Alexander Woollcott started inviting people to meet for lunch in the hotel's comfortable restaurant. Originally, the cozy group of writers and actors dined in the back, at a long, rectangular table presided over by a surly waiter named Luigi, so they called themselves the Luigi Board. But once the group gained notoriety, the hotel's manager understood how valuable the fame was to his business, and moved the luncheon to a large round table in the lobby, where they could be seen and quoted, as they often were. And while they took to calling themselves the Vicious Circle—a term Dorothy Parker had coined—the newspapers referred to them as the Algonquin Round Table, and the name stuck.

In her later years, Dorothy Parker attacked the group and everyone in it, with lines like "Most of them are dead now, but they weren't too alive then." Yet there was no denying the impact it had on her life. For an entire decade, the Algonquin Round Table was a pop-culture phenomenon that came to symbolize the wit and sophistication of the nation's most cosmopolitan city. And at the center of it was the tiny woman Tallulah Bankhead had called "the mistress of the verbal hand grenade," Dorothy Parker.

Though Mrs. Parker was well known for her critical assaults—such as describing Katharine Hepburn's performance in a play as "running the gamut of emotions from A to B," or explaining that a certain scientific book had been "written without fear and without research"—even her close friends at the Algonquin Round Table didn't escape her lashing. About Harold Ross, founder of *The New Yorker*, she said, "His ignorance was an Empire State Building of ignorance. You had to admire it for its size." Once, when a boisterous actress at the table was described as outspoken, Mrs. Parker said, "By whom?" And when another woman had been said to speak eighteen languages, Dorothy Parker remarked, "And can't say no in any of them."

It was a time when Americans were in love with words and enamored of writers. Dorothy Parker was one of the most admired women in the country back then—and certainly the most quoted. It saddened Violet to know that her friend grew bitter about those glamorous years, and she wondered whether her idol was being disingenuous when she condemned her Round Table friends and her role in the group.

"Can you tell me something interesting about those years I might not know?" Violet said.

"There *was* nothing interesting about those years, my dear. They were dreadful."

"But at the time," Violet had said, tearing pieces of lettuce and dropping them into a colander, "at the time it was fun, wasn't it?"

"Fucking your best friend's husband is fun," Mrs. Parker said, "but it's not something you look back on with any particular pride."

"But those were your friends."

"Mr. Benchley was my friend. The rest were awful."

"But witty, talented . . ."

"Please. There's a hell of a difference between witty and wisecracking. And talented? Hardly."

"You liked and admired them back then, didn't you?"

"They amused me. That was all."

Violet finished with the lettuce and wiped her hands on a towel, as she weighed her next statement. Dorothy Parker had spent ten years having lunch with these people. There had to be more to it than her friend was admitting. Something drove her bitterness and soured the memory.

"Do you miss them?" she asked.

Instead of answering, Mrs. Parker refilled her glass and took a long drink. Violet waited. Clearly, her friend intended to ignore the question. Or maybe she was getting too drunk to respond. But Violet pressed on. "You do, don't you?"

Mrs. Parker bent to pick up Cliché, who was at her feet, and nearly fell off the chair. Violet rushed to her side and helped her get settled in the seat.

"You okay?" Violet asked.

Mrs. Parker waved away her concern. "They really thought I was something," she said, as she stroked the little dog.

"Of course they did—you were. You *are*."

"I never did a single great thing. Not one. I came close when I got arrested for protesting that sham of a trial. Those poor men."

Violet knew she was talking about Sacco and Vanzetti again. "You should feel proud for trying."

"They were executed. Innocent men."

"It wasn't your fault," Violet said. "You did what you could."

"But what did I accomplish?"

"Tons. I don't even know where to begin."

"Perhaps I can help," Mrs. Parker said. "Let's see. I drove my husband to suicide. I steered my stepmother to the grave. I fueled my own mother's death." She paused to consider what else she could add.

"None of those things were your fault."

"This is exactly what I can't abide about the modern world. You people don't believe in personal responsibility."

"That's not true."

"Isn't it? Psychotherapists are as ubiquitous as screenwriters and just as loathsome. Everywhere you turn, there's a headshrinker on a mission to convince guilty souls they're not to blame for their own awful behavior."

"People are just trying to understand themselves," Violet said.

"Rubbish."

"Point is, you need to give yourself credit for all your achievements."

"I achieved nothing."

"Your poetry—"

"Light verse. And not even good light verse at that. I was just trying to follow in the footsteps of Edna St. Vincent Millay, unhappily, in my own horrible sneakers."

"Aren't you proud of your short stories, at least?"

"Entrails," Mrs. Parker said.

"But you won an O. Henry Award."

"Writing one passable short story is a feeble body of work."

Violet shook her head. "Even your reviews are still being read today."

"I suppose malevolence will always have its fans."

Violet sighed, pulled out a chair, and sat. It was hopeless. She simply could not convince Dorothy Parker that she deserved any kind of happiness in life, or even in death.

"Can't you give yourself credit for *anything*?" Violet asked.

"Why should I?"

Because, Violet thought, if you recognized even an ounce of self-worth, you wouldn't be afraid to cross over into the light. And then, instead of suffering this terrible space between life and death, you'd find love.

But she knew it wouldn't help to say it. Dorothy Parker would have to discover it on her own.

Chapter 28

On Saturday morning, just after Violet headed off to get Delaney from her grandparents' house, she heard her cell phone's text-message alert, so she pulled over to read it. As she suspected, it was from her niece.

Slept @ friend's hse in Syosset. Pik me up here. 122 Laurel Dr.

Violet set her GPS for the address and texted back:

B there in a few. Did u take yr meds?

The reply came almost immediately:

Yes. Duh.

A short time later, she turned onto a pretty block in southern Syosset. She found the address—a pale yellow cape—and rang the bell. The door opened, and Violet reeled in surprise.

"Michael?"

He was smiling. "Hello, Violet."

"What are you . . . Is this your . . . She didn't tell me this was your house. I . . ." She paused to get her wits about her. "I thought you lived in Plainview."

The smile melted from his face. Clearly, he hadn't anticipated her reaction, and at once Violet understood: he thought she knew she was ringing his bell.

"I . . . I do," he stammered. "This *is* Plainview, but I told Delaney she should tell you to program it in your GPS as Syosset because it's on the town border. I figured she would let you know it was my house."

Violet shook her head. "She didn't."

"I'm sorry," he said, and there was an awkward pause. "Will you come in?"

Violet stepped into the entryway, feeling like she had been ambushed. Kids. What was Delaney thinking? Were the girls cavorting in some kind of *Parent Trap*–inspired plot to bring them back together?

The worst part of it was that Michael was feeling as uncomfortable as she was. He had looked so happy to see her when she approached the door. But now that he realized she was there on false pretenses, he barely knew what to say.

"I never told her to lie to you," he said. "I hope you know that."

They were at the bottom of a staircase, and Violet could hear the girls moving around upstairs. Michael looked freshly showered, with wet hair and a close shave. He leaned his back against the banister and stuck his hands in the front pockets of his jeans. She had never seen him self-conscious before, and it made her feel awful. But the worst part of it, she thought, was that he smelled so damned good.

"Do you want a cup of coffee or something?" he asked, pointing toward the kitchen with his head.

"No, I have to—"

"Okay, I'm not, you know, pressuring you or anything."

"I'm so sorry about coming here, about . . ." She trailed off, hoping he understood that she meant she was sorry she broke it off the way she did, and that she just couldn't explain it to him.

"Violet," he began, and she knew there was some kind of a speech coming that would put her on the spot. She wished she could vaporize.

"Michael, I—"

"Listen," he said, "I'm sure you've been getting my phone messages, but I need to say this to your face: I have no idea what I did to freak you out. And if you don't feel comfortable telling me, that's okay. I hope one day you will, and that you'll give me the opportunity to straighten it out."

"But—"

"Wait," he said. "I need to finish. I want you to know that I'm going to stop calling you. I don't want to cross the line into harassment. Just know that I feel terrible that I upset you in some way."

"Michael, please. I meant it when I said you didn't do anything wrong. It's just . . . I'm sorry I can't explain it, but it's . . . it's just not right."

"I must have done *something* wrong."

"You didn't. I swear."

He nodded, as if he were finally believing her. "Then is it—" He stopped himself.

"What?" she asked.

He took a deep breath. "Carl," he said. "Is it Carl? Are you still in love with him?"

"God, no!"

"Really? Because you can tell me."

Violet swallowed hard. It would be such an easy lie. It would end everything so neatly and without question. It would take him off the hook. He'd be free to think it wasn't his fault after all, and that she was just some kind of awful person who slept around while she was still hung up on someone else.

"Yes," she said. "That's what it is. I'm sorry."

He placed a warm hand on her shoulder, and she nearly melted under his touch.

"Okay," he said.

Violet fought back the urge to cry. Had she done the right thing?

He stared at her face, as if he were discerning something vital, and for a moment she thought he was going to kiss her. It would be wonderful, she thought. One last sublime kiss.

But he took a step back and called upstairs to the girls. Within seconds they came bounding down, side by side, plugged in to the same iPod.

"We want to go out for frozen yogurt," Delaney said.

"All four of us," Kara added.

"Maybe another time," Violet said.

"C'mon, Aunt V. I'm starving."

"We have things to do, and it's almost lunchtime."

"Please!" Delaney said. "There's a new place, and they have sixteen toppings, and Kara-bon has a coupon."

"Not today, kiddo."

"When?"

Violet tsked. "We'll talk about it in the car."

It took about fifteen more minutes of arguing, but Violet, frayed and exasperated, finally got her niece packed up and buckled into the passenger seat.

"So unfair," Delaney protested.

"I know."

"Just because you and Groucho broke up or whatever . . ."

"Stop it. There are about ten different reasons I'm not taking you out for frozen yogurt."

"But one of them is because of him, right?"

Violet sighed. "It's complicated, Del."

The girl folded her arms. "First my parents get killed, and then I get stuck in the middle of my aunt's messy breakup. My life sucks."

"Don't you think you're being a little dramatic?"

"I really *like* her."

"I like her, too. I'm not going to get in the way of your friendship. I promise."

Delaney folded her arms and stared out the window. Violet decided to let her sulk until she was ready to talk again. When she finally did, it was with well-calculated manipulation.

"I want you to take me to another screening. In the city."

"To make up for not taking you out for frozen yogurt?"

"To make up for getting me caught in the middle of your stupid breakup."

"So you're playing the guilt card?"

"Yes."

Violet laughed and considered the request. "Okay, that honesty deserves a reward. As it happens, I'm going to see a PG movie next Friday, and I'll take you. But on one condition."

"What's that?"

"You have to promise not to make a fuss tomorrow when your grandfather comes to pick you up for your piano lesson."

Delaney snorted. "Do I have to?"

"That's the deal. Take it or leave it."

The girl let out a long sigh. "Okay."

"Seen any good movies lately?" Malcolm said the next morning, when he came to get Delaney. Violet laughed and told him he smelled good. She was buttering him up for the favor she was about to ask.

He smiled, baring his blue-white teeth. "Scarface," he said.

"Excuse me?"

"It's the name of my cologne."

"There's a cologne called Scarface?" Violet asked, trying to reconcile the information with the Brian De Palma film flashing through her mind.

"Comes in a bottle shaped like a pepper mill," he said.

In other words, Violet thought, a phallic symbol. "I can see why," she said. "It's spicy."

Delaney came bounding down the stairs with her piano lesson binder. "He smells like rotting fruit."

"Be nice," Violet said.

The girl rolled her eyes. "Can we just *go*?"

"Wait a second," Violet said. "I have to ask Malcolm a favor."

He grinned. "Anything!"

Violet picked up the large Macy's box that was sitting on the side table, and launched into the story Dorothy Parker had invented. "I have a friend who lives near you out in Smithtown, and it's hard for her to get into the city. So I did her a favor and picked something up for her."

"What is it?" Malcolm asked.

"It's . . . uh, an antique book she had appraised downtown. If I give it to you, can you bring it home? She lives close by and can come get it tomorrow."

It was all a lie, of course, and the last part would require one last bit of deception. Violet planned to come by the next morning to pick up the book herself, making up some excuse for her "friend," who got unavoidably detained.

"Sure," Malcolm said. "That's no problem."

Violet carefully handed over the book and thanked him. "Just one more thing," she said. "It's very delicate and can't be exposed to humidity for too long, so whatever you do, don't leave it in the car."

"Don't leave it in the car?" he said.

"Please," Violet said.

He seemed to think about that for a second, and Violet held her breath. Finally he agreed, and so she kissed her niece on the top of the head and said good-bye.

She watched them walk toward Malcolm's RAV4.

"Notice that I'm getting in without a fight!" Delaney shouted to her aunt as she opened the car door.

"Great!" Violet said. "I'll keep my part of the bargain, I promise!"

Violet felt a strange lump in her throat as Malcolm placed the box in the backseat of his car. For some reason, she felt like she was saying good-bye to a very dear friend she might never see again.

As if reading her mind, Malcolm shouted, "Don't worry! I'll take good care of your antique!"

Violet wiped her nose on her sleeve. I hope so, she thought.

Chapter 29

"Over a hundred comments in the first hour," Buck said, "and almost all of them furious. Then another three hundred posts before eleven a.m."

Violet sat across from her boss in his office. She couldn't believe she was actually getting chewed out.

"You know how these things are," she said. "People get crazy. It's the *Internet.*"

Her review of *A Foundling's Story,* posted on the magazine's Web site that morning, had struck a chord. People were passionate about the movie. Sure, there were a few who hated it, but most of the commenters were rabid fans who thought Violet deserved disemboweling for the negative stance she took. There was nothing particularly unusual about this—people were always using the site to vent. But the numbers were impressive. To Violet, it merely meant that the film had scores of devoted fans. The same thing had happened to Travis when he had dared question the lasting resonance of the *Twilight* franchise.

The irony, of course, was that these angry hordes wanted to string her up for panning the film, while she thought she had been pretty soft on it.

"Not *this* crazy," her boss said. "And not that many of them."

Buck had a philosophy about these things. A lot of attention was good, but if too much of it was angry, he got nervous. He kept glancing at his phone, which Violet surmised was a bad thing. He was probably waiting for the publisher to call and give him hell.

He loosened his collar. Though it was a pretty casual office, Buck always wore a suit, usually with a striped tie. He was old-school preppy. Literally.

"Tell me the truth," he said. "Are you letting your personal life affect your work?"

"What?" Violet was stunned. How could he think such a thing?

"I know you have a lot going on. And if it's affecting your reviews—"

"It's not! I swear, Buck. I'm a professional, you know that."

"Because if you need some time off—"

"Wait, are you saying my job is in jeopardy?"

He sighed and sat back in his chair. "These days, whose isn't?" He shook his head and leaned forward. "Look, just keep it in perspective. Travis is our crotchety old critic. You're supposed to be the young, fresh voice here."

"But this isn't even a young person's movie. I don't understand."

"It's about . . . relevance. We need you to be relevant."

Relevant? That didn't even sound like Buck. What was really going on here? Violet folded her arms and looked hard at her boss. "Did Sylvie say something to you?" she asked, referring to Sylvia Merrill, publisher and president of *Enjoy.*

He sighed. "Sylvie's not happy."

"With me?"

"She insists this is just the kind of thing that scares away advertisers," he said, pointing to his computer screen, which was open to the web page with her review.

That was a bomb. A massive, too-close-for-comfort bomb. "So my job *is* in jeopardy? Are you kidding?"

"You know I'll fight tooth and nail for you, Violet, but just . . . tread carefully these next few weeks. Things are tight here, and everyone's looking for a scapegoat."

"Me? A scapegoat?"

"Unfortunately, between this review and the one you passed off to Andi, you've made yourself an easy target."

"I'm in trouble for that, too?"

"Sylvie questioned whether the kid was ready. And frankly, I did, too."

"No one's ready when they first start out," Violet said. "You know that as well as I do."

"I'm just saying you need to be careful. Don't court controversy."

"But you don't want me to compromise my reviews—"

"Of course not."

"I just don't understand what I could do differently," she said. "I was being fair, Buck. I stand behind that review."

"Do you?"

"Of course."

"Good. That's what I needed to hear. Then just keep that up and . . . I can take care of Sylvie."

"You promise?"

"I'll do my best."

Damn Sylvia Merrill. Violet didn't need this added stress in her life—not now, when so much was at stake. Her custody case was hanging on by a thread. Hell, probably less than a thread. And if she lost her job, well, she didn't even want to think about it.

But she did. And it kept her up almost all night. So when the phone rang at a quarter to six—right after she had finally fallen asleep—Violet felt like crying. Why? Why today? All she wanted was a few more hours of sleep.

She picked up the phone, hoping it was a wrong number.

"Ms. Epps? This is Jacqueline Connor from *Good Morning America*?"

Violet shook herself awake and sat up, wondering why she was on the phone with one of those young women who ended every statement with a question mark.

"Who?" Violet said.

"*Good Morning America*? Jacqueline Connor? I just wanted to tell you that your car service will be there in thirty minutes?"

"Car service?" Violet had no idea what this woman was talking about.

"We confirmed it with your office yesterday?"

"I don't understand. Why are you sending a car for me?"

"We have you scheduled for the seven-thirty segment, and you had requested car service?"

"I did?"

"I'm looking at your e-mail right now?"

"Are we talking about an appearance on *Good Morning America*?" Violet said. It couldn't be, she thought. It just couldn't.

"We are," said Jacqueline Connor.

A statement. This was serious. "Today?"

"You wrote a very gracious e-mail?"

"E-mail?" Violet said, and then went ice-cold as it became clear.

Andi.

She must have written to them accepting the invitation, after Violet had specifically told her to turn it down. That bitch. That conniving, lying, two-faced little shit. Just when Violet was starting to trust her! This was a living nightmare.

"I'm sorry," Violet said. "There's been a misunderstanding. I . . . I can't possibly do your show today."

"But we *confirmed*."

Not just a statement, but an emphatic one. Violet looked out the window, where she could see the sun rising behind the house across the street. The world was changing from dark to light, and all she wanted was to go back to sleep before the transformation was complete.

"I understand that," she said, "but—"

"It's live television, Ms. Epps. We ran a promo for your segment. And your publisher is already here in the studio."

"My publisher?"

"Sylvia Merrill? She's very excited about the segment."

Until that moment, Violet had never really understood the term *cold sweat.* But now she got it, as a chill swept her flesh, raising goose bumps in ugly, angry peaks and triggering a drenching, full-body sweat that almost made her drop the handset.

With all her heart and soul she did not want to do this television appearance. She could picture the cameras, the ice-cold studio, the pressure. Millions of people would be watching, judging. Some of them were already readers who would tune in to see what the snarky critic was really like. It was all too much.

"Ms. Epps? Are you still there?" Jacqueline Connor asked.

Violet had to hold on to the phone with both hands. "What should I wear?" she said.

Violet sat in a sage-green padded chair on set and held still as a stagehand wearing headphones clipped a small microphone to the lapel of her olive suit.

"Didn't they tell you not to wear green?" he said.

Violet cleared her throat and then coughed into her hand, as she felt like her larynx had been coated in a thick, voice-proof mucus.

"It was all I had," she croaked.

"I hope you don't disappear," he said.

If only, she thought.

He adjusted her mike. "This is very sensitive, okay? You don't have to bend your head to talk into it. Just speak normally."

Violet coughed again. Her throat was not cooperating. "I understand," she said.

"Can someone get the guest a glass of water, please?" he said into his mouthpiece, and then patted her shoulder. "You'll be great," he said. "Don't worry. Wendy's a pro."

At that, a striking African American woman walked onto the set. She was all poise and confidence—the kind of person who couldn't wait for the cameras to get rolling so that she could glimmer and glow for all the world to see.

"Wendy Whitney," she said, extending her hand.

Violet, of course, already knew who she was. "Violet Epps," she said, and cleared her throat again. "Nice to meet you."

"So glad you agreed to come."

Violet glanced over to the left, where she saw her boss's boss, Sylvia Merrill, chatting with the show's executive producer. They were both uncommonly tall. Sylvie was dressed in her combat uniform—a bright red blazer and straight skirt in a black-and-white houndstooth print. The producer, John Dower, was in a dark pin-stripe suit with the kind of print shirt-and-tie combination you saw only on Englishmen and formidably prosperous WASP businessmen. Individually, they were intimidating. Together, they looked like a gorgeous middle-aged power couple conspiring to take over the world.

Violet swallowed hard. Talk about pressure. She wasn't just appearing on live television before millions of people. She was auditioning for a woman who was one pen stroke away from firing her.

She took a deep breath to the count of four, held it for a count of four, and released it for a count of four. It was a calming technique she had learned in kung fu class.

You can do this, she told herself. *You know these films.*

Since it was a segment on romantic comedies, Violet had made notes in the car on the way to the studio, preparing herself for any questions that might come up. She had even scribbled down a few pretty good sound bites. If she could remember to say them, she might actually come off okay. She pulled an index card out of her pocket and read over what she had written.

"Two minutes, Wendy," said a young woman crouching in front of the camera.

The newswoman took her seat and turned to Violet. "I'll be on camera first, doing the segment intro. Then we'll go to camera two and I'll introduce you."

"Great," Violet said. "Are you showing any clips from the movies?" She was hoping for at least a quick heads-up on what films they would be discussing. The producer had declined to tell her, saying the segments worked best when they were spontaneous.

"Movie," Wendy said. "Not movies."

"I . . . I thought we were discussing romantic comedies."

"Not anymore."

"Not anymore"? What did that mean? Violet's blouse went damp under her jacket.

The crouching woman held up her hand and counted down with her fingers. "And live in five, four, three . . ." She trailed off, signaling the last two seconds in silence, and pointed at Wendy.

The woman came alive like a lit fuse. She stared into the camera, intense and focused. "Once in a while, a movie comes along that takes everyone by surprise, touching the hearts of both the tender and the strong. *A Foundling's Story* isn't a big-budget Hollywood blockbuster. There are no car chases, no violence, no sex, no modern cynicism. And yet moviegoers are drawn to it in droves, and leaving in tears.

"The critics, by and large, have had an entirely different reaction, calling the movie maudlin, manipulative, sappy. Why the disconnect? I'm here today with *Enjoy* film critic Violet Epps to see if we can get some answers.

"Violet, welcome. Let's start with a simple question. Why did you hate this movie?"

This wasn't really happening, was it? Surely it was a nightmare she would awake from at any second. Violet stared straight ahead at the massive camera in front of her. It was, she knew, capturing her image. The sweat forming on her upper lip was being viewed from kitchens and living rooms, from hospital beds and office chairs. She was being watched by housewives in Idaho, teachers in New Jersey, scientists in Colorado, carpenters in Tennessee, politicians in Washington, construction workers in Maine, magazine publishers in New York. Violet glanced to her left, where she had seen Sylvia Merrill, but the lights reduced everything behind the cameras to darkness.

She held tight to the arms of her chair to prevent an out-of-body experience. Violet needed to stay put, to answer the question. Everything depended on it.

Everything.

If only she had known. If only they had told her they would be discussing *A Foundling's Story*, she could have prepared some notes. But she was blank. Violet didn't have a single thing to say.

She replayed the question in her mind. *Why did you hate this movie?*

She hadn't hated it, had she? Didn't her review make that clear? She had admitted that it made her weep.

She took a deep breath and offered a weak smile. She immediately sensed that it was a failed attempt at charm.

Everyone was waiting for her to stay something. She picked up her water and took a sip. Bad move, she knew. It was the classic stall, the action of someone who knows they're in the hot seat and simply can't handle it. Worse yet, her hands were trembling.

She tried to remember what she had written on her index cards. Was there anything that could help her? Could she possibly make one of her clever sound bites work here?

Damn. There was nothing.

Wendy Whitney stared her down expectantly. She had to say something. There was simply nothing worse than dead air time.

"I didn't hate it," Violet finally said.

"The public certainly thinks you did. Let's take a look at some of the comments moviegoers posted on *Enjoy*'s Web site."

Violet glanced at the monitor, where Wendy's face had been replaced with an image captured from the comments section of the magazine's online review page.

"A commenter who calls herself AnnapolisMom says, 'How could you call the direction cloying when you admit it made you cry? That is completely hypocritical! This is a sweet, beautiful movie, and I don't understand why critics can't just admit that.'

"And that was one of the kinder ones," Wendy continued, as a different post appeared on the monitor. "Another commenter says, 'Violet Epps is a moron. *A Foundling's Story* is the movie of the year!'

"And here's one that poses the question 'What do you call a thousand movie critics at the bottom of the ocean? A good start.' "

The monitor now showed the newswoman and Violet on the set.

"How do you respond to this?" Wendy asked.

"Um . . . people are entitled to their opinions?" Oh, no. Had she really just done that? Had she really intoned her statement as if it were a question? It was like a goddamned virus.

"Is that a question?" Wendy asked.

"What?"

"Are people entitled to their opinions or not?"

"That's what I said."

"All *I* heard was a question."

God, this was a train wreck. "People are entitled to their opinions," Violet repeated. "Definitely."

Wendy Whitney laughed. "Very democratic of you! Okay, let's talk about your review. It sounded as if you liked *A Foundling's Story* but didn't want to admit it. Is that a fair assessment?"

"Yes. I mean no. I didn't really *like* the movie."

"Didn't it make you shed a tear or two?"

"Certainly, yes."

"But you thought it was terrible."

Violet took a deep breath. She knew she had to stop equivocating and say something with conviction, even if it was controversial. After all, Dorothy Parker would.

"Yes," Violet said. "Objectively, it was a terrible film, with too many flaws to count."

"A terrible film that touched your heart. It makes me wonder what a movie has to do to get a *good* review."

"It has to live up to its potential," Violet said, pleased with herself. That sounded good. Her brain was actually working. Was it possible Dorothy Parker's mettle was actually rubbing off on her? "And I think there's some solid material in *A Foundling's Story*. But it could have been much, much better."

"So what do you say to the people who think it's perfect as is?"

"Like I said before, they're entitled to their opinion."

"Which isn't as valid as yours because you're a movie critic?"

Violet took a deep breath. They were looking for controversy, and she was going to give it. She was paid good money for being a person with opinions, and, damn it, she had them.

"In a way, yes. And if that sounds condescending, I apologize, but I'm a professional reviewer. I studied writing; I studied film. I'm paid to understand what makes a movie work or not work. So I stand behind my review of *A Foundling's Story*. It's not a perfect movie—far from it. And if the public disagrees, that's okay. I still contend that it's easy to make people cry. A good filmmaker needs to do much more than that."

"To please *you*, perhaps." Here, Wendy Whitney turned from Violet to face the camera. "For the rest of us, *A Foundling's Story* is a gorgeous testament to the human spirit. As for the critics? Well, people like Violet Epps might *claim* they're not condescending, but I'll let her words speak for themselves. Here's a direct quote from *Enjoy* magazine . . ."

The monitor showed a paragraph from Violet's review, but it wasn't an image captured from the magazine's Web site. It appeared in a crisp, fancy, scrolling typeface, which Wendy Whitney read out loud:

> . . . [I]f you're eager for a good cry despite obvious manipulation and single-note characters, go see A Foundling's Story. *You might not feel proud of yourself for losing control when the violins swell (yes, violins—I meant it when I said there were no surprises), but you'll have handfuls of tissues to hide your embarrassment.*

Wait a second, Violet thought. That's out of context. Where was the part where she admitted that she had cried right along with the rest of them? Without that, the review did indeed sound condescending. It changed the entire tone of the paragraph. Her self-deprecating charm had given way to judgmental arrogance.

"Excuse me," Violet said, but her mike had been turned off. The camera was now on Wendy Whitney, who was speaking directly to the audience.

"Fortunately, as Violet Epps so democratically stated, you're entitled to an opinion, too. So make your voice heard. Visit the Web site at enjoymagazine.com and let the critics know what you think. Violet Epps, thank you for joining me. I'm Wendy Whitney."

There were two long seconds of silence, and then the lights went off. Wendy unclipped her microphone and dropped it in her chair.

"Thanks so much," she said to Violet, extending her hand. "That was fabulous. You'll get tons of responses."

Violet remained in her chair, head down, almost catatonic. What had just happened? That went by so fast.

Ambush, she thought. I was ambushed.

She felt someone looking at her and knew it had to be Sylvia Merrill. Would she fire her on the spot, or would she make Buck do it?

Violet got busy unclipping her mike, just to have an excuse to avoid facing Sylvie.

"Ms. Epps?" said the young man with the headphones. "You can go now. It's over."

That's what I'm afraid of, Violet thought, but when she looked up, Sylvia Merrill was gone.

Chapter 30

Violet needed to see Dorothy Parker and talk to her about what had happened on live television. She knew her mentor would have some words of wisdom, and hoped to be inspired by her courage. She wanted to be able to walk into the Enjoy office the next day ready for battle, armed with ten reasons why they shouldn't fire her. And if it didn't work, if nothing she said made a difference, she wanted to find the strength and dignity to leave with her head high and her spirits intact.

Also, she needed an outlet for her fury over what Andi—the lying, two-faced little shit—had done to her, and knew Dorothy Parker would be a perfect sounding board. No doubt her friend would share her outrage over Andi's audacity in accepting the TV appearance on her behalf, when she had expressly told her to turn it down. This wasn't just insubordination. This was betrayal. This was *All About Eve* with Wi-Fi.

As she merged onto the highway, heading out to the Webers' house, where she would pick up the guest book and reunite with her mentor, Violet remembered a conversation they had had about getting fired. Dorothy Parker was incredulous that Violet had never lost a job.

"Not once?" she had said. "You've never been fired in your whole life?"

Violet thought about her summer jobs as a kid and about her professional résumé, which wasn't very long, as she had worked for only four companies. With one notable exception, she had hunkered down and made each office her home.

"Never," she said. "Though I did quit one job after only five months."

It was her second employment out of college. Her first had been as an editorial assistant for a small academic book publisher. The pay was terrible, but she enjoyed learning about the business and made some good friends. Then an acquaintance told her about a powerful PR executive who was looking for an assistant, and got her an interview. The salary was nearly double what she had been making, so she took it. But she soon learned that her new boss was a brute and a narcissist. In fact, the whole company was like that. From the first day, Violet knew it was a mistake, but it took five months of nearly suffocating under the pressure of all those giant egos before she worked up the gumption to hand in her resignation. From there, she took a pay cut to work for a local magazine, but it was the best move she ever made, as it led to her career as a movie critic for one of the nation's biggest entertainment weeklies.

"So you've never made mischief?" Mrs. Parker asked.

"I don't think I have it in me."

"My dear, I've read your reviews. You have barrels of it. In fact, you have so much of it, it scares you."

As usual, Dorothy Parker saw right through to the truth. Violet had never even told her about the childhood trauma with Ivy that scared her into shutting down, but the legendary writer intuited her fear.

"How do you do it?" Violet asked. "How do you feel free enough to say what's on your mind?"

"Drinking helps."

Violet frowned. Here was a chance to learn something she had always yearned to know, and her mentor was being evasive. "Is that a wisecrack?"

"Loathsome, aren't I?"

"So what's the real answer?"

"The real answer is that it's very much like drinking, as it's intoxicating. Standing tall, opening your mouth, and saying exactly what's on your mind makes you feel more powerful than a hundred soldiers and a thousand kings."

Maybe, Violet thought, but if she tapped into that power, would she resurrect the horrid child within her—the one who spoke without regard for feelings? The one who could inflict enough pain with her words to cripple the relationship with the person whose love she most coveted?

On some level, Violet knew it was possible to be courageous and outspoken without turning into a monster. She even knew the secret to finding that balance was somewhere inside her, obscured by the complex tangle of anxieties about losing the people she loved. But she couldn't uncover it on her own.

Violet parked her car in front of the Webers' house and thought about Dorothy Parker. Soon they would be face-to-face again, and Violet would open up about the childhood trauma with Ivy that had frightened her into submission. She felt certain that her friend's searing intelligence would see right through to the truth, and help free Violet of her demons.

She approached the house and rang the bell. Malcolm answered the door wearing a sweatshirt and the skinny jeans Delaney had warned her about. Violet tried not to stare. Or cringe.

"This is a pleasant surprise," he said. "We saw you on TV this morning."

Violet winced. "It was a train wreck."

"You were great!" He turned and shouted toward the back of the house, "Wasn't she great on TV today?"

"Her suit was the same color as the chair!" came Sandra's voice.

"Don't listen to her," he whispered. "You're a star."

"Thanks," Violet said, and left it at that. She wasn't very well going to tell him that the next time he saw her she would probably be unemployed.

"Are you here for Delaney?" he said. "Because she's at school."

"I know," she said. "I came to pick up that box I gave you. My friend who was supposed to pick it up got sick. I'm, uh . . . going to bring it to her."

"She was already here," he said.

"What?"

"The woman. She came by this morning and picked it up."

"But that's impossible."

"You can ask Sandra. She showed up just after your TV appearance. In fact, it was kind of strange. She just appeared in the doorway. We didn't hear her ring the bell or even knock."

A woman who appeared out of nowhere? It couldn't be . . . could it? Violet went cold.

"Did she say her name?"

"Daisy something. Petite thing with dark hair and a dress that looked . . . What's the word? Retro? But very authentic. She must have bought it at a thrift shop."

Violet had to hold on to the door frame, as the truth became clear. Of course. As long as the guest book was inside something, Dorothy Parker could carry it anywhere. Violet remembered watching her walk into the 7-Eleven carrying it in the tote bag. And now she was walking free in the world. She could be absolutely anywhere, doing anything.

A wave of anxiety gripped Violet, as she tried to imagine the trouble Mrs. Parker could get into. Worse, it occurred to her that she might never see her idol again. She held back tears. Did she have to lose yet another person in her life? It was so unfair.

"Are you okay?" Malcolm said. "You look a little ill."

"Do you know where she went?"

He shrugged. "Didn't say. Is there some kind of problem?"

Sandra showed up behind him. "If you find that woman, I want to have words with her."

"You do?"

"Sixty dollars went missing from my wallet, and I think she took it."

"She didn't even step inside the house," Malcolm said to his wife. Then he turned to Violet. "She just forgot what she spent it on."

"I know what I spent!" Sandra said.

"So how do you suppose this woman stole from you?" he asked. "You think she went invisible when you weren't looking?"

"What are you talking about?" Sandra said. "That doesn't even make sense. If someone goes invisible, it doesn't matter if you're looking."

"It doesn't *have to* make sense," he said. "People can't *go* invisible."

"I know that. You think I don't know that?"

"So then why did you say—"

"I was just pointing out how illogical you are!" Sandra said.

"*Me?* You're the one who thinks an invisible woman stole your money."

Sandra growled. "He's impossible," she said to Violet.

"I . . . I have to go," Violet said. "Are you sure you don't know where she went?"

Sandra shrugged. "No idea. But I sure would like to talk to her."

Violet said good-bye and turned to leave.

"Wait a second," Malcolm said, "I just remembered something. She asked me if there was a train station in walking distance. I thought that was kind of odd. Doesn't she drive?"

"Uh . . . no. She doesn't."

"I never heard of someone living out here without a car. Doesn't she have trouble getting around?"

Violet swallowed against a lump in her throat. "Apparently not."

Chapter 31

When Violet arrived at her office, Andi was already there—dressed in black boots, black tights, and a black miniskirt with a red-and-black-striped top—holding a steaming coffee cup. Violet stared at the girl, seething. How could she look so nonchalant after what she had done?

"Buck is looking for you," Andi said.

Violet dropped her handbag onto her desk and took the coffee. "Of course he is."

"And there was a woman here, waiting for you. I don't know where she went. She was here yesterday, too."

Violet was too angry to look Andi in the eye. She picked up the pile of mail that had been dropped in the middle of her desk and riffled through it. She felt like she might explode. "What woman?"

"A Mrs. Buchanan? Short lady with dark hair. Cool dress—very vintage."

At least there's that, Violet thought. At least her friend was looking for her and would probably turn up again soon. Still, it wasn't going to keep her from getting fired. She threw the mail aside.

"Sit down," she said. "We need to talk."

Andi sat and tucked her blue-black hair behind her ears. "What's up? Should I get something to write with?"

Violet felt like her heart might thump right out of her chest. How dare this little shit sit there and pretend nothing was wrong!

"You are one cold, calculating bitch," Violet said. She didn't measure her words. She didn't worry about their power to harm. She was too furious to be frightened.

Andi blinked. "What?"

"A bitch," Violet repeated. "A liar. A bottom feeder. A filthy, manipulating piece of garbage."

Dorothy Parker was right. This was intoxicating. She deserved this anger.

Andi looked stunned. "I don't understand."

"Is that the tactic you want to employ right now? That you don't know what I'm talking about?"

"But I *don't.*"

"That e-mail you sent to ABC," Violet said. "Right after I told you to turn them down!"

"Violet . . . uh, Ms. Epps, I never—"

"Don't lie to me! You're making it worse."

"I'm not lying."

"I have irrefutable proof, Andi! They got an e-mail from you accepting the appearance on my behalf."

"Not from me, from *you.*"

"That's ridiculous," Violet said.

"But it came from *your* e-mail account."

"What are you talking about?"

"You told me to send them an e-mail turning them down, but when I checked my in-box, there was an e-mail from you to that *Good Morning America* producer saying you'd be delighted. You CCed me. I figured you changed your mind. I didn't want to make a big deal about it, because I know you get nervous about these things."

"But I never wrote to them!" Violet insisted.

"Check your out-box."

Violet turned on her computer and stared, waiting for it to boot up. Her anger, a simmering cauldron, was now a confused and messy soup.

"I swear," Andi said. "I didn't do it. I wouldn't. I know I can be a snotty little bitch sometimes. My mother says I get it from my dad, who's a total prick. But I'm not like him. I just, you know, show off. I'm *not* a backstabber."

Violet's screen came to life, and she opened her e-mail. Sure enough, there was a message from her to the producer of *Good Morning America*:

What a charming invitation. Thank you for thinking of me; I'd be delighted. I accept your offer for car service. Please contact my staff for the correct address.

Yours,
Violet Epps

"Oh, God," Violet whispered, as she felt herself dissolve. She read the message again, but there could be no other conclusion. The language, the grammar, the meticulously placed semicolon—it all made one thing abundantly clear. Someone had indeed betrayed her, but it wasn't Andi. It was Dorothy Parker.

But how had she done it? And when?

Then Violet remembered. Mrs. Parker had been buzzing around the office on the day she had given Andi instructions on how to handle the invitation. When Violet stepped out for a meeting, her wicked friend must have materialized and typed the message.

Violet put her head in her hands. Why had she ever shown Dorothy Parker how to send an e-mail?

"Are you okay?" Andi asked.

"No."

"Do you need anything?"

Violet shook her head. "Just leave. And shut the door."

"But Buck is—"

"Waiting for me," Violet said, without looking up. "I know. Tell him I need a few minutes."

"Are you sure I can't get you anything?"

"Just go. Please."

Andi left and closed the door behind her. Alone, Violet put her head down on her desk and wept. Dorothy Parker had been her mentor. She was supposed to help her . . . to make her better, braver. Instead, she had wrecked her chances with a man she was falling in love with, put her career in jeopardy, and, worst of all, nearly obliterated any chance she had of gaining custody of her niece.

"How could she!" Violet cried.

Don't be so dramatic. It was for your own good.

"Huh?" Violet looked up, and there, in the chair where Andi had been sitting, was Dorothy Parker. "Where did you come from?" she said.

Mrs. Parker pointed to the floor beneath the credenza. Violet leaned forward and saw it—the large Macy's box containing the Algonquin guest book. "I've been here the whole time," the legendary writer said. "You did a hell of a job chewing out that ghoulish girl."

Yes, she had been vicious. Brutal. This was what happened when she finally uncorked. "Poor Andi," she said. "What have I done?"

"It was quite amusing."

Amusing? She thought this was *amusing*?

"I should close that damned guest book and bury it!" Violet said.

"You'll wind up thanking me."

"Trust me, I won't."

"You were actually quite good on that television program, once you settled in."

"You saw it?"

"With that awful couple. I knew you would need reassurance, so I materialized, picked up the box, and left. I considered taking your advice to visit my mother's grave, but I knew that could wait, as she's likely not going anywhere. So I came straight into the city to look for you."

"Did you steal sixty dollars from the Webers?"

"More than that, I would think," Mrs. Parker said.

"So you were here yesterday, in this office?"

"For a short time, then I left to wander the city. Never did make it back to the Algonquin, though I long to see the old girl. But I learned quite a bit about the modern world. Did you know there's not a bar in Midtown that lets a lady have a cigarette?"

How could she be so casual when Violet wanted to scream? "Did *you* know I'm about to get called into my boss's office to get fired? I'm sure you don't think that's any big deal. Hell, you probably *wanted* me to get fired. I bet that was your goal. You think it's character-building or some bullshit."

"It most certainly was *not* my goal. But now that you mention it, I don't think it would be the worst thing in the world. One day, you might even find an amusing way to talk about it."

"This is my life!" Violet shouted. "It's not some colorful anecdote destined to become cocktail-party chatter! It could be the end of my career and a very sorry day for a little girl who deserves a chance to come home."

"Oh, come now—"

"Don't!" Violet said. "Don't you dare try to convince me I'm overreacting! There is nothing adorable about your mischief. You are a reckless and dangerous woman."

"I've been called worse."

"Spare me your glib comebacks." Violet put her head in her hands again. "What am I going to do?"

"You're taking this awfully hard."

"Shut up."

"You don't even know if you're going to get fired. Why don't you save your hysteria for—"

"I said, *shut up!*"

"Not in my nature, dear. But here's a thought. Perhaps I could spy on your boss before you go in there. Certainly, it would help if you knew what he had planned."

Violet's phone rang, and she ignored it. "I don't want any more of your 'favors.' "

"Aren't you going to answer that?"

Violet snatched her phone from the receiver. "Hello!"

"Hi, Aunt V."

"Delaney. What's the matter?"

"What time are you picking me up today?"

"Picking you up?" Violet asked.

"For the screening."

"That. Oh, God. I'm sorry, hon, we can't—"

"But you promised!"

"I know. It's just a very, very bad time."

"Did you forget? It sounds like you forgot."

"There's a lot going on here right now."

"We had a deal!" Delaney said. "You can't back out. You *can't!*"

"I'm sorry."

"I knew this would happen! I knew you would forget about me!"

"Delaney, I could never forget about you. You're the most important thing in the world to me."

"Liar!" Delaney said, her hysteria mounting. "If I was so important, you'd take me like you promised."

"Honey, look. There's a lot of trouble here right now. It's serious."

"What do you mean? Like at your job?"

"Yes, at my job."

"Are you getting fired or something?" the girl asked.

"I don't know, sweetie. Maybe."

Delaney started crying.

"It'll be okay," Violet lied. "I promise."

She paused for a response, but all she heard was sniffling.

"Delaney—"

"Second-period bell," she said. "I have to go to class."

"Are you all right?"

Silence.

"Delaney?"

She was gone. Violet hung up the phone and looked up. Dorothy Parker was gone, too.

Chapter 32

Dead man walking.

As Violet moved through the corridor toward Buck's office, she remembered the Sean Penn film that had so effectively conveyed what it felt like for a death-row inmate to take that final walk toward his ultimate fate.

Violet pictured Buck's somber face as he delivered the news. His hands would be folded on his desk. *I'm sorry,* he would say. *Not my decision.* He would throw around phrases like *current environment* and *skittish advertisers.* He probably even had another reviewer waiting in the wings to take her job. Maybe, in the final twist of irony, it would be Andi. How perfect. Would they expect Violet to pack up and leave today? Would he be willing to give her a letter of recommendation?

Movie critic jobs were scarce, and there was little chance she'd find another one anytime soon, if at all. And she doubted the family-court judge would look kindly on her if she was unemployed. What could she find quickly? Were there people she knew who could set her up with a job? She would, of course, take anything if it meant improving her chances at custody. But what could she do that would give her the flexible hours she needed to spend time with her troubled niece?

She closed her eyes for a moment and remembered a conversation with her sister. It was early in Violet's ill-fated pregnancy, and she was still blissful and dreamy. She and Andrew had decided to keep the news private for a few more weeks, but as she was shopping with Ivy in a children's clothing store, looking for something special for Delaney to wear for her eighth birthday, they passed the baby department and Violet couldn't resist fingering one of the tiny outfits.

Ivy stopped cold and stared. "Do you have something to tell me?" she said.

Violet shook her head, and Ivy smiled.

"You do, you dirty liar!"

Violet laughed, and it was just the signal Ivy needed to confirm her hunch. "You're going to be a great mom," she said, hugging her sister. "You really are."

At that joyous moment, she believed it. And maybe she would have been. But right now, it looked like she was failing Delaney in every possible way.

Violet continued her walk toward Buck's office. Nothing worked out as it should have. Ivy should be alive. Violet should have a five-year-old boy named Nate getting into trouble at preschool or learning to read or begging his mom for the latest video game.

No crying, she told herself. Just get through this.

When she rounded the corner, Violet heard voices and saw that Buck was not alone in his office. Sylvia Merrill was in there with him. So was Owen Weiss, the executive vice president of their online division, and Sam Lee, the advertising director.

Dear God, it was a firing squad. Dizzy, she paused, leaning against the wall.

She took a few long, slow breaths and coached herself to be brave. Then she marched in.

"Violet!" Buck announced, and they all clapped.

Clapped?

"Brava!" said Sylvie, beaming with delight.

Violet felt like she had just short-circuited. "What's going on?" she asked.

"We've gone viral!" Owen said.

"Viral?"

"Your TV appearance sparked the hottest online debate we've ever seen," said Buck. "We were flooded with readers who hated the movie and wanted to support you."

"They're duking it out with the people who loved it," said Owen.

"It's brought out the worst in *everyone*!" Sylvie gushed.

"And this is a good thing?" Violet asked.

"The hits are through the roof," said Sam. "Advertisers love this kind of controversy."

"I . . . I thought they hated controversy."

"Not when there's this many eyeballs," Sam said.

Buck leaned back and folded his arms. "Violet, you're a hero."

Chapter 33

The meeting lasted less than thirty minutes. There was a lot of backslapping, and a bit of brainstorming about how to use social media to keep the controversy going. Buck wondered whether Violet would be willing to go on television again. (She would!) And Sam Lee made predictions about increases in ad sales. Violet, feeling bold, joked that it might be a good time to ask for a raise. Buck sucked air nervously and glanced at Sylvia Merrill, who nodded almost imperceptibly, and said annual reviews would be here before you know it.

It looked very, very good.

There was talk of going out for drinks after work, but Violet took a rain check, as she had a screening that afternoon, and a girl on Long Island to pick up first.

Back in the office, she looked under the credenza, but the box was gone, which meant she couldn't tell Dorothy Parker the good news. She hoped her friend would show up soon, because she wanted to forgive her. Maybe not completely. She had crossed the line again and again. But this time, at least, it was indeed working out for the best.

Violet considered going out to look for Dorothy Parker, but was it ridiculous to even try? She had only a couple of hours before she needed to head out to Long Island, and her friend could be anywhere.

But hadn't she said something about longing to visit the Algonquin? Did it pay to take a walk over there?

Ridiculous, she told herself. As much as she wanted to bend Dorothy Parker's ear, she wouldn't go on a wild-goose chase looking for her. Besides, she had no desire to run into Barry Beeman, whom Andi was still maneuvering in a game of phone tag.

Meanwhile, she wanted to focus her attention on poor Delaney, who had been so disappointed about missing the screening. Fortunately, there was still plenty of time to take the train to Long Island, pick up the girl, and take her back to the city for the film. Delaney loved surprises, and this would be perfect.

First, though, there was someone else Violet hoped would forgive her. She stopped at Andi's desk on her way out.

"I want to apologize," she said.

Andi shrugged. "It's okay."

"It is?"

"Sure."

Violet paused to let that wash over her. She had unleashed the worst of herself on this young woman, and yet the sun hadn't gone dim and the moon hadn't turned black. Despite all her fury and unjustified accusations, Andi was . . . okay. The very idea made Violet so giddy she almost laughed. This troublesome young lady was the last person in the world she thought she might learn from.

"It isn't okay," Violet said. "I made some awful accusations, and I'm so sorry."

"Don't sweat it. That was tame compared to the shit that gets said at my house."

"I wish you didn't have to deal with that."

"Me, too."

Violet gave Andi's shoulder a squeeze and turned to leave. Then another thought stopped her. "You have time for a cup of coffee?"

At Starbucks, Andi saved a table while Violet went to the counter to place their orders. As the barista moved about, pouring coffee and steaming milk, Violet felt a warm sense of irony. She liked the idea that the coffee-fetching tables had turned. What better way to make amends to her protégée?

"Let me apologize one last time," Violet said, as she handed Andi her cup. "I really lost my temper today, and you didn't deserve that."

"Whatever," she said, sipping her hot drink. "Everyone's an asshole once in a while."

Not me, Violet thought. I always hold it in. "Well, I feel bad," she said.

"Forget it."

"You're really fine about this?"

"Of course."

As Violet stirred her coffee, which was still too hot to drink, she tried to picture the environment Andi grew up in. She imagined flaring tempers and unbridled fury—parents, children, and extended family lashing out with every vicious thought that crossed their minds. It seemed so ugly, so selfish. And indeed, Violet believed that there was something decidedly egotistical about releasing one's anger. It said, *I'm more important than you, and I have the right to cut you down.* And yet, in families like Andi's, people unloaded their rage and it all worked out. They apologized or they didn't. Either way, everyone moved on.

"I guess your family's pretty free with their feelings," Violet said.

Andi took a big gulp. "That's a nice way of putting it," she said.

Violet ventured a small sip and almost burned her tongue. "There's a lot of yelling?"

"If by *a lot* you mean *always*, then yeah."

"How do you feel about that?"

Andi shrugged. "I'm used to it."

Violet blew into her latte. "Doesn't it bother you?" she asked.

"I guess."

"You don't seem as troubled by it as I would expect."

Andi put down her cappuccino and wiped the froth from her mouth with the back of her hand. "That's because you're from one of those quiet homes where the kids say things like, 'Father dear, may I please watch my television program now?' and the parents say, 'Why, certainly, my little buttercup; here is the remote control. What else may I get for you?'"

Violet laughed. "We weren't quite that well mannered."

"So your parents yelled, too?"

"Not much. But my sister and I fought when we were small."

"The one who died?"

"Ivy," Violet said. "My only sister."

Andi looked down. "Tough break," she said.

Violet nodded. "She was my best friend."

Andi fidgeted with the paper sleeve on her coffee cup, and Violet could tell she was uncomfortable. The kid might be tough as nails about flaring tempers, but it seemed that tender emotions frightened her.

The young woman peered into her drink and shifted into joke mode. She waved her hands over the cup like a fortune teller. "The caffeine goddesses tell me you were the baby sister."

"And how do they know?"

"It's obvious," Andi said. "Your sister bullied you."

If someone else had said it, Violet might have reacted defensively. But she didn't think Andi was being judgmental of Ivy. It was just her acknowledgment of the natural order.

"I don't know if I'd call her a bully," Violet said. "But she was kind of overbearing when we were young."

"Everything you said was stupid, right? And embarrassing? Like she almost couldn't bear the thought that anyone might hear your remarks"

"I guess you could say she really didn't appreciate it when I opened my mouth."

"But you don't call that bullying?"

"Doesn't matter. She grew out of it."

"Still," Andi said, "you must have been pissed for a long time."

"Not really."

"Seriously? You were never furious?"

"I'm not an angry person, Andi."

The young woman chewed on her black-painted lips as she considered that. "I want to tell you a story, but you have to promise not to be judgmental, okay?"

"Of course."

"I have a little brother named Stephan. He's eighteen now, but once, when he was about fifteen, he snuck into my room and stole this joint I'd been saving to share with my friends over the weekend." She peered at Violet here for a reaction, but she just shrugged. There was nothing particularly shocking about the idea of Andi getting high.

She continued. "He knew I was saving it, too, the little prick. Normally, I would have broken his neck over something like that. But he'd had a really shitty week. He lost his iPod and got kicked out of advanced math, and my father was giving him a hard time about *everything.* So I cut him some slack and let it go."

"That was . . . sisterly of you," Violet said, unsure of where Andi was going with the story.

"I guess it was. But here's the thing. We stopped getting along after that. I mean, everything he did infuriated me. I just had no patience for him. One day my mom asked what was going on between us, and I said, 'Nothing.' But the more I thought about it, the more I realized that it had to do with that joint." She paused to drink a few gulps of her coffee.

"And the point is?" Violet asked.

"The point is that I couldn't forgive him, since I never let myself be mad at him to begin with." She sat back and folded her arms.

"I see," said Violet.

"Do you?"

"You think I need to get mad at Ivy before I can forgive her."

"Something like that," Andi said. "But what the fuck do I know, right?"

A lot, Violet thought, as she rode home on the Long Island Rail Road. You know a lot.

It had never occurred to Violet, but maybe she really did need to get angry with Ivy before she could forgive her. Maybe that was why so many negative memories of her sister were now floating to the surface. But what was she so angry about?

Her friend Jill, who read a lot of self-help books, had once suggested that Violet was angry at her sister for dying. She said it was a common psychological phenomenon, however illogical. Violet understood, as she had experienced that when her father died, and even more when she lost her mother. But with Ivy, the explanation never felt quite right.

What would Dorothy Parker say? Violet had never really opened up to her about Ivy. She never even told her about the childhood incident that had been so traumatic. Would Mrs. Parker agree that Violet had been a mean and terrible brat? Probably. But would she also think Ivy had been a brat for reacting so dramatically?

No, Ivy couldn't help it. She had been so hurt, hadn't she?

Violet stared out the train window. They were past the Jamaica station, picking up speed as they barreled through Queens toward Long Island. Soon the landscape would change from dingy factories and bland apartment buildings to tiny houses built close together. As they continued east, the homes would get larger and the plots would expand—the suburban dream spreading its wings as the city receded farther and farther into the horizon.

She was manipulating you.

The voice came from Violet's own head. It was what she knew Dorothy Parker would say about her sister. But was it true? Had Ivy's reaction been more about punishment and manipulation than hurt feelings?

And why did simply thinking about it make tears spill down Violet's face as she stared out the window?

No, she thought. It couldn't be. Ivy was just a young girl whose feelings were hurt. She wasn't trying to control her little sister. The proof was that she had spent so much of her adult life trying to get Violet to be bolder, to speak up for herself, to overcome her fears.

Again, Violet could almost hear Mrs. Parker's voice: *She was compensating, my dear.*

Violet didn't want to believe it. She just wanted to love Ivy with all her heart, and to honor her memory by missing her every hour of every day. But the pain of this realization formed such a terrible lump in her throat Violet felt she might choke.

Worst of all, she no longer had Ivy in her life to love *or* to fight with. She couldn't pull out her cell phone and press two on her speed dial to talk to the one person who always made time for her. "Are you busy?" Violet would say, and her sister would understand that it was shorthand for *I need you.* "Always," Ivy would answer, "but what's up?"

And on those occasions when she couldn't talk because she was in the middle of paying the cashier at Waldbaum's or walking into

Delaney's school concert or trying to hear over the noise of a car full of loud, excited kids, Ivy would always call back. No matter what was going on, she made time for Violet.

And maybe Ivy *had* been a brat. Maybe there were mountains of things to be angry with her about. But she loved Violet with everything she had. And the loss of that was almost too much to bear.

Violet felt a terrible chill of loneliness. Who was left for her? She no longer had a mother, a father, or a sister. Dorothy Parker had disappeared. Even Delaney had slipped from her grasp. And Violet had distanced herself from most of her dear friends.

She pulled out her cell phone and ran her fingers lightly over the keypad. There was a great big hole inside her that needed to be filled by hearing the voice of someone who loved her.

Her finger hovered above the two, where Ivy's number was still programmed in the speed dial. Once, while she sat by Delaney's bed in the hospital shortly after the accident, she had called it just to hear her sister's recorded voice. It was a stupid thing to do when she was already in so much pain, but grief does that to you. When things get that excruciating, you're compelled to pick at the wound, as if it might offer some relief. But of course it doesn't, and hearing Ivy's voice just about ripped her apart. She had never done it again, but she didn't want to erase it. Ever. One day, she just might need to hear it again.

Violet considered reaching out to one of her old friends, like Jill, but it was the middle of a workday, and she would be too busy for a heart-to-heart. She could call her friend Heidi, who was home with her two small kids, but someone was always crying in the background.

Of course, there was someone in her life she could call. Someone she wanted to talk to, needed to talk to. Someone who would understand her pain.

But she had pushed Michael away, too.

Was it too late to make things right? Could she call him now and open a dialogue?

Never too late, Mrs. Parker might say. But how would he react to hearing her voice? She had treated him so unfairly. She couldn't just phone him out of the blue and tell him she needed to talk, as if they were old friends. As far as he was concerned, she was some unbalanced woman who toyed with him, taking him to bed while she was in love with someone else.

Violet stared at her phone and thought about telling Michael the truth. Or the important part of the truth, anyway—that she really *wasn't* in love with Carl, that she wanted another chance with him.

I'll do it, she thought. I will! But her cell phone battery was running low. If she called him and got only halfway through the conversation, that would be worse than not calling at all.

No excuses, damn it! Just place the call.

This time, the voice wasn't Dorothy Parker's but her own.

She opened up the contact list, scrolled down to Michael's name, and pressed the call button. She stared at the display, waiting for it to connect, but the screen went black.

Her cell phone was dead.

After the train pulled into the Oyster Bay station, Violet got into her car and held tight to the steering wheel. The plan was to go home, take Woollcott for a walk, and leave him some food before heading out to the Webers' to pick up Delaney for the screening. But she had enough time for one important detour. The question was, did she have enough courage?

If you can do a push-up, you can do anything.

She put the car in gear and headed off.

––––––––––

"Hello?" Violet called, when she entered the Red Dragon Kung Fu Academy studio. There were no classes going on, and the place seemed empty.

"Hello!" she called again. She stood in the middle of the waiting room, her hands trembling.

She heard a sound from the back, and then there he was, in his black silk Chinese jacket—the one he wore to greet students.

"Violet!"

She tried to read his face. He was surprised, for sure. But did he also seem glad? Her heart raced.

"My cell phone died," she said.

"Tragic," he said. "I would have sent a card, but—"

Was he being snide, or was that just one of his goofy jokes? His face was unreadable.

"What I mean is," Violet said, "I was going to call, but I couldn't. Is it a bad time?"

"Not at all."

Violet wiped her hands on her slacks, hoping this wasn't a mistake. Sure, he was being polite, but where was the warmth?

It was gone. Of course. It was silly of her to assume it could be otherwise. She had treated him horribly. I should just go, she thought. This was a bad idea.

"Is everything okay?" he asked.

"Yes, fine. Better than fine, actually. I started the day thinking I was going to be fired, but . . . I made a splash."

"Congrats," he said. "I'll order a fresh bouquet from 1-800-paper-towels."

Another corny joke, but maybe he was warming up. It was an opening, anyway. She continued, "I wrote a review that got a ton of negative attention—"

"*A Foundling's Story,* right?"

"You read it?"

"I read all your reviews."

That felt like an electric charge. Violet tucked her hair behind her ear and went on. "I was ambushed about it in a TV appearance. Then I got called into my boss's office and was *sure* I was being fired. Turns out . . ." She paused, almost embarrassed to say it. She took a deep breath. "Turns out I went *viral.*"

She braced herself, expecting him to say something like, *Can you take anything for that?* But she hoped he wouldn't. She needed him to be happy for her. If he made another dumb joke now, she would know he was shut down and that she had no chance.

"That's wonderful," he said. "I'm glad you came to tell me."

"Thanks," she said, and paused, wondering how to say what she had really come for.

"Is there something else?"

Violet nodded and fidgeted. She glanced toward the darkened training hall they called a *mo gwoon,* and pictured herself going through exercises in there. *Kick, punch, kick, punch.* It had always made her feel so strong.

"I wanted to clear the air about something I said to you," she announced. "Something I've been feeling bad about." She looked down—this was just too hard to say straight to his face. "Remember the other day, when I told you I was still in love with Carl?"

"Violet—"

"I just . . . I need to say this. It was a lie. I'm sorry. I'm sorry I lied to you."

"Relax," he said. "I already knew."

She looked into his eyes. "You knew it was a lie?"

"I'm guessing you don't play much poker."

"Am I that obvious?"

"Sorry to break it to you," he said.

It sounded like a joke, but his eyes were nothing but earnest, and it made her pulse throb with crazy affection. Why had she gone so far to sabotage this?

"You must think I'm terrible," she said.

"I think you're scared."

"I'm trying not to be."

"I know."

She looked toward the *mo gwoon* again, trying to channel it all—the lessons she learned there, the courage of Dorothy Parker, and the wisdom that was right in her own heart.

She could do this. Violet took one long breath . . . and then she said it. "Can we start over?"

"Start over?"

"Us, I mean. I . . . I'd like to try this again from the beginning, take things one step at a time." She stared hard at his face, looking for a reaction. "What do you think?"

He went silent, pensive, and Violet swallowed hard. Was he groping for a kind way to reject her?

A woman can handle being maimed or blinded better than she can handle being rejected, Dorothy Parker had said to her. And maybe she was right, but Violet knew it was a risk worth taking. Whatever happens, she thought, at least I tried.

He took her hand. "What are you doing tomorrow night?" he asked.

Chapter 34

Violet drove home, imagining a brighter future than she had been able to picture in a long time. She saw her career becoming stronger and stronger as she got braver about making television appearances. She saw herself in a happy, healthy relationship with Michael. And best of all, she pictured winning custody of her niece and settling into a life that would pave a promising path for the girl.

She remembered a conversation she'd had with Dorothy Parker about her hopes for Delaney. They were sitting in the study, and her guest, as usual, was sipping a glass of gin.

"What do you think will happen to the girl if she has to stay with those people?" Mrs. Parker had asked.

"I don't know," Violet said. "It's hard to think about."

"Are they monstrous?"

"Clueless, is more like it."

"An odd turn of phrase," Mrs. Parker said. "What does it mean?"

"It means they don't have a clue how to handle her."

"So you think they could ruin her?"

Violet sighed. Her heart felt so heavy. "Yes, and that scares me. I mean, I know they love her and want what's best for her. But they're just not the right people to raise her. They can't give her what she needs. I even feel like there's something disingenuous about their desire for custody, but I can't quite put my finger on it."

"Kind of like the stepmother who raised me," Mrs. Parker said, "except for the loving-and-wanting-what's-best-for-her part."

"That's the thing," Violet said. "They really do love her. But it's not enough. She's such a fragile kid."

"She might be stronger than you think."

Violet shook her head. "Sometimes she seems strong, but she's not. And my fear is that she'll grow up wounded, bitter, and unhappy."

"I resemble that remark."

Violet squinted at Mrs. Parker, trying to remember where she had heard that joke. "Isn't that a Groucho line?"

Her friend didn't respond.

"What's the matter?" Violet asked. "You didn't like Groucho?" She had never read anything about the two of them not getting along.

"It's not that," Mrs. Parker said.

"What, then?"

"Never mind. I'm just being wretched again."

"Tell me," Violet pressed.

"I've been known to bristle over matters small and petty," Mrs. Parker said, "and this is no exception. I'm certainly not proud of myself. It's just that our vicious little group was so competitive, always arguing over who was the first to coin a phrase or invent a joke. But does it even matter? Maybe Groucho said it first. Or maybe George Kaufman wrote it and Groucho just read it. Or perhaps Mr. Benchley said it first and I repeated it and Kaufman wrote it and Groucho made it famous. But who really cares? In the end, does any of it matter?"

Mrs. Parker was sounding particularly morose, even for her.

"Are you okay?" Violet asked.

"I'm dead, my dear child, so the answer to that is unequivocal—I am most definitely *not* okay."

"I just meant—"

"Don't worry about *me*," she said, waving away Violet's comment. "The damage is already done. But I'd hate to see your niece grow up to be a writer of light verse and unimportant short stories, remembered only for her wisecracks and her last drunken years."

Violet could have argued with Mrs. Parker about the lasting value of her writing, which was still being read all over the world, but she knew this wasn't really about that.

"Do you think . . . if someone had been there to help you cope with the death of your mother—"

"Please," Mrs. Parker said.

"I mean it," Violet said. "Maybe if you'd had someone to help you deal with it—"

"Does one ever 'deal' with the death of one's mother? Did *you*?"

Violet was acutely aware that being motherless was something she shared with Dorothy Parker and Delaney. But since the day Mrs. Parker had called her "lucky" for having a mother until she was well past childhood, Violet had avoided bringing it up, as she sensed her friend would resent the comparison. So even though the pain of it was as primal as anything she had experienced, she knew Dorothy Parker would see it as an entirely different kind of loss.

Violet thought hard about how to answer.

"Yes," she finally said. "I think you do. I think you learn to deal with it. Not that the wound ever really heals—you just find a place to store the pain so you can get on with your life. I hope that doesn't sound facile. I know it's different for a child. If there isn't an adult to help you process it, and to make you feel safe—"

"Then you're left to cope all alone on a hard cot at boarding school . . ."

"Or in a big soft bed in your grandparents' house," Violet added.

"And either way," Mrs. Parker said, "your heart turns to brittle stone. We can't let that happen to your niece."

"No," Violet said. "We can't."

Violet threw her keys on the hall table and greeted Woollcott, who was literally jumping for joy, as he did every time she came home. She refilled his water bowl and was pouring dry food into his dish when the doorbell rang three quick times followed by serious pounding. It sounded like an emergency. Violet wiped her hands and rushed to open the door.

There stood Sandra, looking hysterical. A police car was parked at the curb. Violet went numb in confusion.

"Where is she!" Sandra demanded, before Violet could get a word out.

"What? Who? Delaney?"

Sandra pushed her way into the house and looked around. "Is she here?"

"Of course not. What's going on?" Violet watched as two police officers emerged from the cruiser.

"Do you know where she is?" Sandra said. Her eyes looked wild and impenetrable.

Violet's heart pounded in alarm. "Didn't she come home from school?"

"Why do you think I'm here!" Sandra screamed.

"Start from the beginning," Violet pleaded, hoping this was just a matter of Sandra's tendency toward hysteria. "I don't know what you're talking about."

"Where have you been!" the older woman demanded.

"What do you mean? I was at work."

"I called there, and they said you left hours ago. And you didn't answer your cell phone."

"The battery died, and I stopped someplace on the way home. Sandra, what's going on? Did you call the school?"

"Do you think I'm stupid? Of course I called. They said she didn't go to any of her classes after first period."

First period. That must have been when Delaney called her about the screening. Violet felt like she was going to be sick. This was serious.

"And . . . and the school didn't call you earlier in the day?" Violet asked.

Sandra waved away the comment in a fury. "My idiot husband left the phone off the hook."

"Did you try her cell phone?"

"There you go again! Of *course* I called—I'm not stupid. She didn't answer."

As belligerent as Sandra sounded, Violet knew it was fueled by terror. And that made her own heart seize in fear. She fished her cell phone from her purse to see if there was a message from Delaney. Meanwhile, the two officers walked toward the house.

"What are you doing?" Sandra shrieked at Violet. "This is no time to check your e-mail!"

"I want to see if she tried to reach me," Violet said. "I need to plug it into the charger."

"If you know where she is, you'd better tell me *right now*."

"You think I would *hide* her?"

Two policemen were now in the doorway. The shorter one, who had a stocky build and black hair, introduced himself as Officer Goncalvez. The taller one, who looked barely old enough to shave, was Officer Valentino.

Officer Goncalvez explained that a detective was at the school, investigating, and that it would help if the ladies could start calling all of Delaney's friends to see if anyone had any information.

"*She* has some very strange friends!" Sandra said, pointing a finger at Violet. "One of them stole sixty dollars from my wallet."

Violet froze. The last thing she needed now was to have any sort of suspicions cast on her. Desperate, she turned it right back on Sandra.

"A woman who was never even in your house?" she said, and then addressed the officers. "Even her husband said she imagined it."

"I think it would be best if we all just cooperated," Goncalvez said.

Violet tried to focus and walk down a rational path of thought. Where could Delaney be? Maybe she went to friend's house and didn't call because she lost her cell phone or the battery went dead. Maybe she cut out of school with a girlfriend and went to the mall, and just hadn't called because she didn't want to get in trouble. That had to be it—something simple like that. But even as she tried to believe it, something deep inside told Violet this was terrifyingly real.

The officers walked back to the squad car to listen for updates on their two-way radio, while Sandra and Violet went into the kitchen to make calls. Sandra sat at the table, and Violet handed her the landline phone. "You call the kids she knows from Smithtown, and I'll try her old friends." She opened the cupboard, took out the thick phone book, and dropped it on the table. The thud made her jump.

Don't fall apart, she coached herself. Just get through this and ignore the paranoia. In all likelihood, the officers will get a message any minute that Delaney is home, safe. Or that she was found at the frozen-yogurt shop with a friend. Goncalvez will burst back inside and give them the news. All of this will be over.

But the door didn't open again. And Violet was alone in the kitchen with Sandra.

"I don't *know* who her friends are," Sandra said. She was sounding less angry and more frightened.

"You must know one or two."

"I know there's some girl named Alexis."

"Rayburn," Violet said. "She calls her X-ray."

"Delaney and her damned nicknames," Sandra said, and started thumbing through the pages of the phone book. Violet nodded. Sandra was filtering her fear through anger, and likely wouldn't calm down until they found Delaney. And they *would* find her. They had to.

Violet opened her cell phone—now plugged into the charger—and looked through her contact list, where she had stored most of the numbers of Delaney's old friends.

"Where's Malcolm?" Violet asked, as she scrolled through the list.

"He stayed home in case she shows up."

Violet pulled a pad and pencil from the drawer and pushed them toward Sandra. "Try to get the names and numbers of some of her other friends."

"What are you, the expert?"

Violet reached out and covered Sandra's hand. "I'm as scared as you are," she said.

Sandra responded by pulling her hand away and frantically fanning herself—channeling her emotional energy into physical movement so she wouldn't cry.

Violet nodded, a tacit understanding acknowledged. She started making her own calls, trying to keep her voice steady and even. *Please,* she thought, as she explained the situation to each person who answered, *don't react hysterically. I need to hold it together.*

By the fourth or fifth call, she had perfected a little speech with rote responses: *This is Violet Epps, Delaney's aunt. We're a little concerned because she didn't come home from school today and we don't know where she is. By any chance, have you heard from her? Can you ask your daughter if she has any ideas where Delaney might be? If you hear anything, please give me a call back.*

A half hour later she had no results other than a dozen offers of help and some text messages from Delaney's friends, who said they were passing around the info.

Violet rubbed her forehead and stared out the window, trying to imagine where the girl could have gone. Soon the sun would set and things would get even more terrifying.

I already came close to losing her once, Violet thought. That's not going to happen again. It can't.

She remembered sitting at her niece's bedside in the hospital the night of the accident. Delaney was in the ICU, one arm in a cast and the other attached to an IV. She was hooked up to monitors that fed information to the nurses' station for constant surveillance. Still, Violet wouldn't take her eyes off the screen that showed the girl's vital signs. She didn't know what all the numbers meant, but the doctor had explained that Delaney had suffered a heart contusion that could be life-threatening if her pulse rate became too fast or irregular. So as her niece slept, Violet stared at the monitor, watching the girl's heartbeats displayed as an illuminated green line, jumping up and down in regular peaks that scrolled across the screen. Next to it, the number of heartbeats per minute blinked 83, 83, 84, 83, 83.

Meanwhile, she held her niece's wrist, feeling for the pulse the way a kind nurse named Cathy had shown her. But she didn't take her eyes off the screen.

By then, Ivy and Neil were already dead, and grief bore down on Violet like a relentless storm. But she couldn't even react to it. She had to let it pelt and punish her as she watched and waited: 82, 82, 80, 83, 83, 83, 84.

She was tired and thirsty and hungry. The nurses had been so kind, offering her food and suggesting she get some rest. But she couldn't. She wouldn't. As the hours ticked on, the fear and exhaustion began to obliterate her reason. She couldn't think or focus. She floated in a strange, detached space where the only things in the world were the pulse she felt in her niece's delicate wrist, that jagged green line, and those blinking numbers.

And then . . . the green line went chaotic, and the numbers went haywire, blinking 83, 79, 55, 87, 88, 91, 109, 155, 156. A high-pitched alarm blared from the monitor. Violet wanted to cover her ears, but she held on to Delaney's wrist, feeling for the regular rhythm. It was getting fainter.

What was going on? And where was Delaney's pulse? Was she dying?

The green line teased her, jumping even more erratically, while the number rose: 155, 161, 166, 181.

She willed the display to come back to normal. Meanwhile, Delaney's pulse was undetectable. Violet tried to find it with her sweaty fingers, but it seemed to be gone.

No pulse? Violet leapt from her chair, and Cathy, the kind nurse, appeared at the door. She rushed to Delaney's bed and looked at the monitor. She turned toward the door, where another nurse now stood. "Atrial fibrillation," Cathy said. "Call Dr. Marciano."

Cathy put her stethoscope to Delaney's chest and listened. Within moments, the doctor was at her side.

"She's in afib?" he said. "What's her BP?"

"One-twenty over eighty-two."

The doctor listened to Delaney's chest with his own stethoscope.

"What's happening?" Violet said. "Is she dying? Why can't I feel a pulse?"

"She has a pulse," Cathy explained. "It's just faint."

The doctor pressed his knuckles into the girl's shoulder. "Delaney, wake up. Delaney? Can you hear me?"

"Leave me alone," Delaney said, without opening her eyes. Her voice was thin as vapor.

"How do you feel?" the doctor asked. "Are you dizzy?"

"I just want to sleep."

The doctor spoke to the nurse. "Put her on oxygen," he said. "And then I need a twelve-lead EKG."

The other nurse, a tiny dark-haired woman, came back in and told Violet she would have to wait outside.

"Is Delaney going to be okay?" she pleaded to all three of them.

"We're doing everything we can," the petite nurse said. She led Violet into the hallway and tried to coax her into the waiting room, but the distraught aunt refused to go. She didn't want to leave Delaney.

"I can't lose her," Violet said to the nurse, as she thought of her father, her mother, her sister. It was too much to bear. "I can't. I can't lose her. I can't."

"You'll be more comfortable," the nurse said.

"No. No, no, no," Violet said. She felt sure that if she went into the waiting room, there was only one thing that could happen next: The Talk. She imagined a doctor coming in, smelling of blood and sweat. It would be obvious he was there to deliver bad news, and everyone in the waiting room would be thinking the same thing: *Please, not me. Let him be here for someone else. Dear God, let someone else be dead.*

But he would say Violet's name. He'd put his hand on her shoulder and apologize. And it would all be over.

"I can't lose her," Violet said to the tiny nurse. "Don't you understand?"

"Of course. But the hallway is busy. There's equipment. And the waiting room—"

"I won't go."

"I promise we'll come and get you the minute there's any news."

Violet remained immobile. The double doors to the unit opened, and a rolling bed appeared, being pushed by two orderlies. On top was an old woman who looked awake but blank.

"You see?" the nurse said. "We have to move."

Violet let herself be led away, feeling like she had no choice but to sacrifice her niece for the old woman on the stretcher. It was irrational, of course, and she soon got the news that Delaney had stabilized, but she never forgot the feeling of sitting in that cold room, thinking her niece was dead and that in some way it was her fault.

And now? Now it just might be her fault for real.

What had she said on the phone that morning that would have upset Delaney enough to make her run away? Was the girl so furious about missing the screening? No, that wasn't it. Violet had admitted her job was in danger. Delaney was bright enough to understand what that could mean for the custody case. She had run away because she had lost hope that she would ever get to move back home.

But where could she have gone?

Violet wanted to tell Sandra about that morning's phone conversation so that they could put their heads together and figure out where Delaney might be. She knew there was no way to phrase it that wouldn't make Sandra lose control, so she just took a deep breath and spit it out.

"She called me this morning from school—wanted me to pick her up and take her to a screening. I was having a bad moment and told her I couldn't."

"Why didn't you tell me that?"

"I'm telling you now."

Sandra slammed the table. "This *is* your fault!"

"You're not *helping*."

"If it wasn't for you," Sandra said, "she would be home right now, safe and sound!"

"If it wasn't for *you*, she wouldn't want to run away in the first place."

The terror in Sandra's eyes told Violet everything she needed to know—this grandmother *did* think it was her own fault. That was why her defenses were on high alert. But Sandra would do anything to keep from admitting that to anyone . . . especially herself.

Violet heard someone open the front door, which she had left unlocked for the police officers.

"Hello?" It was Malcolm's voice.

"We're in the kitchen!" Violet said.

He rushed in, holding up a pill bottle.

"Why are you here?" Sandra said. "You're supposed to be home. What if she turns up?"

"Rita is there," he said, referring to his sister, whom Violet had met a few times.

"Rita!" Sandra said, and rolled her eyes, implying that she was the most ridiculous choice Malcolm could have made.

"What's this?" he said, showing Sandra the pill bottle.

"You know what it is," she said. "It's Delaney's medicine."

"Why doesn't she have it? She's supposed to carry it with her, just in case."

"Where did you find that?" Sandra demanded.

"Where you hid it," Malcolm said. "On the top shelf behind the Metamucil."

"You *hid* Delaney's medicine?" Violet said.

Sandra stood. "For her own good! Don't gang up on me!"

"How is hiding her medicine for her own good?" Violet demanded.

"She's very responsible about taking it," Sandra said. "I just . . . I thought if she couldn't find it she wouldn't run away."

So this was the terrible truth Sandra had been hiding. It was worse than Violet had imagined. She looked at the clock. It was just a few hours until Delaney was due for her next dose. If she didn't take it, her heart could go into atrial fibrillation again. And without immediate attention she could pass out, or worse—have a deadly stroke.

Violet's flesh prickled in fear as she ran out of any shred of sympathy for Sandra. "Do you have any idea how dangerous this is?" she said.

Malcolm rattled the pill bottle at his wife. "You shouldn't have hid this!"

"You really thought hiding her medicine would stop her from running away?" Violet asked.

"I'm doing my best!" Sandra said. "Which is more than I can say for you—taking her to nudie shows and putting ideas in her head. Who *knows* where she went off to after the kind of things you expose her to?"

"Don't put this on me!" Violet said. "You're the one who drove her away, and you're the one who hid her medicine. And guess what? I *do* think you're stupid!"

"And I think you're *dangerous*!"

"Don't talk to me about dangerous when you're the one who hid her heart medication! If she strokes out, it will be *your fault*."

"I was only trying to protect her!"

"From what?" Violet said.

"From *you*!"

"Liar! You *know* she belongs with me, but you'll do anything to keep that from happening."

"Of course!" Sandra said. "I don't want her living with a single woman who's never even raised a child."

Violet went cold. "What are you saying?" she asked quietly.

"I'm saying that a woman whose baby died before it even had a chance to be born can't be much of a mother."

Violet was aghast. There was no longer any way to contain her fury. "No wonder Delaney hates you!"

"She might hate me," Sandra said, "but at least I can provide a stable, two-parent household."

"With a husband who cheats," Violet said.

"What?"

"Go ahead—ask him! Ask him who he goes to visit when Delaney is taking her piano lesson! Your husband is cheating on you, Sandra. So much for a stable household!"

Sandra turned to Malcolm. "Is this true?"

Malcolm's face reddened beneath its orange glow. "Uh . . . no. Of course not."

"Then whose house is he parked at every Sunday?" Violet asked.

"I thought you just drove around," Sandra said. "You told me you just drove around."

"I . . . uh . . . Why are we talking about this now?" Malcolm said. "Delaney is *missing*."

"Oh, my God!" Sandra said. "It's true! Who is she?"

"It doesn't matter. I mean . . . we can't do this now. Sandra—"

"How could you! How could you do this! Is that what the manicures are about? And the tanning? And the teeth? Oh, God!"

Violet heard the front door open again, and the two police officers entered the kitchen.

"We've got a lead," Goncalvez said. "A girl matching Delaney's description was seen at the Smithtown train station."

The train station? Violet shuddered. Delaney could be anywhere.

Chapter 35

Sandra and Malcolm agreed on a temporary détente and accompanied the officers to the depot to show Delaney's picture to everyone they could. Meanwhile, the detective on the case was reviewing security tapes, and Violet stayed behind to make more phone calls.

She had sent several text messages to Delaney, but of course there had been no response. She tried again:

You don't have your meds. Wherever you are, call me and I'll bring them to you.

She hit send and stared at the screen. Nothing.

Poor Woollcott was at the front door, whimpering, as she still hadn't taken him out. Violet stuck her charged cell phone in her pocket and grabbed his leash.

As they walked down the block, Violet tried to focus on where Delaney might have gone by train. Almost everyone who boards at a Long Island station is headed to Manhattan. But would Delaney have done that? And if so, where was she going? Did she have any favorite spots? A museum? A restaurant? Did she have a friend in the city Violet didn't know about? Had she met someone online?

Please, God, Violet thought, don't let it be that.

Her cell phone rang, and Violet grabbed it from her pocket. It was an unfamiliar number.

"Is this Violet?" a woman asked.

"Yes. Who's this?"

"My name is Sherry Pierce. I live about four blocks from the Webers, and my daughter gave me your number. She said all the kids are texting about Delaney. Are you still looking for her?"

"Yes!" Violet said, her heart racing. "Did you see her?"

"I don't know what time it was. Late morning, maybe? I remember thinking it was strange that she wasn't in school. I saw her walking down Redwood toward the train station. Someone probably reported this already, right?"

Violet sighed. "Yes, but thank you. Thank you very much. It's good to have it corroborated."

"I wish there was something I could do."

"I appreciate that."

"I would have asked her where she was going, but since she was with an adult—"

Violet stopped walking. "She wasn't alone?"

"No, she was with a petite woman with dark hair. A teacher, I figured."

Woollcott tugged on the leash, but Violet remained frozen. It couldn't be, could it? "What was she wearing?"

"The woman? A dress, I think. Yes, definitely. Definitely wearing a dress—something old-fashioned. And she was carrying a box."

Dorothy Parker! Dear God, what was she doing with Delaney? And was this good news or bad?

Violet thanked Sherry Pierce and rushed back home, certain Mrs. Parker and Delaney had headed into the city. Beyond that, she had no ideas. But she knew she had to locate them before the Webers got wind that Delaney had been seen with Violet's strange friend. Once that happened, Violet would be suspected of masterminding some kidnapping scheme. And she was damned sure no one would believe her explanation of who the strange woman really was.

Violet grabbed her car keys, determined to drive into the city and find a troubled thirteen-year-old girl and a mischievous older woman. But where should she look? Manhattan was a big place, and they could be anywhere. Think, Violet coached herself. Would they have gone someplace Delaney wanted to go? Or would Mrs. Parker be the tour guide?

Delaney had wanted to go to the screening, but that wasn't possible. She had no idea where it was and wouldn't be able to get in without Violet's pass. Mrs. Parker had mentioned there was still one place she wanted to visit—her old haunt, the Algonquin. Violet shuddered. It was the last place she wanted to show her face again. There had to be a more likely spot she could check first.

The only other place that made sense was the screening. Could the partners in crime have found a way to get in? Perhaps Mrs. Parker sneaked back into Violet's office, found the pass, and took Delaney to the private showing. Yes, that made some sense. She would start there.

Just after Violet merged onto the Long Island Expressway heading west toward the tunnel into Manhattan, her cell phone rang. The caller ID showed that it was the Suffolk County police.

"Miss Epps? This is Detective Diehl."

He was the lead investigator on the case, and Violet had spoken to him by phone earlier, before the Webers left for the train station. He had a deep voice, and a careful, measured way of speaking.

"Is there any news?" Violet asked.

"Where are you now?" he asked.

"I'm in my car, why?"

"We'd like you to come down here and look at these security tapes."

Uh-oh.

"Why? What did you see? Is Delaney in danger?"

"She was seen with an individual who was identified as someone you might know."

Shit.

"Really? Who?" Violet's stomach was in a knot. She hated lying, especially when the man on the other end of the phone was trained to know when people were being dishonest.

"I'd like you to come down and take a look for yourself."

"When? Now?"

"As soon as possible," Detective Diehl said. He gave her the address of the Suffolk County police headquarters and told her to ask for him at the front desk.

"I'll be there as soon as I can," Violet said. Then she got off the phone and continued west toward New York City.

"It's in progress, Ms. Epps," said the young intern at the desk situated in the hallway in front of the screening room. The girl wore a name badge that said BROOKE, and Violet remembered her from previous screenings. She had been working for the studio for several months, and did a good job memorizing the critics' names.

"I know," Violet said. "I'm not here officially. I think it's possible my niece sneaked into the theater. By any chance did you see a girl about thirteen years old go inside?"

Violet hoped Brooke might remember seeing someone that young, as there weren't many kids at these things. Critics were entitled to bring a guest, but they rarely brought children. Sometimes, when there was a family feature, the studios gave out promotional passes to the public and a few kids might be in attendance, but this wasn't one of those films.

Brooke shook her head. "I haven't been here the whole time. Taryn was at the desk, but she had to leave early."

"Can I peek in and look around?"

"It's in *progress.*"

"I know, but . . . this is practically life and death." Violet paused, wondering if Brooke would take that as hyperbole. She was having a hard time believing it herself. But the chill that prickled Violet's skin reminded her it was very, very real. "The kid ran away without her medication," she said.

"Oh, shit. Okay, go in, but watch out for Buzz."

"Buzz?" Violet asked.

"Security."

"Right," Violet said. There was always one very serious security guard at these screenings, as the studios were paranoid about pirated copies of the films being sold. So a guard stood off to the side, watching the people watching the movie, making sure no one was surreptitiously recording it. If you even took out a cell phone during the screening, you got thrown out.

Very quietly, Violet opened the door to the dark room. She waited a moment for her eyes to adjust, hoping for a brightly lit scene that might illuminate the auditorium enough to look around.

The space was smaller than a regular theater, with plush, oversized chairs upholstered in leather. Violet could make out a very tall figure leaning against the opposite wall toward the front of the room. No doubt that was Buzz, who must have been at least six five. His arms were folded, and while she couldn't make out his face, Violet felt sure he was staring at her.

She glanced at the screen. Two characters were talking in a darkened alleyway—a scene that threw virtually no light into the room. She watched and waited. An off-camera siren sounded, and Violet felt certain she knew what would happen next. Sure enough, a police car pulled into the narrow passage and the scene cut to the headlights from the characters' point of view. This instantly lit the screening room.

Violet rushed along the wall toward the front so she could scan the seats for Dorothy Parker and Delaney. Before she could turn around, she felt a heavy hand on her shoulder. It was Buzz.

"Can I help you, miss?" he whispered.

"Looking for someone," she said, trying to peer around him. He was blocking her view with his massive frame.

"You have to leave."

"I'm a movie critic," she said.

"Then take a seat."

"You don't understand."

"Outside," he said.

"But—" she began, but before she could plead her case, a sound even louder than the siren erupted. It was her cell phone. Every head in the theater turned toward her.

She reached for it as fast as she could, but the room went dark again and she couldn't see what she was doing. She let Buzz usher her out the door into the lobby.

"I'm so sorry!" she said. "Really." She looked at the caller ID on her phone. It was Detective Diehl again. She silenced the ringer and slipped it back into her purse.

Violet explained the situation to the security guard just as she had done with Brooke. "Please," she said. "You have to let me back in to look for her. She might be in there right now!"

Buzz scratched his chin. "I think she is," he said.

"You do? Really? Oh, please," she said, rushing for the door.

He grabbed her arm. "I can't let you back in."

"But—"

"Just wait here," he said. "The movie ends in less than twenty minutes."

"That's too long!" she said. "She needs to take her medication." Violet felt her cell phone vibrating in her purse. "And the police are involved. Everyone's looking for her!"

He sighed. "*I'll* bring her out. You wait here."

Thank God, thank God, thank God, Violet thought, as she paced the hallway, waiting for Buzz and Delaney to emerge. This whole nightmare was about to end. Delaney was safe. Safe! And Violet wouldn't have to worry about being suspected of kidnapping her niece. In fact, she would be a hero for being the one who found her.

She rubbed down the goose bumps on her arms and stared at the door to the screening room. Any minute, it would open and become the happy ending to the terrible story that started on the day of the tragic accident.

Violet thought back again to that day at the hospital, after Delaney had stabilized and regained consciousness. While still groggy, the girl repeatedly asked for her mother, and Violet said the same thing each time, "I'm here with you, sweetheart. It's Aunt Violet. I won't leave you."

But finally, after Delaney had taken her first small meal and was wide awake, Violet knew it was time. She could have called the nurse and asked her to summon the in-house psychologist, who had offered to help break the news, but Violet thought that would only make it worse. It should be just the two of them sharing this quiet, unbearable moment.

"I want to see my parents," Delaney said, when she finished her apple juice. "Where are they?"

Violet took her hand. "You know you were in a terrible car accident, right?"

Delaney pushed her tray away and stared at her aunt. Violet wondered what was going through her mind. Was she remembering? Replaying the terrifying scene? And then something changed. A darkness passed over the girl's eyes, and her spirit seemed to shrivel as tears spilled down her cheeks.

She knew.

"Are they dead?" she asked.

Violet nodded. "Yes."

"Both of them?"

"I'm sorry."

Delaney pulled her slender hand from her aunt's grip. "I wish . . ." she said, and paused. Violet felt her own heart constrict as she waited for her niece to finish the sentence.

Delaney scratched at the corner of the medical tape holding her IV in place. It looked like she was trying to get a grip so she could peel it off. But the cast on her wrist made her efforts clumsy.

"You have to leave that alone, hon," Violet said.

The girl ignored her and kept scratching.

"Del?"

Delaney looked up as if she had forgotten someone was in the room with her.

"I'm going to take care of you," Violet said.

Delaney went back to picking at the tape.

"Del, please," Violet said, laying a hand on Delaney's shoulder.

The girl didn't say anything, but she moved to the side of the bed. Violet took it as an invitation to get beside her for a hug. She lay down and embraced her poor niece. Delaney rested her wet face on her aunt's shoulder. Violet held her close, trying to convey that she loved her and would never leave her, and that it would all be okay.

"I wish I was dead, too," Delaney said.

They had come such a long way since that dark moment. And when the door to the screening room opened at last, Violet was weeping with joy and fear and expectation. But what she saw made her throat tighten. Buzz emerged with a young blond girl who looked scared and confused.

Violet shook her head. "It's not her. That's not Delaney."

Chapter 36

A short time later, Violet pulled into an illegal parking space on West 44th Street, diagonally across the street from the entrance to the Algonquin Hotel, and held tight to her steering wheel. She tried to imagine what would happen if she went inside and Barry Beeman spotted her. Would he accuse her of stealing the guest book? Would he demand that security detain her until the police arrived? And then what? The detective on Long Island probably considered her a kidnapping suspect by now. Once he learned where she was and what she had been accused of, she could well be arrested on felony charges.

This could go very, very badly.

I should just turn around and go home, she thought. If I go straight to the police station now, maybe I can talk my way out of any trouble. But if I get nabbed here, it's all over.

Violet pulled out her cell phone and sent Delaney another text message:

I'm parked in front of the Algonquin. If you're inside, please come out!

She turned the ringer back on and dropped the phone into her purse, not terribly hopeful that Delaney would respond.

While she waited, Violet stared at the entryway, trying to convince herself it would be ridiculous to go inside to look for the pair. But it was no use. Violet had read too many books about Dorothy Parker to underestimate the significance of this place in the life of the legendary wit. And after spending all those decades flitting around the Algonquin only when the book was open—and being at the mercy of whoever might close it—she would likely relish the opportunity to experience the place on her own terms.

Violet's phone rang again. She looked at the caller ID. Suffolk County PD. She dropped it back into her purse.

Courage. This was something she had to do, regardless of the consequences. She got out of the car and approached the entrance to the Algonquin, putting her face right up against the dark glass doors. She couldn't see much beyond the vestibule, where there was another set of dark glass doors leading to the hotel lobby.

"Can I help you, miss?" the doorman asked.

"Maybe you can," Violet said. She took out her cell phone and scrolled to a recent picture of Delaney. "I'm looking for my niece," she said, handing it to him. "Have you seen this girl within the last couple of hours? I think she may have gone into the hotel."

He adjusted his hat as he looked at the image. "I don't think so," he said. "But a lot of people come and go." He gave the phone back to Violet. "Maybe somebody at the front desk saw her."

She nodded and moved toward the door.

"You going to leave your car there?" he asked, pointing across the street.

"I'll only be a few minutes," she said. "You think I'll get a ticket?"

He held the door open for her. "Fifty-fifty," he said. "Try not to take too long."

Violet hesitated, worried. And then scoffed at her own stupid knee-jerk anxiety.

"And I doubt you'll get towed," the doorman added.

"It's a tow-away zone?" Violet asked.

"I've only seen them tow one car in all the time I've been working here."

"That's a relief," Violet said, and then thought to add, "How long have you been working here?"

"Almost four weeks."

Great. Just when she thought this day couldn't get any worse.

"I'll be quick," she said, and stepped into the darkened interior of the Algonquin Hotel.

Normally, Violet loved entering the historic hotel. But today, instead of feeling charmed by the place's rich history and antique decor, she was almost nauseated by a chill of foreboding. The past felt like a threat to her now—a physical thing that could swallow Delaney whole.

Violet did a quick scan for Barry Beeman, who was nowhere in sight. Matilda, the Algonquin's famous cat, sat at her perch on the front desk, looking bored. She seemed to glance at Violet contemptuously, as if she knew about the stolen guest book.

The maître d' at the lectern was not the handsome Middle Eastern man who had been on duty the day she had created a scene and made off with the guest book, but a short, portly man with elegantly lush white hair—someone who wouldn't know her connection to the missing artifact. Thank goodness, Violet thought, as she approached.

She showed him her niece's picture on her phone. "Have you seen this girl?" Violet asked.

"I don't think she's arrived yet," he said, clearly assuming she was meeting Violet there for dinner. "Would you like to look around?"

She said that she would, and threaded her way through the armchairs and sofas to the back of the room, glancing at every face. No Delaney. No Dorothy Parker. Likewise, she didn't find them in the Oak Room, a supper club off the lounge.

Violet boldly approached the front desk and showed the cell-phone picture of Delaney to a uniformed woman who looked like a round-faced Cindy Crawford.

"Have you seen this girl?" she asked. "She's my niece, and I think she might be here."

The woman passed Violet's phone to the other two people behind the desk, but none of them had seen her. Violet asked where the hotel's corporate office was located.

"Second floor," the attractive woman said. "Is there someone I can call for you?"

Second floor—just as Violet had feared. Contrary to popular belief, the Algonquin suite Dorothy Parker most fondly remembered was not the one on the eleventh floor named in her honor, but, as she had once informed Violet, a more obscure room on the second floor. It was the only place in the hotel Violet wanted to scout out, but it was also where she was most likely to run into the general manager.

This was going to be tricky, but Violet knew what she had to do.

"Would you mind buzzing Barry Beeman and asking him to come down?" she said. "Tell him Violet Epps is here."

The woman picked up the phone at the front desk and relayed the message.

"He'll be with you in a moment," she said to Violet. "He'd like you to wait right here."

"Of course," Violet said, but as soon as the woman looked back at her computer screen she inched away, finding a place to position herself in the shadows on the other side of the elevator bank, near the closed stairway. She wedged herself tightly against the cabinet holding the fire hose, and hoped Barry Beeman didn't glance to his right before approaching the front desk.

Within moments, the elevator dinged and opened, and Violet watched as several people emerged. Barry Beeman was not among them. Then the door to the stairwell opened, almost hitting her in the face.

And there he was, tall and rigid in his dark suit. He charged right to the front desk without seeing her, and Violet slipped into the stairwell.

She went straight to room 209, which had been Dorothy Parker's residence for several years after she and Edwin Parker, her first husband, split up.

She knocked on the door. There was no answer. She tried again.

"Delaney?" she called. "It's Aunt Violet. If you're in there, please open up."

Nothing. Violet pressed her ear to the door but couldn't hear anything. She knocked again and waited. A chambermaid pushing a housekeeping cart turned the corner, and Violet wondered if she would be able to talk the woman into opening the room for her. It would take a bit of fiction. Violet didn't know if she had the acting chops to pull it off, but it was worth a try.

Violet knocked again on the door and called, "Honey? Open up, it's me."

"You lose your key, miss?" asked the chambermaid.

Yes! Just the reaction she had been hoping for. Violet was grateful for her newfound courage.

"I . . . left it in my room. Thought my husband would be here, but I guess he went out." Violet paused and waited. Was her story compelling enough for the woman to break the rules and let her in?

"They help you at front desk," the woman said. "You get new key-card."

Damn.

"Okay, thanks," Violet said. "I'll do that." She turned to go and affected a pronounced limp that she figured wasn't very convincing. But once she was committed, she knew she had to do it all the way down the hall. She felt like an idiot.

"Miss, wait," the chambermaid said, opening the door with her master key. "I let you in."

Violet turned. "That's very kind of you," she said.

Violet shut the door behind her and looked around. It was indeed a suite. The living room was clean, spare, and modern—clearly nothing like it had been in Dorothy Parker's day. There was a closed laptop on the desk, a copy of *The Wall Street Journal* on the coffee table, and a John Grisham novel on the orange leather armchair.

"Hello?" Violet called, just to be sure the room's actual resident wasn't there.

There was no answer, so she quietly stepped into the empty bedroom. The bed was made but rumpled, as if someone had been sitting on it. A few art museum brochures were spread out on the dresser, and three pairs of men's shoes were neatly lined up in the corner. Violet opened the door to the bathroom. There were toiletries on the counter— a small tube of Colgate Total, Speed Stick deodorant, shaving cream, and a razor—and a damp towel on the floor. The shower curtain was half closed. Violet hesitated before looking behind it, the murder scene from Hitchcock's *Psycho* too vivid to shut out.

This isn't a horror movie, she reminded herself, as she pushed the curtain aside. Of course, no one was there.

Violet wanted to take a quick look around for the Macy's box before leaving, but she heard voices in the hallway. She stood, frozen, trying to imagine what kind of excuse she could give if the man entered the room. Fortunately, the footsteps passed right by the door and Violet let out a long, relieved breath.

She quickly looked through the drawers, the closet, and under the bed, but the Macy's box wasn't there. So that was it. Delaney and Mrs. Parker were not in the hotel.

She lowered herself onto the sofa in the living room area of the suite and cried. There was no place else she could think to look for her niece. And now she had to drive to the Suffolk County police headquarters and face Detective Diehl. What would happen? Would she be arrested? Placed in handcuffs? Thrown into a cell? More important, were they going to find Delaney?

They had to. They simply had to.

She rose. No time to wallow in self-pity. She would face the detective and would do whatever it took to find her niece.

First, though, she had to figure out a way to get past Barry Beeman.

The corporate offices were in a suite facing the elevator bank. She knocked lightly on the open door, and a middle-aged woman in reading glasses looked up.

"Can I help you?"

"Is Barry Beeman in?" Violet asked. "I need to speak with him about something."

"I believe he's at the front desk."

"Do you think he'll be back soon?"

"I can call if you like," she said, picking up the phone.

Violet nodded and waited as the woman spoke softly into the receiver. She covered it with her hand and looked at Violet.

"What is your name?" she asked.

"Violet Epps."

She spoke into the receiver again for a few moments, but Violet made sure to slip away before she looked up again.

Violet almost laughed at she got into the elevator. This was so much easier than they made these things look in the movies. Barry Beeman would take the stairs up and she would take the elevator down, and they would miss each other entirely. Easy peasy.

The doors opened on the first floor, and Violet stepped out of the elevator, congratulating herself on outwitting the general manager. Maybe her luck was changing. But then a hand landed on her shoulder from behind.

"Ms. Epps," said Barry Beeman.

Violet turned to face him, and his eyes said it all. He knew she'd stolen his guest book and would be only too happy to call the police and have her arrested.

Don't panic, she told herself. You can do this. Just think fast and you can lie your way out. Surely, her background in dissecting so many hundreds of movie scripts would serve her well now. Besides, if Andi could so easily lie, she could, too. Her heart pounded.

"There you are!" she said. "I've been looking all over for you."

"You have?"

"My apologies for what happened with your guest book," she said. "I was so delirious that day I passed out. I don't even know how it wound up in my purse. Anyway, I'm glad my assistant returned it. So sorry it took so long. I've been convalescing."

"She returned it?"

"She left it with someone at the front desk yesterday. Didn't they give it to you?"

"What time was that?"

"I don't know," she said. "Sometime in the morning."

"Do you know who she left it with?"

"Um . . . no." She glanced over at the Cindy Crawford look-alike, who seemed tense. Violet wanted to let her off the hook. "A man, I think."

"Jonathan?"

"Maybe."

Exasperated, Barry Beeman turned to the woman at the front desk. "Where's Jonathan?" he asked.

"He got off at three today."

Violet's cell phone rang, and she begged the manager's pardon, telling him she had to take the call. Then she slipped out the front door and dashed across the street to her car, which, mercifully, was still there. She put it in gear and drove away, an orange parking citation beneath her wiper flapping in the breeze.

Chapter 37

Violet's cell phone stopped ringing, and almost immediately started again. She didn't want to answer it, because she couldn't even think of what she would tell the detective. He wouldn't believe the truth and wouldn't buy her lies. There was no way she could win.

Violet imagined that once she got to the precinct, she would be shown the surveillance video from the train station and asked if the petite woman seen with Delaney was a friend of hers. She wouldn't be able to deny it, as both Sandra and Malcolm had already met her, and her neighbor, Candy Baker, had seen them together.

How could Violet possibly explain who the woman was? If she told them she was actually the ghost of Dorothy Parker, they'd lock her away in a psych ward.

Was there any way out?

Violet couldn't take it for another second. When she stopped at the next red light, she grabbed her phone and answered it, ready to tell the detective she was on her way.

"It's me," said the caller.

"Michael?" she said. "What's going on?"

"I've been trying to reach you," he said. He sounded agitated.

"Sorry, I . . . I thought it was someone else." The light turned green, and she stepped on the gas. "Did you hear anything?" She had phoned him earlier about her niece, so she knew he was on high alert.

"Kara got a text from Delaney."

"What! When?"

"Just a few minutes ago. Kara had texted her three times asking where she was. Delaney finally responded."

"What did it say?" Violet's heart was thumping. This meant the girl was okay. This meant they would find her! "Read it to me."

"I'm with my aunt's friend," he read. *"She's taking me to see my mother."*

"Her mother?" Violet stepped on the brake, and a cold sweat dampened her shirt. "That's all she wrote?"

"Don't panic," he said.

"You don't understand!"

"Violet—"

"Michael, please! The woman she's with is obsessed with death and dying. She tried to commit suicide three times!"

"Take a deep breath," he said. "It might not be what you're thinking."

"Did she say where they are?" This was a nightmare. An ugly, black, terrifying nightmare.

"Just a few minutes ago, but before you freak out, listen. I don't think it's a suicide pact. You once told me that Delaney had never visited her mother's grave. If she was upset enough to run away, that's where she would have wanted to go. She probably wanted her mother so very desperately that she finally needed to see where she was buried."

Could he be right? Were Delaney and Dorothy Parker visiting Ivy and Neil's graves? That would explain their appearance at the train station. They could have been traveling to the cemetery.

Violet got off the phone and pushed her way through Midtown traffic as fast as she could. She went through the Queens–Midtown Tunnel to the Long Island Expressway and sped toward the New Montefiore Cemetery on Long Island.

When she got to the gatehouse, a guard in uniform came out and told her he was sorry, but they were closed.

"Closed?" She peered past the iron gates and saw several cars driving along the cemetery's narrow interior roadways. She saw families and couples walking among the tombstones. He followed her gaze and explained that there were still people inside, but that the entrance gate was locked every night at six-thirty.

"I can't let anyone else in," he said. "Sorry."

"You don't understand," Violet said. "My thirteen-year-old niece is in there, and she could be sick. She forgot to take her medicine, and I have it with me. Please!"

"I have to check with my boss," the man said, and picked up his walkie-talkie. He squeezed the control several times and talked into it but got no response.

"I'm going to have to go look for him," he said.

Did he even believe her? Violet was frantic. "I'm running out of time!" she said. "Just open the gate. I promise I'll find her and come right out." She dug into her purse and took out a twenty-dollar bill, which she held out the window. "Her parents are buried here. They died last year in a car accident. Drunk driver. She's just a kid, and she needs me. Please!"

The guard's expression changed. Did he realize she was telling the truth? Violet held her breath.

"Keep your money," he said, and pushed the button to open the gate. "Just don't stay too long . . . and don't tell anyone I let you in this late."

Violet stepped on the gas and sped through the gate. She drove along the marked narrow streets of the massive cemetery to the corner plot where Ivy and Neil were buried. She got out of her car and looked toward the grave. The sun was low in the sky, and she could see the silhouette of a young tree and two moving figures. Violet wept as she watched them. A breeze pushed its way across the broad terrain, and the delicate tree swayed toward the couple. The more slender of the figures crouched and laid her hands upon the earth. The other stood very still.

Violet pulled a tissue from her purse and blew her nose. Then she took out her cell phone and called Detective Diehl.

"I found her," she said. "I found Delaney. She's okay."

"Where are you!" he barked.

"At the cemetery," she said, and told him that Malcolm and Sandra would be able to direct him to the plot. Then she dropped her phone back in her purse and took a few steps toward her niece, whose head was bowed toward the earth. Violet didn't want to break whatever meditation Delaney was in, so she stood and waited for the girl to look up and notice her.

Violet thought about the day Ivy called to tell her Delaney had been born. The phone rang at four in the morning, and she knew it was her sister, because she had called the night before to say she was in labor and heading to the hospital.

"News?" Violet said, instead of hello.

"She's here," Ivy said.

"You have a daughter?"

"Delaney Bea."

A girl! Violet started to cry. "What is she like?"

"You have to see her. You have to hold her. She has these lips. This tiny little perfect mouth. It doesn't seem possible for anyone to be so beautiful."

"I'll be right there."

Now Violet looked up toward her niece, still crouched on her mother's grave. This was so damned unfair.

She tried to pull herself out of her despair. This was a happy moment. She had found her niece. She looked around the cemetery at the endless rows of tombstones. So many people. So many stories. So much misery. Violet couldn't help remembering something Dorothy

Parker had once said to Samuel Goldwyn when he complained that the script she had written for him ended on a sad note. "I know this will come as a shock to you, Mr. Goldwyn, but in all history, which has held billions and billions of human beings, not a single one ever had a happy ending."

She looked back at her niece and knew that Dorothy Parker was wrong. Some stories did have happy endings. The girl looked up and spotted her. "Aunt Violet!" she cried, and ran into her arms. "I'm sorry I ran away. I'm so sorry!"

Violet held on to her niece, feeling like she would never let her go again. "I know," she said.

"You must want to kill me."

"I'm just glad you're okay."

"I should have called," Delaney said.

"Yes."

"Your friend Daisy told me not to. She said we needed to visit the grave first."

"She's not always the best influence," Violet said, looking past her niece at the figure by the tombstone. Mrs. Parker waved to her. Violet waved back.

"You must have been here for hours," she said to her niece.

"No, we walked around for a while, went out to eat. Talked. She's pretty smart. Funny, too."

"I know."

"I was so upset. I was thinking about . . ." Delaney trailed off and shook her head, as if she just couldn't say it.

Violet's stomach clenched. She pulled her niece away so she could look into her face. "Thinking about what?" she asked.

The girl looked down.

"Delaney—"

"I was angry," she said. "Furious. I wanted to cut my wrists and bleed all over Sandra and Malcolm's stupid pink bathroom rug. I wanted them to feel terrible for taking me away from you."

"Oh, honey."

"They deserve it," Delaney said, but didn't sound that convincing. Clearly, her anger had dissipated.

"And you were mad at me, too," Violet said.

"Not so much about the screening," the girl said. "For fucking up at work, for getting fired and ruining everything."

Delaney paused, and before Violet had a chance to explain about her job, the girl continued. "But I guess it wasn't your fault," she said. She took a long, jagged breath and let it out. "It was good to come here. It made me think about them more. I've been trying so hard not to."

"I understand."

"I needed to be sad."

"Of course you did."

"I miss them so much."

"Me, too," Violet said. They were both crying now.

"My mother wouldn't want me to kill myself," Delaney said. "I need to stick around. For them. For me."

"It's all going to be okay, you know?"

The girl nodded and hugged her aunt again.

"And guess what?" Violet said, as she stroked her niece's hair. "I didn't get fired. In fact, I'm some kind of viral phenomenon now. How do you like that?"

"*Awesome*, Aunt Violet."

"That's the second time you've called me Aunt Violet in the last five minutes."

Delaney nodded. "I know."

"I shouldn't have told you my job was in jeopardy," Violet said.

"And I shouldn't have ditched school," Delaney said.

Violet watched as Dorothy Parker walked slowly to a wooden bench and sat, holding the Macy's box on her lap.

She looked back at her niece. "I love you," Violet said.

"I'm a brat," said the girl.

"You're not."

"Your friend Daisy said it was okay. She said if I couldn't be a brat at my age, when *could* I be?"

"At her age," Violet said, laughing. She looked back at Mrs. Parker, who seemed to be opening the box.

Delaney followed her aunt's line of vision, then reached into the pocket of her jeans and pulled out a folded page. "She told me to give you this," she said, handing it to Violet.

"How did she know I'd find you?"

"She said after I texted Kara you'd figure it out."

Violet had to smile. Dorothy Parker wasn't content to just leave a clue to bring her to Delaney but had to orchestrate a connection that would bring Michael and Violet together. She unfolded the note and read it.

My Dear Ms. Epps,

> *I'm writing this as I watch your precious niece sitting cross-legged on your sister's grave, tearing tufts of grass as if she's trying to claw at tiny pieces of her mother's soul. Don't know that I've ever seen anything more heartbreaking.*
>
> *But the damned thing of it is, I get it now. She's a hell of a kid. But even when she's not—even when she's being a smartass (bless her soul)—I can imagine that her mother loved her. Maybe imagine isn't the right word; it's more like something I sense. Yes, in fact, I just closed my eyes and there it was—your sister's ridiculous heart. And*

now I know that even in her worst moments, like when she was operating on no sleep and needed to get out of the house and the baby had just thrown mashed peas and crapped in her diaper and overturned her bowl of pabulum, your sister would have laid down her life for the kid.

For so long, I couldn't imagine my mother ever felt that way about me. I just assumed I was a born shit. And maybe I was, but even so, I can see that my mother loved me. She didn't have a choice, poor thing. And all this time, she's been waiting behind that white light so she could tell me herself. What an idiot I've been.

So you see, you were right. But don't tell anyone I said that.

One more thing before I shuffle off this mortal coil once and for all, as you're probably wondering how I knew your niece would be in peril. While I was floating around that awful house (Who decorated that place, anyway? It looks like the regurgitated contents of Busby Berkeley's storage closet), I heard Delaney tell a friend that if she thought you wouldn't win custody, she would kill herself. That's why I left your office after you had that terrible telephone conversation with her—I knew she would need some help.

How do you like that? Maybe I have done some good after all.

You can thank me when we meet again, my dear friend. Meanwhile, take care of that girl.

Love and farewell, and love,
Dorothy Parker

"What does it say?" Delaney asked.

"Grown-up stuff," Violet said, as she refolded the note and stuck it in her own pocket. She glanced over at the bench where Dorothy Parker had been sitting, but she was gone.

Chapter 38

 Gone?

Frantic, Violet glanced around the cemetery and finally saw Mrs. Parker walking up a small hill.

"Wait!" she shouted, but her friend didn't seem to hear. Violet watched as Dorothy Parker reached the top, laid the box on the ground, and stared into the distance.

It's the light, Violet thought. She's going to walk into the light.

Violet felt a rising panic. She wasn't ready to let go—not yet. There was still so much to say.

"You need to talk to your friend?" Delaney asked.

"I do," Violet said, crying.

"I'll wait in the car."

Violet hugged her niece and then ran toward the hill. "Mrs. Parker!" she shouted.

At last her friend heard her and turned around.

"I have to go now, Ms. Epps," she said, waving good-bye.

"Please wait," Violet said. She reached the top of the mound and bent to catch her breath.

"Was there something you wanted to ask me?" Mrs. Parker said.

Violet straightened and looked into her friend's dark eyes, thinking hard about what final wisdom she hoped to glean from this woman. There was so much she still needed to talk about. She wanted to tell her that things were working out with her career, that she had boldly reached out to Michael, that she finally understood that her relationship with her sister had been at the root of her fears all along.

"I don't know where to start," Violet said.

"Perhaps that's because there's nothing more to say."

"There is," Violet insisted. "I never really told you about my sister."

"What about her?"

Violet closed her eyes. There was so much to explain, but she sensed that Mrs. Parker wouldn't have the patience for a protracted conversation. She was so ready to cross over she was practically gone already. Violet needed to boil the point about her sister down to its essence.

"She wasn't . . . perfect."

"And this is news?"

"What I mean is, it's all her fault. When we were small she . . . she pushed me around so much it made me afraid of my own voice."

Mrs. Parker shrugged, as if it were barely significant. "My dear, in the history of the world, I doubt there's been a family that wasn't every bit as awful as it was wonderful."

Violet sniffed. "I suppose."

"Look," Mrs. Parker said, "if she were here now, what do you think she would say to you?"

Violet knew the answer with such certainty it surprised her. "That she was sorry."

"And what would you say back?"

That I forgive her, Violet thought. But she couldn't get it out. A roiling wave of tears pushed up from her center and overtook her before she could speak. Of course she forgave her. How could she not? Ivy was a mere child when she tortured Violet with silence—just a jealous little girl consumed with sibling rivalry. Violet had to hold herself equally responsible for not realizing all of this years ago.

Dorothy Parker seemed to understand. "You need to forgive yourself, too," she said.

Violet caught her breath and wiped the tears from her face. "Are you leaving now?"

"It's time," she said, peering into the distance as if she were looking at something specific, something Violet could see only as a soft shimmer in the air. "I have my own bratty big sister waiting. My mother, too, of course. And it seems the old Algonquin friends have a seat saved for me. They'd better have decent gin over there."

Violet took a step toward her mentor and gave her a hug.

Mrs. Parker returned the embrace and then backed away. "I hate dramatic good-byes," she said.

Violet smiled. "I'll miss you, too," she said.

"The kid's going to be okay," Dorothy Parker said, as she stepped into the shimmering light.

"I hope so," Violet said. "And thank you. Thank you, Mrs. Parker . . . for everything."

"Dorothy," her friend corrected, and then vanished.

Chapter 39

Violet leaned against the wall in the narrow hallway outside the courtroom of Judge Anita Jacobs, fanning herself with a magazine. Her lawyer, Allison Oliveri, had already briefed her on what to expect, and now tried to make small talk to calm her nerves. It wasn't working. The Webers and their bear of an attorney, John Gibb, stood just a few feet away. And while everyone else got jostled as people made their way through the hot, crowded passageway, no one dared make contact with the intimidating Mr. Gibb, who looked more like he belonged in the corridors of power than the cramped hallway of this dingy makeshift courthouse.

Violet stared at him. He wore a pin-striped European suit that had to have been custom-made for his massive frame. His bald head looked as shiny as it did the last time she saw him, and she imagined that he shaved it daily as some kind of pre-battle ritual. She could smell his cologne from where she stood.

Allison followed Violet's line of vision and read her mind. "Don't worry," she said. "He's all form and no substance."

"He scares the shit out of me," Violet whispered. For all her new-found courage, she couldn't help slipping back into her old pattern of fear with this terrifying figure.

"Don't let the expensive suit fool you," Allison said. "These New York City lawyers tend to get too cocky for their own good." She put a slender hand on Violet's shoulder. "We'll eat him for lunch."

A whole *village* couldn't eat him for lunch, Violet thought.

She couldn't get a good look at Malcolm and Sandra, who were mostly blocked by their attorney. Occasionally, though, the nosy Sandra craned her neck to watch the parade of humanity pass through the hallways. Violet could see that her hair had been beauty-parlor coiffed for the occasion.

The door to the courtroom opened, and the uniformed court officer appeared. "Epps versus Weber!"

"Showtime," Allison whispered.

They filed into the courtroom, which was blessedly cooler than the cramped hallway, and stood behind a long wooden table, scarred by years of note-taking, pen jabs, and other assaults. Judge Anita Jacobs entered. She was in her late forties, with narrow features and dark hair wound into the kind of tight curls that could come only from a perm.

"If everyone's ready," she said, after the attorneys stated their names and affiliations, "let's take a seat and begin. Mr. Gibb?"

"Yes, Your Honor." He spoke so loudly Violet thought he was trying to project through the walls, down the hallway, and clear across the pillars of justice. He called Sandra Weber to the stand, where she was sworn in by the court officer. Then John Gibb proceeded to ask her routine questions about how long she had been married and living at her current address. He established that she was the girl's grandmother and had known her since birth. This was followed by a series of questions about the house she lived in, what kind of accommodations the girl had, and what a typical day was like.

"And how long have you been married?" her lawyer asked.

"We just celebrated our forty-fifth wedding anniversary," Sandra answered.

"Forty-five years!" John Gibb said, as if he were surprised by the answers. "Congratulations. I imagine it must be tough to keep a marriage going that long. How do you do it?"

"Like any couple, we have our ups and downs, but we talk and we work it out."

"So you have no plans to get divorced or separated?"

"No, never. Absolutely not," Sandra said.

The warrior attorney told the judge he had no further questions, and Violet's lawyer approached for cross-examination.

"I understand you believe a two-parent household is a better environment for raising a child than a one-parent household," she said. "Is that correct?"

"Yes, definitely."

"Under *any* circumstances?" Allison pressed.

"Well, maybe not *any* circumstances, but if the marriage is solid—"

"What kind of issues might make a marriage less than solid, Mrs. Weber?"

Sandra put her hand to her throat. "I . . . uh . . ."

"What if one of the spouses was cheating? You think that might create a less-than-ideal environment for a child?"

"It depends," Sandra said. "If the couple can work it out—"

"But couples can't always work it out, can they?"

"We're going to counseling!" Sandra said. "We're fine. Everything is fine."

"You're seeing a *marriage* counselor?"

"Yes."

"And why is that?"

"Because . . . because we want to be sure our marriage is strong." Sandra leaned back, pleased with herself.

Violet looked across the table at Malcolm, whose head was down as he picked at his no-longer-manicured nails. He looked almost as nervous as she felt, though Violet sensed he was more worried about Sandra's wrath than about losing custody.

"Did something happen to threaten your marriage, Mrs. Weber?" Allison Oliveri asked. "Did one of you have an affair?"

Sandra mumbled her response.

"Excuse me?" the lawyer said. "I didn't hear you."

"My husband," she said.

"Your husband had an affair?"

"Yes."

"Since you're so sure your marriage is on solid ground, it must have happened a long, long time ago. How long ago was it—more than ten years?"

"No," Sandra said, her voice soft.

"More than five years?" the lawyer asked.

"No."

"More than one year ago?"

"No."

"No? Surely it was more than six months ago?"

"Objection!" barked Gibb.

"Sustained," said the judge.

"I beg your pardon, Your Honor," said Violet's attorney. She turned back to Sandra. "When, exactly, did you learn of your husband's affair?"

"Two months ago."

"So about eight weeks," Allison Oliveri said.

"More or less."

"I see. That must have been devastating. And still so fresh. When did you go into marriage counseling?"

"Last month."

"And how long was your husband's affair?"

"About a year, I guess."

"So just to be clear, your husband had a yearlong affair you found out about eight weeks ago, and you just started marriage counseling last month to try to work things out. Is that right?"

"We're dealing with it," Sandra said.

"Thank you," said the lawyer. "No further questions, Your Honor."

John Gibb called Malcolm to the stand. As he was sworn in, Violet was finally able to get a good look at him. With a few extra pounds and the orange tint of his spray-on tan faded away, his face looked gray and doughy. And even in his new suit, there was a shabbiness about him. Violet thought he looked defeated.

He took the stand, and John Gibb launched right into his questions. "I understand you've been married to your wife, Sandra, for forty-five years, is that right?"

"Yes."

"And during all those decades, have you ever moved out of the house and separated from her?"

"No, never."

"Have you ever contacted a divorce attorney?"

"No. We have a good marriage."

John Gibb folded his large arms and affected a somber expression. "But I understand the relationship has had some serious issues lately," he said.

"Yes," Malcolm said.

"You had an extramarital affair?"

Malcolm looked down. "I did."

"Was it your first?"

"And my last," Malcolm said, glancing up. "It was a terrible mistake. I love my wife."

"Thank you," John Gibb said. "No further questions."

That was quick, Violet thought, and she guessed that John Gibb knew that the less Malcolm said, the better.

Allison Oliveri approached him and smiled. He grinned right back, the big dope, and Violet couldn't help feeling just a little bit sorry for him. Not that he didn't deserve the thrashing he was about to take. Violet wrung her hands as if she could squeeze out her ambivalence.

"I understand you're sorry for your infidelity," Allison said gently to Malcolm.

"*Very* sorry."

"I imagine you must feel guilty for cheating on your wife."

He nodded. "I do."

"I guess that's why you went to her and confessed your sins on your own accord," she said. "You did confess on your own accord, didn't you?"

"On my own accord?"

Allison was going in for the kill. Violet leaned forward.

"I'll clarify," said the attorney. "Did you go to your wife and confess the affair before she had any idea of what was going on?"

"Not exactly."

"When, exactly, did you finally tell her the truth?" Her tone was getting harsher, and Malcolm looked shaken, as if a new friend had suddenly turned on him.

"Well, she . . . she found out. But right away I was totally honest. I didn't try to cover it up or anything."

"I see. You were caught. And then, once your lie was exposed, you confessed. Is that about right, Mr. Weber?"

"I really felt bad," Malcolm said.

"Yes," Allison Oliveri said, "people who get caught usually do. Good luck with your marriage. No further questions, Your Honor."

Malcolm left the stand wearing an embarrassed grin, and Violet squirmed. But as hard as this was, she knew the worst was yet to come. And indeed, after she was called to the stand, sworn in, and questioned by her own attorney about how she would support the child, as well as the particulars of taking possession of the house Delaney had grown up in, it was John Gibb's turn to cross-examine. Violet felt her armpits go damp beneath her summer suit. She held her trembling hands on her lap. Do not slip, she coached herself. You've come so far. Don't let him scare you.

"*Ms.* Epps—" he began, emphasizing the pronunciation of the form of address as if it were ludicrous. "You do prefer *Ms.*, don't you?"

Already, a lump was forming in her throat. Keep it together, she coached herself. You can do this.

"Yes."

"Well, then, *Ms.* Epps, can you tell the court what you do for a living?"

"I'm a movie critic."

"A critic?"

"Yes."

"So I assume people read your reviews to decide whether or not to go see a particular movie?"

"Yes."

"And do parents sometimes read your reviews to decide whether a movie is appropriate for a child?"

"Sure," she said quickly, and started to understand where he was going with this. She wished she still had that magazine to fan herself.

"And do you think this is an important, responsible thing for a parent to do—to make sure the movie is appropriate before bringing a child to see it?"

She took a deep breath and tried to center herself. *You are not going to bully me,* she thought.

"Well," he pressed, "do you?"

"Yes."

"For instance," he said, "if there's full frontal male and female nudity, a responsible parent would understand that it's an adult film, is that right?"

"Well, it would be rated NC-Seventeen, so—"

"NC-Seventeen? Isn't that what used to be called X?"

"That was a long time ago."

"But either way, if a movie shows a man's genitalia it gets that rating, correct?"

"Yes."

"So the Motion Picture Association of America has determined that no one under the age of seventeen should see entertainment showing a man's genitals, is that right?"

Violet swallowed hard. "Yes."

"And wouldn't it be terribly irresponsible, if not downright dangerous, for a parent to take a child to an X-rated movie?"

"NC-Seventeen," Violet corrected.

He paused and smiled theatrically, as if he thought that was funny. An evil grin, Violet thought, not meant to charm but to intimidate.

"Yes, of course," he said. "Excuse me, I'll rephrase. Wouldn't it be irresponsible and dangerous for a parent to take a child to see a movie rated NC-Seventeen?"

"The child wouldn't even be allowed in."

"Oh, yes, that's right. These performances are so objectionable it's not even left to the parent's discretion. Children under seventeen are not allowed in the theater under any circumstances, is that right?"

"Yes."

"And what is your opinion of this rule?"

"Mine?"

He looked around and held up his hands. "Who else would I be asking?"

Violet felt herself blush. It wasn't enough to pummel her—he had to embarrass her, as well. Fortunately, her lawyer objected and the judge sustained.

"I'll repeat the question, Ms. Epps," said John Gibb. "What is your opinion of the MPAA's authority over age limits?"

"I think it's necessary," she said.

"So you agree that if a man's genitalia is shown on screen no one under the age of seventeen should be permitted to see it?"

"Usually, yes."

"What if it was a live performance and not a movie? Is there any reason why that would be an exception?"

Violet's face broke out in a sweat, but she knew it would be worse to wipe it off than to just let herself dampen. So she just licked her lips and responded. "Mr. Gibb, it was an honest mistake."

"Just answer the question, Ms. Epps. Is there any reason why full frontal nudity in a live, theatrical performance would be *less* objectionable than the same nudity in a film?"

"No," Violet said. "There isn't."

"And yet you took your thirteen-year-old niece, Delaney, to just such a show last May, didn't you?"

"I was under the impression that—"

"Yes, of course. You didn't know it was X-rated. But you didn't bother to check, did you? You just subjected your innocent young niece to a pornographic performance."

"It wasn't pornographic." She was doing it. She was standing up for herself, refusing to be intimidated.

"I guess that's a matter of opinion, isn't it? The Motion Picture Association of America would classify it as pornographic, but Violet Epps, famous film critic, thinks it's perfectly suitable for a child."

"That's not true."

"So you agree that the performance was unsuitable for a child?"

"I would never have taken Delaney to the show if I had known. I made a mistake when I assumed it would be family entertainment."

"Would it be safe to say it was an error in judgment?" he asked.

Violet cleared her throat. It was so hard to know how to answer when she couldn't tell what he was setting her up for. She glanced at her attorney, who gave her a small nod.

"Fortunately," Violet said, "the girl wasn't traumatized."

"And how did you determine that, Ms. Epps?"

"We spoke about it. She's fine."

"You *spoke* about it. I see. Are you a licensed child psychologist?"

"I . . . uh, no."

"Are you a therapist?"

"No."

"Are you a social worker? A school counselor? Have you done any fieldwork with troubled teens?"

"No, but—"

"Then I'll repeat my earlier question. Would it be safe to say that taking Delaney to a live performance with full frontal female and male nudity was an error in judgment?"

"I . . . uh, yes. I guess it was."

"Seems you make a lot of errors in judgment," John Gibb said. "What can you tell us about a woman named Daisy Buchanan?"

"She's a character from *The Great Gatsby*."

"Very amusing," he said, without smiling. "It's also the name of a friend of yours, isn't it?"

"Well, I, um . . . I knew someone who went by that name."

"And how did you know this woman?"

"We met . . . at the Algonquin Hotel. She's a fellow critic. Or was. She hasn't written for a long time."

"But this is the same woman who was seen with your niece the day she disappeared, is that right?"

"Yes."

John Gibb took a long pause, as if he had to think hard about his next question, but it was pure theatrics. He was going for a long, uncomfortable silence after determining that Delaney had disappeared with Violet's friend.

"How long was the girl missing?" he finally said.

"All day—about ten hours."

"Ten hours. That's a long time for a child to be lost."

Violet closed her eyes for a moment, and the black terror of that day came back. "It felt like weeks," she said.

"Did you call the police?"

"No, but—"

"It was the girl's grandparents who called the police," he said, pointing to the Webers. "Wasn't it?"

"Well, of course. She didn't come home on the school bus. How could I have known—"

"They spent the entire day wondering if the girl was dead or in danger, right?"

"And so did I."

"Really? That's very interesting, since the girl was with your friend the entire time."

"I didn't know!"

"Is that so?"

"Of course."

"Isn't it true that you were worried about your custody case, especially after your error in judgment regarding the pornographic performance was revealed?"

"Yes. I mean, it wasn't pornographic, but of course I was worried. I love Delaney, and I want her to come home."

"Is that why you arranged to have your friend kidnap her?"

"That's ridiculous!"

"You realize, of course, the girl could have died without her medication."

"It was Sandra's fault she didn't have her medication. She hid it."

"Is that why you changed your mind at the last minute and pretended to discover the girl at the cemetery?"

"Objection!" yelled Violet's lawyer.

"Sustained," the judge said, and then addressed John Gibb. "Counselor, you're on thin ice."

Gibb nodded and looked back at Violet. "Ms. Epps, can you please tell the court what happened to the mysterious friend of yours who goes by the name Daisy Buchanan?"

"She disappeared."

"Into thin air?"

"As far as I know, yes."

"And the police have been unable to find her for questioning, is that right?"

"Yes."

"And you have no idea where she is?"

"Like I said, she disappeared. But she didn't commit any crime. In fact—"

"No further questions," John Gibb said, and turned to walk back to his seat.

Violet looked at her lawyer, who made no move to rise and tell the judge she wanted to redirect. Please, Violet thought, you can't just let this pass! I have more to say! Everything is riding on this.

"Thank you, Ms. Epps," said the judge. "You're excused."

Violet's heart thumped so hard it felt like a prisoner trying to beat its way out of her chest. She could barely breathe.

"Wait a minute," Violet said, sounding winded. "I'm not finished."

John Gibb did the slowest, foulest, meanest, most deliberate turn toward her. He seemed to twist from the bottom up: his massive frame, his head, and finally his glowering eyes, which fixed on her with a fury that tried to suck out her courage and spit it on the floor. It was working, too. Violet's spirit disappeared behind the rush of fight-or-flight hormones compelling her to get the hell out of there so she wouldn't have to face this charging mammoth.

He pointed at her face. "You're *excused!*"

Violet's reptile brain heard *Run! Run or I'll eat you!* She tried to fight it and find her center again, but she was dizzy from hyperventilating.

"Just a minute, Counselor," Judge Jacobs said. "I'd like to hear what Ms. Epps has to say."

John Gibb folded his arms and stared Violet down. She averted her eyes and tried to find her courage by remembering the heady feeling she got when Dorothy Parker had entered her.

She thought back, recalling the day she lost her nerve on the phone with Carl, and Dorothy Parker took over. She had been so brave then, so powerful. Why couldn't she conjure that now? Why was this fear so paralyzing?

She closed her eyes.

Delaney, Violet thought. *Delaney.*

Violet held up her hand to let everyone in the courtroom know she needed a minute. As she had been taught in kung fu class, Violet took a long, slow breath to the count of four, held it to the count of four, and released it to the count of four. Then she repeated the whole process until finally she was ready to speak. And when she did, the courage that pulsed through her wasn't Dorothy Parker's. And it wasn't play-acting. It was nothing but her own true strength.

"My friend," she said, "did not kidnap the girl. She saved her life."

"Your Honor," John Gibb said, "this is absurd."

The judge shot him a look. "Please finish, Ms. Epps."

"Delaney was feeling suicidal, only I didn't know it. Sandra and Malcolm didn't know it. No one did. Except for . . . for Daisy, who, well, had a sense for these things. If she hadn't gone to her when she did and spent the day talking to the girl, listening to her, taking her to visit her parents' grave, who knows what might have happened."

"Why was Delaney suicidal?" the judge asked.

"Because she thought I would lose this case," Violet said. "That's how badly she wants to come home. She needs me, Your Honor."

"Hearsay!" said John Gibb.

"You can ask her yourself," said Violet, who knew Delaney was waiting in the judge's chamber with her court-appointed attorney for the child.

Judge Anita Jacobs rose from her bench. "I will," she said. "Thank you, Ms. Epps. You are excused."

Chapter 40

On a bright Saturday in late September, more than a year after she had gained custody of Delaney, Violet sat next to Michael behind an exhibitor's table at a local street fair. The sign above them said RED DRAGON KUNG FU ACADEMY. Michael had rented the space so that he could promote his business, and Delaney and Kara had cheerfully volunteered to work the booth, giving out lollipops to the kids, refrigerator magnets to the adults, and discount coupons to anyone who would take them. But after putting in several hours, the girls asked if they could take a walk around, so now it was just the two of them.

A middle-aged woman approached. Her hair was dyed pink and blue, and she wore long dangling feather earrings. She was at least fifty but dressed like a teenager in a pop-star T-shirt and short denim skirt. If Violet had to guess, she would have pegged the woman as the owner of multiple cats.

"What are you giving away?" the likely cat owner asked.

Violet knew the type. People like this often came to these fairs looking for anything they could get their hands on for free, no matter how useless.

"Are you interested in learning kung fu?" Violet asked.

"Depends," the woman said.

"On?"

"On what you're giving away."

"Would you like a refrigerator magnet?" Violet asked, holding one up. It wasn't exactly exciting swag—just a magnetized version of the Red Dragon Kung Fu Academy business card.

"Can I have five?" the woman asked.

"You can have two," Violet said, smiling. "And a coupon for a free lesson. How's that?"

"I can get a free lesson?"

"Yup."

The woman squinted at the coupon, trying to read it. She moved it farther from her face. "Can I bring my boyfriend?"

"The more the merrier."

"Thanks," she said, shoving the coupon and two refrigerator magnets into her purse. Then she grabbed a handful of lollipops and disappeared into the crowd.

"You suppose she sells the stuff on eBay?" Michael asked.

"I prefer to imagine a house full of shoe boxes crammed with crap she intends to make into jewelry one day but never does."

Michael gave her a kiss, and Violet smiled. She didn't have Dorothy Parker in her life anymore. She didn't have her parents or her sister. She would miss them forever, of course, but she had figured out how to enjoy and appreciate all she did have—Michael, Delaney, and her own powerful voice. Not that she didn't backslide into fear every once in a while, but those regressions were getting less and less frequent.

Violet decided to take a walk around the fair and see if she could find the girls before they filled up on too much popcorn, cotton candy, and funnel cakes. A few things caught her eye as she made her way through the aisles, but the booth that attracted her most was the one selling antique and collectible printed materials, including books, magazines, and postcards.

She went through a stack of old battered hardcovers, most of which were missing the book jackets, and was surprised to discover a first edition of *Enough Rope*, Dorothy Parker's first poetry collection.

"How much?" she asked the proprietor.

"Twenty," he said.

Violet knew the damaged volume wasn't exactly a collector's item, but she thought she might enjoy owning it. Then again, she wondered if a small part of her wasn't succumbing to wishful thinking, hoping there might be another book out there that could bring back her friend. Of course, it wouldn't. She knew that. Dorothy Parker had gone into the light where she belonged, and now all that was left of her were her words.

"Aunt Violet!"

She turned and saw Delaney and Kara walking toward her, holding massive tufts of cotton candy on paper tubes.

"How much junk have you girls eaten?"

The teenagers exchanged looks.

"Not that much," Delaney said. "But listen, you're not going to believe who's here. Vincent van Loser!"

"Carl?"

"He's selling those little painted chairs again, only now they've got kind of an antique country look."

"He called it *Americana*," Kara added.

"We told him you were here," Delaney said. "I hope that's okay."

Violet paused to think about that and realized she had no nervous tension about seeing Carl. "Of course it is."

"He said you should stop by and say hi," Kara said.

Delaney seemed excited. "He asked us to find you," she said. "But if you don't want to talk to him—"

"No, it's fine," Violet said, still holding the book. She looked over at the man who managed the booth, but he was talking to another customer.

"Excuse me," Violet called. "I'm coming back for this." The man waved his assent, and Violet placed the book on the table. "Where is he?" she asked her niece.

Giggling over the gossip-rich situation they were orchestrating, the girls led Violet to Carl.

"She's going to rip his head off," Delaney said to Kara, and then pulled her away so they could watch from a distance.

Of course, Violet knew she would do nothing of the sort. She greeted him like an old friend, and the girls, bored and disappointed by the lack of drama, walked off.

"You look great," Carl said. "Different, but great."

That was, in a nutshell, exactly how she felt. "You, too," she said, and meant it. He had lost a little weight and seemed happy.

"I've been seeing you on TV. My girlfriend can't believe I used to go out with someone who's on television. We liked your review of that three-D movie."

So he has a girlfriend, Violet thought. Smooth how he worked that in. "Thanks, Carl. Sounds like things are working out well for you."

"After we broke up I started dating a neighbor, Bonnie. She's awesome—older but very cool, and a sculptress. We live together now."

Violet latched right onto the word *older*, as Carl had clearly been looking for a mother figure, and she guessed he found one.

"I'm glad for you," she said. "Where are you living?"

"Just around the corner from my old place."

In other words, he moved into his girlfriend's house.

"And you've got a whole new esthetic," she said, pointing to his painted chairs, which no longer bore kitschy sixties-inspired designs. "I like it. It's . . . earnest."

"Yeah? Thanks." He was, she could tell, genuinely pleased. "Delaney tells me she's back home now, living with you. That's awesome."

Violet smiled. "It's been a hell of a year."

"How did Sandra and Malcolm react? They must have freaked."

"They did, at first," she said, recalling the hysteria in the court-room after the judge announced the verdict. *You've ruined everything,* Sandra had shouted at Violet. *Everything!*

"And then?" Carl asked.

"Then they wound up separating."

Carl's eyes widened. "Malcolm and Sandra?"

"Turns out the marriage had been shaky for a long, long time. I think that deep down, the real reason they wanted custody was because they thought it might help glue the marriage together. But the split was inevitable."

"Are they doing okay now?"

"Malcolm got to keep his new car, which was really all he wanted. He moved in with his girlfriend."

Carl looked stunned. "Malcolm had a *girlfriend*?"

Violet smiled. "The best part is how Sandra transformed. She sold the house and most of that horrible stuff, and moved into a small place on the North Shore. She went back to work as a medical receptionist and she actually has *friends.* I've never seen her so happy."

"Please tell me she sold that life-sized ceramic Weimaraner."

"Phil," Violet said. "She calls him Phil, and he's the closest thing she'll ever have to a pet, so no. She kept that."

Carl laughed, and then focused on something in the distance over Violet's shoulder. "There's Bonnie," he said, waving. "I'd like you to meet her."

Violet turned around to see Carl's new girlfriend, the older woman artist whose house he had moved into. And when she saw the short denim skirt and the hair dyed pink and blue, she had to smile. It was the freebie-hunting woman she had pegged as a cat owner.

After spending a few moments chatting, and listening to Bonnie apologize for not having recognized her earlier, Violet said good-bye and went back to the booth selling antique books and magazines, as she desperately wanted the Dorothy Parker collection. It would, she thought, be a meaningful memento, something she would enjoy owning. She pictured sitting in the study with Delaney as they read the poems to each other.

"Too late," the man at the booth said. "Someone just bought it."

"But I told you to hold it for me!"

"I'm sorry," he said. "I didn't know if you were coming back."

Violet's disappointment felt physical, like a little piece of her heart had been taken. Dejected, she went back to Michael's booth, where the girls were busy handing out goodies as a couple of teenage boys stood nearby, flirting.

"Where's your father?" Violet asked Kara.

"He went to get drinks," she said.

Sure enough, a short time later Michael returned with a tray of refreshments. He handed a bottle of water to Violet, who offered a weak smile as she thanked him, trying to get past her sunken spirits.

"I bought you something else," he said, and gave her a small paper bag with a book inside.

It couldn't be, she thought, could it? She pulled out the slim volume. Sure enough, it was the first-edition Dorothy Parker book.

"How did you know?" Violet asked, running her hands over the smooth surface of the cover.

"Delaney said you were looking at it."

She threw her arms around him. "Thank you."

He returned her embrace and she almost couldn't let go. When they finally pulled apart, he looked at her face. "You're crying," he said, laying a cool hand on her cheek.

"I'm happy."

"Because of one little book? You must be a hell of a Dorothy Parker fan."

Violet opened the volume and scanned the verses Mrs. Parker had written so long ago. It seemed remarkable that every single one was about love or death. More amazing, though, was that most of them were as vibrant, funny, and insightful as they were in 1926.

She looked up and saw Delaney laughing at something one of the teenage boys said to her. Not a fake, flirty giggle, but a genuine, deep-in-the-gut laugh she couldn't control. Violet closed the book and wiped her nose. Though her voice was now as strong and as brave as she ever dared dream, she knew that sometimes the loudest comment need only be whispered.

She looked back at Michael and smiled. "I am."

Author's Note

J. D. Salinger once said that writers should get very still and ask themselves what piece of writing in the whole world they would most want to
read if they had their heart's choice, and then sit down shamelessly
and write the thing themselves.*

That is precisely how this book came about. One day, as I was not-
ing that Jane Austen, whom I love, had dozens of novels written in her
honor, it occurred to me that someone should do the same for the one
writer I had always worshipped and adored with gushing abandon:
Dorothy Parker.

Then, in a moment of giddy excitement I thought, *Me! I'll write it!*

Almost immediately my skittish ego hit the brakes. How could
I possibly tackle such a thing? Dorothy Parker had one of the wittiest
and most beguiling voices of the twentieth century. Who did I think I
was, anyway?

But the truth is, I wanted so badly to read a book in which the
ghost of Dorothy Parker came back to life that it trumped my insecurity. So I took Salinger's advice and drove forward to write the thing
myself.

Of course, that process involved rereading all of her poems

---

* Paraphrased from J. D. Salinger; "Seymour; An Introduction," *The New Yorker*, June 6,
1959.

and stories. But it was her other writing—the essays, reviews, and letters—that unlocked for me the distinct voice of this unique and audacious woman.

And now here it is, presented with equal doses of pride and humility. I hope that it will please those who, like me, have been Dorothy Parker fans for a long time, as well as anyone just discovering the irreverent wit.

The only apologies I offer are for the liberties I took with the facts of Dorothy Parker's life for the sake of my fiction. Parker scholars may notice certain discrepancies, some as small as her preferred drink (scotch, not gin), and others as large as changing the name of the proprietor of the Algonquin Hotel during the Round Table years (Frank Case, not Percy Coates). Most of the broader facts, like losing her mother at a young age and her passionate commitment to justice and civil rights, are true.

Still, this novel should in no way be considered a factual account of Dorothy Parker's life, and anyone who wishes to know more about this important writer should read one of the many fine biographies written about her. In particular, I recommend *Dorothy Parker: What Fresh Hell Is This?* by Marion Meade. Related readings, some of which are sadly no longer in print, include *The Algonquin Wits* by Robert E. Drennan; *Dorothy Parker: In Her Own Words*, edited by Barry Day; *George S. Kaufman: An Intimate Portrait* by Howard Teichmann; *Smart Aleck: The Wit, World, and Life of Alexander Woollcott* by Howard Teichmann; *The Vicious Circle* by Margaret Case Harriman; *Wit's End* by James R. Gaines; *You Might as Well Live* by John Keats; and *A Journey into Dorothy Parker's New York* by Kevin C. Fitzpatrick.

Of course, my highest recommendation is to read Dorothy Parker herself. You'll find a wonderful collection of her stories, poems, reviews, essays, and letters in *The Portable Dorothy Parker*, edited by

Marion Meade. I think you'll agree that she was not only a master of acerbic barbs but a keen observer of the human heart and a writer of uncommon gifts.

> *I find at the end I'm not scared.*
> —Dorothy Parker[*]

---

[*] Radio interview with Studs Terkel, 1959.

Acknowledgments

I was knee-deep in another project when I got the idea for this book, but I was too excited to put it on the back burner. And so I hurried into Manhattan for some face time with my agents to get their opinion. Their reaction was even better than I had hoped, and I began writing *Farewell, Dorothy Parker* that very day. So for their wild enthusiasm and nonstop encouragement, huge thanks to Andrea Cirillo and Annelise Robey, as well as to Peggy Gordijn, Mike McCormack, and the rest of the wonderful folks at the Jane Rotrosen Agency. A special shout-out to Joel Gotler, too.

To my erstwhile editor, Rachel Kahan, who not only embraced the book but provided a brightness that lit the path, a deep and humble bow of gratitude. You knew exactly what this story needed.

A very special thanks to every member of the extraordinary team at Putnam/Berkley, including Katie Grinch, Lydia Hirt, Caitlin Mulrooney-Lyski, Kate Stark, Shannon Jamieson Vazquez, Meaghan Wagner, Alexis Welby, and, of course, Ivan Held.

Thanks, too, to my talented and generous beta readers, Myfanwy Collins and Saralee Rosenberg, and to my fellow traveler and lunch mate, Susan Henderson. Your guidance and friendship are everything. Additional thanks to all the supportive lit pals who were always there with helpful advice and encouragement, including Mary Akers, Don Capone, Ron Currie, Katrina Denza, Susan DiPlacido, Pamela Erens, Kathy Fish, Kelly Flanigan, Carol Hoenig, Debbi Honorof,

ACKNOWLEDGMENTS

Andrew Gross, Brenda Janowitz, Elinor Lipman, Pam Mosher, Michael Palmer, Ellen Parker, Patricia Parkinson, Jordan Rosenfeld, Robin Slick, Maryanne Stahl, and Alix Strauss. And a heartfelt salute to the late Louis Catron.

I owe a huge debt of gratitude to Tony Iovino, who gave so generously of his time and expertise to help me understand the intricacies of family law in New York State. And to the doctors, movie critics, Algonquin staff, and other professionals who patiently answered my questions—including Gary J. Budge, Catherine Custalow, Stuart Kanterman, Rik Kellerman, Patricia Latzman, Doomy Midouin, and Max Weiss—a grateful hug as well as an apology for any creative license I took with your accurate and useful information.

Like most authors, I love book club readers, and I am happy to acknowledge the following individuals here: Anita Beall, Ericka, Pamela, Suzanne O'Neil, Moira McGarry, C. Zuniga, Susan Stokes Erichsen, Rozanne Notaristefano, Valerie Nielsen, Carolyn Everitt, Roberta Teer, Beth Gilman, Chav Landau, Melissa Marasciullo, Jessica Brakhage, Tracee Jones, and Kimberly Fisher.

And finally, love and hugs to the four incredible people who make me worry the most and laugh the hardest: Max, Ethan, Emma, and, of course, Mike.